4/11 MOR

Blackpool Council

BUILDING A BETTER COMMUNITY FOR ALL

1 0 MAY 2012

Please return/renew this item
by the last date shown.
Books may also be renewed by
phone or the Internet.

Tel: 01253 478070

www.blackpool.gov.uk

D0281226

Also by Carrie Vaughn
from Gollancz

kitty
TAKES A
HOLIDAY

Carrie Vaughn

The right of Carrie Vaughn to be identified as the author
of this work has been asserted by her in accordance with
the Copyright, Designs and Patents Act 1988.

First published in Great Britain in 2008
by Gollancz
An imprint of the Orion Publishing Group
Orion House, 5 Upper St Martin's Lane,
London WC2H 9EA
An Hachette UK Company

This edition published in Great Britain in 2011
by Gollancz

10 9 8 7 6 5 4 3 2 1

A CIP catalogue record for this book
is available from the British Library

ISBN 978 0 575 10068 8

Printed and bound in the UK by CPI Mackays,
Chatham, Kent

The Orion Publishing Group's policy is to use papers
that are natural, renewable and recyclable products and
made from wood grown in sustainable forests. The logging
and manufacturing processes are expected to conform to the
to environmental regulations of the country of origin.

www.carrievaughn.com
www.orionbooks.co.uk

For Andrea, Denise, April, Melissa, Kevin, and Tim,
who were there at the start.

Acknowledgments

My first readers this time around were Paula Balafas and Jo Anne "Mom" Vaughn. Also, thank you to Paula for the ride-alongs, and to Mom for the road trip.

More thank yous: To Larry "Dad" Vaughn for looking after the dog, and to the rest of the family. To Andro Berkovic for bringing my computing power into the twenty-first century. To the Barony of Caer Galen for the overwhelming support. To Ashley Grayson and Co. for picking up the reins. And as always, to Jaime Levine and the crew at Warner, for believing in Kitty so very, very much.

The Playlist

Blondie, "Hanging on the Telephone"

Go Go's, "Head Over Heels"

The Killers, "Mr. Brightside"

Suicidal Tendencies, "Possessed"

Madness, "Animal Farm"

Pretenders, "I Go to Sleep"

VNV Nation, "Kingdom"

Noel Gallagher, "Teotihuacan"

The Dead Milkmen, "Surfin' Cow"

Andy Kirk & His Twelve Clouds of Joy, "Until the Real Thing Comes Along"

Too Much Joy, "Crush Story"

Bach Collegium Stuttgart, "Sheep May Safely Graze"

Supertramp, "It's Raining Again"

Eurythmics, "When Tomorrow Comes"

chapter 1

She runs for the joy of it, because she can, her strides stretching to cover a dozen feet every time she leaps. Her mouth is open to taste the air, which is sharp with cold. The month turns, and the swelling moon paints the night sky silver, lighting up patches of snow scattered throughout the woods. Not yet full moon, a rare moment to be set free before her time, but the other half of her being has no reason to lock her away. She is alone, but she is free, and so she runs.

Catching a scent, she swerves from her path, slows to a trot, puts her nose to the ground. Prey, fresh and warm. Lots of it here in the wild. The smell burns in the winter air. She stalks, drawing breath with flaring nostrils, searching for the least flicker of movement. Her empty stomach clenches, driving her on. The smell makes her mouth water.

She has grown used to hunting alone. Must be careful, must not take chances. Her padded feet touch the ground lightly, ready to spring forward, to dart in one direction or another, making no sound on the forest floor. The scent—musky, hot fur and scat—grows strong, rocketing through her brain. All her nerves flare. Close now, closer, creeping on hunter's feet—

The rabbit springs from its cover, a rotted log grown over with shrubs. She's ready for it, without seeing it or hearing it she knows it is there, her hunter's sense filled by its presence. The moment it runs, she leaps, pins it to the ground with her claws and body, digs her teeth into its neck, clamping her jaw shut and ripping. It doesn't have time to scream. She drinks the blood pumping out of its torn and broken throat, devours its meat before the blood cools. The warmth and life of it fills her belly, lights her soul, and she pauses the slaughter to howl in victory—

My whole body flinched, like I'd been dreaming of falling and suddenly woken up. I gasped a breath—part of me was still in the dream, still falling, and I had to tell myself that I was safe, that I wasn't about to hit the ground. My hands clutched reflexively, but didn't grab sheets or pillow. A handful of last fall's dead leaves crumbled in my grip.

Slowly, I sat up, scratched my scalp, and smoothed back my tangled blonde hair. I felt the rough earth underneath me. I wasn't in bed, I wasn't in the house I'd been living in for the last two months. I lay in a hollow scooped into the earth, covered in forest detritus, sheltered by overhanging pine trees. Beyond the den, crusted snow lay in shadowed areas. The air was cold and biting. My breath fogged.

I was naked, and I could taste blood in the film covering my teeth.

Damn. I'd done it again.

* * *

Lots of people dream of having their picture on the cover of a national magazine. It's one of the emblems of fame, fortune, or at the very least fifteen minutes of notoriety. A lot of people actually do get their pictures on the covers of national magazines. The question is: Are you on the cover of a glamorous high-end fashion glossy, wearing a designer gown and looking fabulous? Or are you on the cover of *Time,* bedraggled and shell-shocked, with a caption reading, "Is This the Face of a Monster?" and "Are YOU in Danger?"

Guess which one I got.

The house I was renting—more like a cabin, a two-room vacation cottage connected to civilization by a dirt road and satellite TV—was far enough out from the town and road that I didn't bother getting dressed for the trek back. Not that I could have; I had forgotten to stash any clothes. Why would I, when I hadn't intended to Change and go running in the first place? Nothing to be done but walk back naked.

I felt better, walking with my skin exposed, the chill air raising goose bumps all over my flesh. I felt cleaner, somehow. Freer. I didn't worry—I followed no path, no hiking trails cut through these woods. No one would see me in this remote section of San Isabel National Forest land in southern Colorado, tucked into the mountains.

That was exactly how I wanted it.

I'd wanted to get away from it all. The drawback was, by getting away from it all I had less holding me to the world. I didn't have as many reasons to stay in my human body. If I'd been worried about someone seeing me naked,

I probably wouldn't have shifted in the first place. Nights of the full moon weren't the only time lycanthropes could shape-shift; we could Change anytime we chose. I'd heard of werewolves who turned wolf, ran into the woods, and never came back. I didn't want that to happen to me. At least, I used to think I didn't want that to happen to me.

But it was getting awfully easy to turn Wolf and run in the woods, full moon or no.

I was supposed to be writing a book. With everything that had happened to me in the last couple of years— starting my radio show, declaring my werewolf identity on the air and having people actually believe me, testifying before a Senate committee hearing, getting far more attention than I ever wanted, no matter how much I should have seen it all coming—I had enough material for a book, or so I thought. A memoir or something. At least, a big publishing company thought I had enough material and offered me enough money that I could take time off from my show to write it. I was the celebrity du jour, and we all wanted to cash in on my fame while it lasted. Selling out had sounded so dreamy.

I put together about a dozen "Best of *The Midnight Hour*" episodes that could be broadcast without me, so the show would keep going even while I took a break. It'd keep people interested, keep my name out there, and maybe even draw in some new fans. I planned to do the *Walden* thing, retreat from society in order to better reflect. Escape the pressures of life, freeing myself to contemplate the deeper philosophical questions I would no doubt ponder while composing my great masterpiece.

Trouble was, you could get away from society and learn to be self-reliant, like Thoreau advocated. Turn your nose up at the rat race. But you couldn't escape yourself, your own doubts, your own conscience.

I didn't even know how to *begin* writing a book. I had pages of scribbled notes and not a single finished page. It all looked so unreal on paper. Really, where did I start? "I was born…" then go into twenty years of a completely unremarkable life? Or start with the attack that made me a werewolf? That whole night was so complicated and seemed an abrupt way to start what I ultimately wanted to be an upbeat story. Did I start with the Senate hearings? Then how did I explain the whole mess that got me there in the first place?

So I stripped naked, turned Wolf, and ran in the woods to avoid the question. As hard as I'd struggled to hold on to my humanity, that was easier.

The closest town of any size to my cabin was Walsenburg, some thirty miles away, and that wasn't saying a whole lot. The place had pretty much stopped growing in the sixties. Main street was the state highway running through, just before it merged onto the interstate. The buildings along it were old-fashioned brick blocks. A lot of them had the original signs: family-owned businesses, hardware stores, and bars and the like. A lot of them were boarded up. A memorial across from the county courthouse paid tribute to the coal miners who had settled the region. To the southwest, the Spanish Peaks loomed, twin mountains rising some seven thousand feet above the plain. Lots of wild, lonely forest spread out around them.

The next afternoon, I drove into town to meet my lawyer,

Ben O'Farrell, at a diner on the highway. He wouldn't drive any farther into the southern Colorado wilds than Walsenburg.

I spotted his car already parked on the street and pulled in behind it. Ben had staked out a booth close to the door. He was already eating, a hamburger and plate of fries. Not much on ceremony was Ben.

"Hi." I slipped into the seat across from him.

He reached for something next to him, then dropped it on the Formica table in front of me: a stack of mail addressed to me, delivered to his care. I tried to route as much of my communication through him as I could. I liked having a filter. Part of the Walden thing. The stack included a few magazines, nondescript envelopes, credit card applications. I started sorting through it.

"I'm fine, thanks, how are you?" I said wryly.

Ben was in his early thirties, rough around the edges. He seemed perpetually a day behind on his shaving, and his light brown hair was rumpled. He wore a gray suit jacket, but his shirt collar was open, the tie nowhere to be seen.

I could tell he was gritting his teeth behind his smile.

"Just because I drove all the way out here for you, don't ask me to be pleasant about it."

"Wouldn't dream of it."

I ordered a soda and hamburger from the waitress, while Ben set his briefcase on the table and pulled out packets of paper. He needed my signature in approximately a million different places. On the plus side, the documents meant I was the beneficiary of several generous out-of-court settlements relating to the fiasco my trip to Washington, D.C., last fall had turned into. Who knew getting kidnapped and paraded on live TV could be so lucrative? I also got to sign depositions in a couple of criminal cases. That felt *good*.

"You're getting twenty percent," I said. "You ought to be glowing."

"I'm still trying to decide if representing the world's first werewolf celebrity is worth it. You get the strangest phone calls, you know that?"

"Why do you think I give people your number and not mine?"

He collected the packets from me, double-checked them, stacked them together, and put them back in his briefcase. "You're lucky I'm such a nice guy."

"My hero." I rested my chin on my hands and batted my eyelashes at him. His snort of laughter told me how seriously he took me. That only made me grin wider.

"One other thing," he said, still shuffling pages in his briefcase, avoiding looking at me. "Your editor called. Wants to know how the book is going."

Technically, I had a contract. Technically, I had a deadline. I shouldn't have had to worry about that sort of thing when I was trying to prove my self-reliance by living simply and getting back to nature.

"Going, going, gone," I muttered.

He folded his hands in front of him. "Is it half done? A quarter done?"

I turned my gaze to a spot on the far wall and kept my mouth shut.

"Tell me it's at least started."

I heaved a sigh. "I'm thinking about it, honest I am."

"You know, it's perfectly reasonable for someone in your position to hire a ghostwriter. Or at least find a co-author. People do it all the time."

"No. I majored in English. I ought to be able to string a few sentences together."

"Kitty—"

I closed my eyes and made a "talk to the hand" gesture. He wasn't telling me anything I didn't already know.

"I'll work on it. I want to work on it. I'll put something together to show them to make them happy."

He pressed his lips together in an expression that wasn't quite a smile. "Okay."

I straightened and pretended like we hadn't just been talking about the book I wasn't writing. "Have you done anything about the sleazebag?"

He looked up from his food and glared. "There's no basis for a lawsuit. No copyright infringement, no trademark infringement, nothing."

"Come on, she stole my show!"

The sleazebag. She called herself "Ariel, Priestess of the Night," and starting about three months ago she hosted a radio talk show about the supernatural. Just like me. Well, just like I used to.

"She stole the idea," Ben said calmly. "That's it. It happens all the time. You know when one network has a hit medical drama, and the next season every other network rolls out a medical drama because they think that's what everyone wants? You can't sue for that sort of thing. It was going to happen sooner or later."

"But she's *awful*. Her show, it's a load of sensationalist *garbage*!"

"So do it better," he said. "Go back on the air. Beat her in the ratings. It's the only thing you can do."

"I can't. I need some time off." I slumped against the back of the booth.

He idly stirred the ketchup on his plate with a french fry. "From this end it looks like you're quitting."

I looked away. I'd been comparing myself to Thoreau because he made running away to the woods sound so noble. It was still running away.

He continued. "The longer you stay away, the more it looks like the people in D.C. who tried to bring you down won."

"You're right," I said, my voice soft. "I know you're right. I just can't think of anything to say."

"Then what makes you think you can write a book?"

This was too much of Ben being right for one day. I didn't answer, and he didn't push the subject.

He let me pay the bill. Together, we headed out to the street.

"Are you going straight back to Denver?" I asked.

"No. I'm going to Farmington to meet Cormac. He wants help with a job."

A job. With Cormac, that meant something nasty. He hunted werewolves—only ones who caused trouble, he'd assured me—and bagged a few vampires on the side. Just because he could.

Farmington, New Mexico, was another two hundred fifty miles west and south of here. "You'll only come as far as Walsenburg for me, but you'll go to Farmington for Cormac?"

"Cormac's family," he said.

I still didn't have that whole story, and I often asked myself how I'd gotten wrapped up with these two. I met Ben when Cormac referred him to me. And what was I doing taking advice about lawyers from a werewolf hunter? I couldn't complain; they'd both gotten me out of trouble on more than one occasion. Ben didn't seem to have any moral qualms about having both a werewolf and a werewolf hunter as clients. But then, were lawyers capable of having moral qualms?

"Be careful," I said.

"No worries," he said with a smile. "I just drive the car and bail him out of jail. He's the one who likes to live dangerously."

He opened the door of his dark blue sedan, threw his briefcase onto the front passenger seat, and climbed in. Waving, he pulled away from the curb and steered back onto the highway.

On the way back to my cabin, I stopped in the even smaller town of Clay, Population 320, Elevation 7400 feet. It boasted a gas station with an attached convenience store, a bed and breakfast, a backwoods outfitter, a hundred-year-old stone church—and that was it. The convenience store, the "Clay Country Store," sold the best home-baked chocolate chip cookies on this side of the Continental Divide. I couldn't resist their lure.

A string of bells hanging on the handle of the door rang as I entered. The man at the cash register looked up, frowned, and reached under the counter. He pulled out a rifle. Didn't say a word, just pointed it at me.

Yeah, the folks around here knew me. Thanks to the Internet and twenty-four-hour news networks, I couldn't be anonymous, even in the middle of nowhere.

I raised my hands and continued into the store. "Hi, Joe. I just need some milk and cookies, and I'll be on my way."

"Kitty? Is that you?" A woman's face popped up from behind a row of shelves filled with cans of motor oil and ice scrapers. She was about Joe's age, mid-fifties, her hair graying and pulled into a ponytail that danced. Where Joe's eyes frowned, hers lit up.

"Hi, Alice," I said, smiling.

"Joe, put that down, how many times do I have to tell you?"

"Can't take any chances," he said.

I ignored him. Some fights you couldn't win. The first time he'd done this, when I came into the store and he recognized me as "that werewolf on TV," I'd been so proud of myself for not freaking out. I'd just stood there with my hands up and asked, "You have silver bullets in there?" He'd looked at me, looked at the rifle, and frowned angrily. The next time I came in, he announced, "Got silver this time."

I went around the shelves to where Alice was, where Joe and his rifle couldn't see me as easily.

"I'm sorry," Alice said. She was stocking cans of soup. "One of these days I'm going to hide that thing. If you'd call ahead, I could make up some chore for him and get him out of here."

"Don't worry about it. As long as I don't do anything threatening, I'm fine, right?" Not that people generally looked at me—a perky blonde twenty-something—and thought "bloodthirsty werewolf."

She rolled her eyes. "Like you could do anything threatening. I swear, that man lives in his own little world."

Yeah, the kind of world where shop owners kept rifles under their counters, while their wives lined healing crystals along the top of the cash register. She also had a cross nailed over the shop door, and more crystals hanging from the windows.

They each had their own brand of protection, I supposed.

I hadn't decided yet if the werewolf thing really didn't

bother some people, or if they still refused to believe it. I kind of suspected that was how it was with Alice. Like my mom—she treated it like it was some kind of club I'd joined. After full moon nights she'd say something like, *Did you have fun at your little outing, dear?*

A lifetime of believing that these things didn't exist was hard to overcome.

"How do you two stay married?"

She looked at me sideways, donned a wry smile, and didn't answer. Her eyes gleamed, though. Right, I wasn't going to press that question any further.

Alice rang up my groceries, while Joe looked on, glaring over his rifle. I had to think of myself as a goodwill ambassador—don't make any sudden moves, don't say anything snide. Try to show him that just because I was a monster didn't mean I was, well, a monster.

I paid, and Alice handed me the brown paper bag. "Thanks," I said.

"Anytime. Now you call if you need anything."

My nonchalance only went so far. I couldn't turn my back on Joe and his rifle, so I backed toward the door, reaching behind to pull it open, and slipped out, to the ringing of bells.

The door was closing behind me when I heard Alice say, "Joe, for God's sake put that thing away!"

Ah yes, life in a small mountain community. There's nothing like it.

chapter 2

The front half of my cabin held a living room and kitchen, while a bedroom and bathroom made up the back half. Only part of a wall separated the two halves, giving the whole place access to the cabin's only source of heat: a wood-burning stove in the living room. The hot-water heater ran on propane, electricity powered everything else. I kept the stove's fire burning to hold back the winter. At this altitude I wasn't snowbound, but it was still pretty darned cold, especially at night.

The living room also had my desk, or rather a small table, which held my laptop and a few books: a dictionary, a dog-eared copy of *Walden.* Shoved underneath were a couple of boxes holding more books and a bunch of CDs. I'd spent my whole adult life working in radio—I had to have something to ruin the quiet. The desk sat in front of the large window that looked out over the porch and the clearing where I parked my car. Beyond that, trees and brown earth climbed up the hill, to blue sky.

I'd spent a lot of hours sitting at that desk, staring out the window at that view. I should have at least made the effort to find some place with a nice mountain vista to occupy my long stretches of procrastination.

When twilight came, deepening the sky to a rich shade of royal blue, then fading to darkness, I knew I'd wasted another day and not written a single decent word.

But it was Saturday, and I had other entertainments. Very late, close to midnight, I turned on the radio. It was time for *Ariel, Priestess of the Night.* I snuggled up on the sofa with a fluffy pillow and a beer.

The front page of *Ariel, Priestess of the Night*'s Web site was all black with candy-apple-red lettering and a big picture of Ariel. She seemed fairly young, maybe my age—mid-twenties. She had pale skin, a porcelain smooth face, dyed black hair falling in luxurious ripples across her shoulders and down her back, and black eyeliner ringing bright blue eyes. That blue, they had to be contacts. She seemed to be in a radio studio, but for some reason the table in front of her was covered in red velvet. She draped herself suggestively across the velvet, her black satin gown exposing not a small amount of cleavage, and leaned toward a microphone as if preparing to lick it. She wore a pentacle on a chain around her neck, silver ankhs on each ear, and a rhinestone nose stud. Animated bat icons flapped in all four corners of the page.

And if all that weren't enough to drive me crazy, the show's theme song was Bauhaus's "Bela Lugosi's Dead."

After a few lines of the song, the woman herself came on the air. Her voice was low and sultry, as seductive as any film noir femme fatale could wish. "Greetings, fellow travelers in darkness. It's time to pull back the veil between worlds. Let me, Ariel, Priestess of the Night, be your guide as we explore the secrets, the mysteries, and the shadows of the unknown."

Oh, give me a break.

"Vampires," she continued, drawing out the word, pronouncing it with a fake British accent. "Are they victims of a disease, as some so-called experts would have us believe? Or have they been chosen, serving as undying ambassadors from the past? Is their immortality a mere quirk of biology—or is it a mystical calling?

"I have with me in the studio a very special guest. He has agreed to emerge from his sanctum to speak with us tonight. Gustaf is the vampire Master of a major U.S. city. He has asked me not to say which, to protect his safety."

Of *course* she wasn't going to say which.

I pouted a little. *I'd* never gotten a vampire Master to be a guest on *my* show. If this Gustaf really was a Master. If he really was a vampire.

"Gustaf, thank you for being here tonight."

"The pleasure is all mine." Gustaf had a low, melodious voice, giving a hint that he might burst out laughing at a joke he wasn't going to share. Very mysterious.

"Hm, I bet it is," Ariel purred. "Tell me, Gustaf, when did you become a vampire?"

"In the year 1438. It was in the Low Countries, what people call the Netherlands today. A very good time and place to be alive. So much trade, commerce, art, music— so much life. I was a young man, full of prospects, full of joy. Then I met... *her*."

Ah, her. Standard dark lady of the night fare. She was exquisite, more intelligent and worldly than any woman he'd ever met. More brilliant, more attractive, more everything.

She'd swept him off his feet, yadda yadda, and here he was, some six hundred years later, and all this time they'd played a game of seduction and mayhem that read like something out of a bodice-ripper.

It was quite the tale of danger and suspense. Out here, alone in a cabin in the woods, with a fire burning in the stove and wind shushing through the pine trees outside, I should have been shaking in my booties.

I'd sure love to give Ariel a *real* scare.

That gave me an idea. A really bad idea.

I retrieved my cell phone from my desk. I dialed the number that Ariel's aggravating voice had seared into my memory.

"You've reached Ariel, Priestess of the Night," said a man. A regular, nonmysterious-sounding man.

"Hi," I said. Oh my God, not a busy signal. I was talking to someone. Was I actually going to get on the show?

"Can you give me first your name and where you're calling from?"

Shit, I hadn't really thought this through. "Um, yeah, I'm... Sue. And I'm from... Albuquerque."

"And what do you want to talk about?"

What *did* I want to talk about? My brain froze. Was this what happened when people called my show? My big mouth took over. "I'd like to talk to Ariel about fear," I said.

"Are you afraid of vampires?" the screener asked.

"Sure."

"All right, if you could please turn off your radio and hold on for a minute."

Crap. Double crap. I turned off the radio.

Instead of hold music, the phone piped in Ariel's show, so I wouldn't miss anything.

Gustaf was talking about the inherent selfless nobility that vampirism conferred upon its victims. "One begins to feel a certain stewardship for humankind. We vampires are the more powerful beings, of course. But we depend on you humans for our survival. Just as humanity has learned it cannot wipe out the rain forests or destroy the oceans without consequence, we cannot rule over humankind with impunity. As we would certainly be capable of doing were we less conscientious."

So people were nothing more than a bunch of endangered monkeys? Was that it? No, vampires would never be able to take over the world because their heads were generally stuck too far up their own asses.

Finally, Ariel made the announcement I'd been waiting for: "All right, listeners, I'm going to open the line for calls now. Do you have a question or a comment for Gustaf? Now's your chance."

I desperately wanted Ariel to put me on the air so I could call bullshit on the guy. She took another call instead. A desperately awestruck woman spoke.

"Oh, Ariel, thank you, and Gustaf, thank you so much for speaking with us all. You don't know how much it means to hear such an old and wise being as yourself."

"There, there, my dear, it's my pleasure," Gustaf said graciously.

"I don't understand why you—I mean you as in all vampires—aren't more visible. You've seen so much, you have so much experience. We could learn so much from you. And I do think the world would be a better place if vampires were in a position to guide us—"

Ariel butted in. "Are you saying, then, that you think vampires would make good world leaders?"

"Of course—they've seen nations rise and fall. They know better than anybody what works and what doesn't. They're the ultimate monarchs."

Great. A freakin' royalist. Ooh, what I would say to this woman if this were my show...

Ariel was maddeningly diplomatic. "You're a woman with traditional values. I can see why the ageless vampires would appeal to you."

"Since the world would clearly be a better place if vampires were in charge—why aren't they? Why don't they take over?"

Gustaf chuckled, clearly amused in a detached, condescending manner. "Oh, we certainly could, if we wanted to. But I think you underestimate how shy most vampires are. We really don't like the harsh light of publicity."

Could have fooled me.

Ariel said, "I'd like to move on to the next call now. Hi, Sue, you're on the air," Ariel said.

Sue—that was me. Wow, I made it. Back on the air—in a manner of speaking. Ha. Here I go—

"Hi, Ariel. Thanks so much for taking my call." I knew the script. I knew how to sound like a fan. I'd heard it enough from the other side. "Gustaf, I don't think all vampires are quite as sensitive and charitable as you imply. Are they stewards watching over the rain forests, or shepherds fattening the sheep for market?"

Gustaf huffed a little. "Every vampire was once a human being. The best of us never forget our roots."

Even if they had to suck those roots dry... "But you give the worst human beings the power and immortality of a vampire, and what do you get? The Third Reich—forever. See, you know why I think vampires haven't taken over the world?"

God, I sounded snotty. I always hated it when people like this called into my show. Crabby know-it-alls.

"Why?" Ariel said.

"Theatrics."

"Theatrics?" Ariel repeated, sounding amused, which irritated me.

"Yeah, theatrics. The posing, the preening, the drawn-out stories of romance and seduction when the reality is Gustaf here was probably just some starry-eyed kid who got screwed over. You take all those petty, backstabbing, power trippy games that happen when you get any group together, multiply it by a few centuries, and you end up with people who are too busy stroking their own egos and polishing their own reputations to ever find the motivation to take over the world."

Aloof, Gustaf spoke. "Have you ever met a vampire?"

"I know a couple," I said. "And they're individuals, just like anyone else. Which is probably *really* why they haven't taken over the world. They couldn't agree on anything. Aren't I right, Gustaf?"

Ariel said, "Sue, you're sounding just a bit angry about all this. Why is that?"

I hadn't expected the question. In fact, I'd kind of expected her to move onto the next call by now. But no, she was *probing*. Which left me to decide: Was I going to answer her question? Or blow it off? What would make her sound like an idiot, without making me sound like an idiot?

I suddenly realized: I hated being on this end of a radio show. But I couldn't stop now.

"Angry? I'm not angry. This isn't angry. This is *sarcastic.*"

"Seriously," Ariel said, not letting it go. "Our last caller practically worships vampires. Why are you so angry?"

Because I was stuck in the woods through nobody's fault but my own. Because somewhere along the way I'd lost control of my life.

"I'm tired of the stereotype," I said. "I'm tired of so many people buying into the stereotype."

"But you're not afraid of them. That anger doesn't come from fear."

"No, it doesn't," I said, hating the uncertainty in my own voice. I knew very well how dangerous vampires could be, especially when you came face-to-face with one in a dark room. I'd seen it firsthand. They *smelled* dangerous. And here she was promoting one like he was a damned philanthropist.

"Then what are you afraid of?"

Losing. I was afraid of losing. She had the show and I didn't. I was supposed to ask the difficult questions. What I said was, "I'm not afraid of anything."

Then I hung up.

I'd turned the radio off, so the cabin was silent. Part of me wanted to turn it back on and hear what Ariel said about my—or rather Sue's—abrupt departure, as well as what else Gustaf had to say about the inherent nobility of vampires. In a rare show of wisdom, I kept the radio off. Ariel and Gustaf could keep each other.

I started to throw the phone, and amazingly refrained. I was too tired to throw it.

Afraid. Who was she to accuse me of being afraid? The one with the radio show, that was who.

* * *

I couldn't sleep. Part of me was squirming with glee at the mighty blow I had struck against my competition. Er, mighty blow, or petty practical joke? I'd been like a kid throwing rocks at the old haunted house. I hadn't even broken Ariel's stride. I'd do better next time.

The truth was, I was reduced to crank calls, followed by bouts of insomnia.

Run. Let me go running.

Restlessness translated to need. Wolf was awake and wouldn't settle down. *Let's go, let's go—*

No.

This was what happened: I couldn't sleep, and the night forest beckoned. Running on four legs for a couple of hours would certainly wear me out to the point where I'd sleep like a rock. And wake up naked in the woods, kicking myself for letting it happen. I called the shots, not that other side of me.

I slept in sweatpants and a tank top. The air was dry with the heat and smell of ashes from the stove. I wasn't cold, but I huddled inside my blankets, pulling them firmly over my shoulders. I pulled a pillow over my head. I had to get to sleep.

I might even have managed it for a minute or two. I might have dreamed, but I couldn't remember about what. I did remember moving through cotton, trying to claw my way out of a maze of fibers, because something was wrong, a smell in the air, a noise that shouldn't have been there. When I should have only heard wind in the trees and an occasional snap of dry wood in the stove, I heard something else . . . rustling leaves, footsteps.

I dreamed of a wolf's footsteps as she trots through dead leaves on the forest floor. She is hunting, and she is very good. She is almost on top of the rabbit before it bolts. It only runs a stride before she pounces on it, bites it, and it screams in death—

The rabbit's scream was a horrible, high-pitched, gut-wrenching, teakettle whistlelike screech that should never come out of such an adorable fuzzy creature.

I jerked upright, my heart thudding fast, every nerve searing.

The noise had lasted only a second, then silence. It had come from right outside my door. I gasped for breath and listened: wind in the trees, a hiss of embers from the stove.

I pushed back the covers and stood from the bed.

Moving softly, barefoot on the wood floor, I went to the front room. My heartbeat wouldn't slow. *We may have to run, we may have to fight.* I curled my fingers, feeling the ghosts of claws. If I had to, I could shift to Wolf. I could fight.

I watched the window for movement outside, for shadows. I only saw the trees across the clearing, dark shapes edged with silver moonlight. I took a slow breath, hoping to smell danger, but the scent from the stove overpowered everything.

I touched the handle of the front door. I ought to wait until morning. I should wait until sunlight and safety. But something had screamed on my front porch. Maybe I'd dreamed it.

I opened the door.

There it was, lying stretched out in front of me. The scent of blood and bile hit me. The thing smelled like it had been gutted. The rabbit was stretched out, head thrown back, the fur of its throat and belly dark, matted, and ripped. The way it smelled, it ought to have been sitting in a pool of blood. It didn't even smell like rabbit— just guts and death.

My nose itched, nostrils quivering. I—the Wolf— could smell blood, the thick stuff from an animal that had died of deep wounds. I *knew* what that smelled like because I'd inflicted that kind of damage on rabbits. The blood was here, just not with the rabbit.

I opened the door a little wider and looked over.

Someone had painted a cross in blood on the outside of my front door.

chapter 3

I didn't go back to bed. Instead, I put a couple of new logs in the stove, poked at the fire until it blazed hot, wrapped myself in a blanket, and curled up on the sofa. I didn't know what bothered me more: that someone had painted a cross in blood on my door, or that I had no clue who had done it. I hadn't seen anything, heard anything after the rabbit's death cry, or smelled so much as a whiff of a breath mint. What was more, I didn't remember if I had only dreamed the rabbit's scream, or if I had really heard it. If it had been real, and crossed into my dream, or if my subconscious had made it up. Either way, it was like someone killed the rabbit, smeared blood on the door, and then vanished.

At first light, I called the police.

Two hours later, I sat cross-legged on the porch—on the far side, as far away from the rabbit as I could get—and watched the county sheriff and one of his deputies examine the door, the porch, the dead rabbit, and the clearing. Sheriff Avery Marks was a tired-looking middle-aged man, with thinning brown hair and a fresh uniform with a big parka over it. His examination consisted of standing on the porch, looking at the door for about five minutes, then crouching by the rabbit and looking at it for about five minutes, then standing on the ground, hands on hips, looking at the whole ensemble for about ten minutes. His deputy, a bearded guy in his thirties, wandered all around the cabin and the clearing in front of it, staring at the ground, snapping pictures, and writing in a notepad.

"You didn't hear anything?" Marks asked for the third time.

"I thought I heard the rabbit scream," I said. "But I was still asleep. Or half asleep. I don't really remember."

"You're saying you don't remember if you heard any-thing?" He sounded frustrated at my answers, and I couldn't blame him.

"I thought I heard something."

"About what time was that?"

"I don't know. I didn't look at the clock."

He nodded sagely. I had no idea what that information could have told him.

"I'm thinking this looks like some kind of practical joke," he said.

A joke? It wasn't funny. Not at all. "Would anyone around here think something like this was funny?"

"Ms. Norville, I hate to say it, but you're well known enough that you may be a target for this sort of thing."

You think? "So what are you going to do about it?"

"Keep an eye out. You see anything suspicious, you see anyone walking around here, let me know."

"Are you going to do *anything?*"

He eyed me and gave the condescending frown that experts reserved for the unenlightened. "I'll ask around, do some checking. This is a small community. Something'll turn up." He turned to the earnest deputy. "Hey, Ted, make sure you get pictures of those tire tracks." He was pointing at the ones leading away from my car.

This man had not inspired my faith.

"How—how am I supposed to clean all this up?" I asked. I was grateful for winter. The smell hadn't become too overpowering, and there were no flies.

He shrugged. "Hose it down? Bury the thing?"

This was like talking to a brick wall.

My cell phone rang inside the house; I could hear it from the porch. "I'm sorry, I should pick that up."

"You do that. I'll let you know when I find something." Marks and his deputy moved toward their car, leaving me alone with the slaughter. I felt oddly relieved by their imminent departure.

I dodged the rabbit, made it through the door without touching blood, and grabbed the phone. Caller ID said Mom. Her weekly call. She could have picked a better time. Strangely, though, I realized I needed to hear her voice.

"Hi," I said, answering the phone. I sounded plaintive. Mom would know something was wrong.

"Hi, Kitty. It's your mother. How are you?"

If I told her exactly what had happened, she'd be appalled. Then she'd demand that I come stay with her and Dad, where it was safe, even though I couldn't. I'd had to explain it a million times when I told her last month that I wasn't coming home for Christmas. I didn't have a choice: the Denver pack had exiled me. If I came back and they found out about it, they might not let me leave again. Not without a fight. A *big* fight. Mom still gave me endless grief. "We're in Aurora," she'd said. "Aurora isn't Denver, surely they'd understand." Technically she was right, Aurora was a suburb, but as far as the pack was concerned, Denver was everything within a hundred-mile radius.

I'd have to try to keep this short. Without lying outright. Damn.

"Oh, I've been better."

"What's wrong?"

"The book's not going as well as I'd like. I'm beginning to think coming here to get away from it all may have been a mistake."

"If you need a place, you can always stay here for as long as you need to."

Here we go again… "No, I'm okay. Maybe I'm just having a bad day." Bad week? Month?

"How are other things going? Have you been skiing?"

I had absolutely nothing to talk about. Nothing that I could talk about without getting hysterical, at least. "No, I haven't really thought about skiing. Everything's fine, it's fine. How are you doing? How is everyone?"

Mom launched in on the gossip. Everyone included Mom, Dad, my older sister Cheryl, her husband and two kids—a regular suburban poster family. Topics included office politics, tennis scores, first steps, first words, who went out to dinner where, which cousins were getting into what kind of trouble, and which of the great-aunts and -uncles were in the hospital. I could never keep any of it straight. But it sounded normal, Mom sounded happy, and my anxiety faded. She kept me in touch, kept me grounded. I may have exiled myself to the woods, but I still had a family, and Mom would call every Sunday like clockwork.

She brought the call to a close, making me promise to be careful, promise to call if I needed anything. I promised, like I did every week, no matter what kind of trouble I was in or what had been gutted on my front porch.

I left the conversation feeling a little better able to deal with the situation.

Hose it down, Sheriff Marks said. I went to get a bucket of water and a scrub brush. And a garbage sack.

The next few nights, I didn't sleep at all. I kept listening for footsteps, for the sound of another animal getting butchered on my front porch. The anxiety was killing me.

Human civilization was becoming less attractive every day. During daylight hours, I didn't even try to pound out a few pages of the memoir. I didn't even turn on the computer. I sat on the sofa and stared out the window. I could go out there and never come back. It would be so easy.

In the middle of another wakeful night, I heard something. I sat up, heart racing, wondering what was happening and what I was going to do about it. But it wasn't footsteps on the porch. Nothing screamed. I heard gravel crunching, the sound of a vehicle rolling up the drive to my cabin. My throat closed—I wanted to growl. Someone was invading my territory.

I got up and looked out the window.

A Jeep zoomed into the clearing, way too fast, swerving a little when the brakes slammed on.

Arms stiff, claws—fingers—curling, I went to the front door, opened it just enough to let me stand in the threshold, and glared out. If the invader challenged, I could face it.

But I knew that Jeep, and I knew the man climbing out of the driver's seat. Thirty-something, with light brown hair and a mustache, he wore a leather jacket, black T-shirt, and jeans, and carried a revolver in a holster on his belt. Cormac, the werewolf hunter. I'd never seen him panicked like this. Even from here I could tell he was breathing too fast, and he smelled like too much sweat.

Leaning on the hood, he came around to the front of the Jeep and shouted, "Norville!" He took a few steps away from the vehicle, glaring at me—challenging me, the Wolf couldn't help but think. His voice was rough. "Norville, get over here. I need your help." He pointed at the Jeep, as if that explained everything.

I didn't speak. I was too astonished. Too wary. He looked like someone getting ready to rush me, to attack, screaming. I knew he could kill me if he wanted to. I didn't move.

"Norville—Kitty, Jesus, what's wrong with you?"

I shook my head. I was caught up in some Wolf-fueled spell. I couldn't get over how weird this was. Suspicious, I said, "What's wrong with you?"

Anguish twisted his features. "It's Ben. He's been bitten."

"Bitten?" The word hit my gut and sent a tremor up my spine.

"Werewolf," he said, spitting the word. "He's been infected."

chapter 4

I ran to the Jeep. Cormac steered me to the passenger door, which he opened.

Ben sat there, relaxed, head slumped to the side—unconscious. Blood streaked the right half of his shirt. The fabric was torn at the shoulder, and the skin underneath was mauled. Individual tooth marks showed where the wolf had clamped its jaw over Ben's shoulder, and next to it a second wound—a messier, jagged chunk taken out of the flesh near his bicep—where the creature had found its grip and ripped. Ben's forearm also showed bite marks. He must have thrown his arm up to try to protect himself. All the wounds had stopped bleeding, were clotted, and beginning to form thick, black scabs. Cormac hadn't bandaged them, yet they were already healing.

They wouldn't have been, if it hadn't really been a werewolf that did this. If Ben hadn't really been infected with lycanthropy.

I covered my mouth with my hand and just stared, unwilling to believe the scene before me.

"I didn't know what else to do," Cormac said. "You have to help him."

Feeling—tingling, surreal, blood-pounding feeling—started to displace the numbness. "Let's get him inside."

I touched his neck—his pulse raced, like he'd been running and not slumped in the front seat for a five-hour car ride. Next, I brushed his cheek. The skin was burning, feverish. I expected that, because that was what had happened to me. He smelled sharp, salty, like illness and fear.

His head moved, his eyes crinkled. He made a sound, a half-awake grunt, turned toward my hand, and took a deep breath. His body went stiff, straightening suddenly, and as he pressed his head straight back his eyes opened.

"No," he gasped and started fighting, shoving me away, thrashing in a panic. He was starting to develop a fine sense of smell. I smelled different and his instincts told him *danger.*

I grabbed one arm, Cormac grabbed the other, and we pulled him out of the Jeep. Getting under his shoulder, I tried to support him, but he dropped his weight, yanking back to escape. I braced, holding him upright and managing to keep a grip on him. Cormac held on to him firmly, grimly dragging him toward the cabin.

Ben's eyes were open, and he stared in a wide-eyed panic at shadows, at the memory still fueling his nerves.

Then he looked right at Cormac. "Kill me," he said through gritted teeth. "You're supposed to kill me."

Cormac had Ben's arm over his shoulder and practically hauled him off his feet as we climbed the steps to the porch.

"Cormac!" Ben hissed, his voice a rough growl. "Kill me."

He just kept saying that.

I shoved through the open front door. "To the bedroom, in back."

Ben was struggling less, either growing tired or losing consciousness again. We went to the bedroom and hauled him onto the bed.

Ben writhed, then let out a noise that started as a whimper and rose to a full-blown scream. His body arced and thrashed, wracked with some kind of seizure. I held down his shoulders, leaning on him with all my weight, while Cormac pinned his legs.

I shifted my hands to hold on to his face, keeping his head still and making him look at me. His face was burning up, covered with sweat.

"Ben! Sh, quiet, quiet," I murmured, trying to be calm, trying to be soothing, but my own heart was in my throat.

Finally, I caught his gaze. He opened his eyes and looked at me, didn't look away. He quieted. "You're going to be okay, Ben. You're going to be fine, just fine."

I said the words by rote, without belief; I didn't know why I expected them to calm him down.

"Kitty." He grimaced, wincing, looking like he was going to scream again.

"Please, Ben, please calm down."

He closed his eyes, turned his face away—and then he relaxed, like a wave passing through his body. He stopped struggling.

"What happened?" Cormac said.

Ben was breathing, soft, quick breaths, and his heart still raced. I smoothed away the damp hair sticking to his forehead, turned his face toward me again. He didn't react to my touch.

"He passed out," I said, sighing.

Slowly, Cormac let up his grip on Ben's legs and sat back on the edge of the bed. Ben didn't move, didn't flinch. He looked sick, wrung out, too pale against the gray comforter, his hair damp and his shirt bloody. I was used to seeing him focused, driven, self-possessed. Not like this at all. I was always the one calling him for help.

How the hell had this happened?

I didn't ask Cormac that, not yet. The bounty hunter looked shell-shocked, his face slack, staring at Ben's prone form. He pressed his hands flat on his thighs. My God, were they shaking?

I unbuttoned Ben's shirt and wrangled it off him, carefully peeling the fabric away where the blood had dried, pasting it to his skin. The adrenaline was fading, leaving my limbs weak as tissue paper. My voice cracked when I said, "What was he saying? About you killing him? Cormac?"

Cormac spoke softly, in a strange, emotionless monotone. "We made a deal. When we were kids. It was stupid, the only reason we did it is because it was the kind of thing that would never happen. If either of us got bitten, got infected, the other was supposed to kill him. The thing is—" Cormac laughed, a harsh chuckle. "I knew if it happened to me Ben would never be able to go through with it. I wasn't worried, because I knew I could shoot myself just fine. But Ben—it was for him. Because he wouldn't have the guts to shoot himself, either. If it happened to him, I was supposed to take care of it. I'm the tough one. I'm the shooter. But I couldn't do it. I had my rifle right up against his skull and I couldn't do it. By that time he was screaming his head off and I had to knock him out to get him to stay in the Jeep."

I could picture it, too, Cormac's finger on the trigger, tensing, tensing again, then him turning away, a snarl on his lips. He was grimacing now.

Even at a whisper, my voice was shaking. "I'm glad you didn't shoot him."

"He's not."

"He will be."

"I brought him to you because I thought, you're a werewolf and you get along all right, and if he could be like you—he'd be okay. Maybe he'd be okay."

"He'll be okay, Cormac."

With his shirt off, Ben looked even more pale, more vulnerable. Half his arm was chewed up and scabbed over. His chest moved too rapidly, with short, gasping breaths.

"We should clean this up," I said. "He'll be out of it for a while. Maybe a couple of days."

"How do you know?" Cormac said.

"Because that's how it was with me. I was sick for days. Cormac..." I stood and moved next to him, reaching out, tentative because he looked like he might break, explode, or tear the room apart. He was the same kind of tense as a cat about to spring on a mouse. He still had the handgun in his belt holster. I had to make him look away from Ben. I touched his shoulder. When he didn't jump, flinch, or punch me, I lay my hand on his shoulder and squeezed.

He put his hand over mine, squeezed back, then stood and left the room, disappearing into the front of the house. I didn't hear the front door open, so he didn't leave. I didn't have time to worry about him right now.

Armed with a soaked washcloth and dry towel, I cleaned up the blood. The wounds, the bite marks and tears in his skin, had all closed over. They looked like week-old scabs, dried and ringed with pink. His skin was slick with sweat; I dried him off as well as I could. Within half an hour, Ben's breathing slowed, and he seemed to slip into a normal sleep. If he'd been in shock, the shock had faded. Nothing looked infected. The lycanthropy wouldn't let him sicken. It wouldn't let him die, at least not from a few bites.

I took off his shoes and covered him with a spare blanket. Smoothed his hair back one more time. For now, he was settled.

I found Cormac in the kitchen, leaning on the counter and staring out the window over the sink. The sun had risen since we'd brought Ben inside. The outline of the trees showed clear against a pale sky. I didn't think Cormac was really looking at any of that.

I started setting up the coffeemaker, being louder than I needed to be.

The strangeness was too much. Cormac gave me this image of him and Ben as kids, talking about werewolves— that wasn't exactly a kid thing to do. At least, not for real. Not meaning it. I'd always suspected Cormac was edging psychotic, but Ben was the levelheaded one, the lawyer. I'd always wondered how he took this world—lycanthropes, vampires, this B-grade horror film life I lived—in such stride, not even blinking. I'd been grateful for it, but I wondered. How long had *he* been living in it? Him and Cormac both?

I didn't know a damn thing about either of them.

I pushed the button, the light lit up, and the coffeemaker started burbling happily. I leaned back on the counter, watching Cormac, who hadn't moved. A minute later, the smell of fresh coffee hit with a jolt.

"Are you hungry?" I said finally. "I have some cereal, I think. A couple of eggs, bacon."

"No."

"Have you gotten any sleep?"

He shook his head.

"You think maybe you should?"

Again, he shook his head. Too bad. My day would be a lot easier if he'd just collapse on the sofa and sleep for the next twelve hours.

The coffee finished brewing. I poured two mugs and set one on the counter next to him. I held mine in both hands, feeling the warmth from it, not drinking. My stomach hurt too much to drink anything.

I had to say something. "How did it happen? How did you let him get—how did he get in a position to be bitten by a werewolf?"

He turned away from the window, crossed his arms, stared across the kitchen. I got my first good look at him since he arrived. He looked gaunt, caved in and exhausted, with shadows under his eyes. He hadn't shaved in days and was developing a beard to go along with his mustache. Dried blood flaked off his hands and spotted his shirt. He smelled of dirt, sweat, and blood. He needed a shower, though somehow I doubted that I could talk him into it.

"There were two of them," he said. "I knew there were two of them. That's why I called Ben, so he could watch my back. But the whole thing was messed up, right from the start. They were killing flocks of sheep, but nobody ever heard anything. I saw a whole field covered with dead sheep, all of them torn to pieces, and the herders sitting in their trailer a hundred feet away didn't hear a thing. Their dogs didn't hear a thing."

"How do you know werewolves did it?"

"Because the family hired me to kill the first one. They told me."

I shook my head. "Whoa, what?"

"The parents, the kid's parents."

"The wolf was a *kid?*"

"No, he was twenty years old! This is all coming out wrong."

"Then calm down. Start over." I held my coffee mug to my face and breathed in the steam. I had to calm down as well, if I expected Cormac to be civil. He was right on the edge.

"They knew he'd gone wolf, knew he was killing sheep, and they were afraid he'd start in on people. Nobody could control him so they called me."

"They just gave up on him? Their own son and they wanted him dead?"

"It's a different world there. Out in the desert, on the edge of Navajo Country. Shit like this happens and they look at it as evil. Pure evil, and the only thing to do with it is kill it. You've seen this kind of thing, you know they're right."

I had, and I did. I just hated to admit it. "What happened?"

"I knew his territory, knew how to find him, because he was going after livestock. But I got out there and found two sets of tracks. Werewolves are tough, but one of them couldn't have done that much damage on his own. His family didn't know there were two of them."

"Him, and the wolf who turned him?"

"Maybe. I don't know. They had no idea who the second one was. Or they wouldn't tell me. That was when I called Ben. The whole job was a mess, I should have just walked away. Too many details didn't fit—like the noise. These two had slaughtered three flocks by the time I got out there. Somebody should have heard something."

"How did you find them?"

"I left Ben by the Jeep, with a gun. He was on the hood, keeping a look out while I went to set bait."

I almost interrupted again. Bait? Is that how he hunted werewolves, with *bait*? But I didn't want to stop him—he might not start the story again.

"I found them right away. One of them. I shouldn't have, it was too easy. And it still wasn't right—the wolf had red eyes. I've seen plenty of wolves, wild ones and lycanthropes, and none of them have red eyes. But this thing—if it wasn't a werewolf I don't know what it was. I sure as hell didn't like it. I aimed my rifle at it—and then I couldn't move. I tried to shout to Ben, and I couldn't move. I couldn't even breathe. I've stared down werewolves before. I've never frozen up like that.

"I'd be dead, I'm sure that thing would have ripped out my throat if Ben hadn't fired just then. Then it was like somebody flipped a switch and I could move. And there was Ben, on the hood of the Jeep, with a wolf on top of him. I don't know if he shot at the thing and missed, or if it was just too fast for him. But it got him. He didn't even scream."

Sunlight covered the clearing outside my house, but Cormac, turned away from the window, was still gray with shadows.

"What did you do?" I whispered. I almost didn't dare breathe.

"I shot the wolf. It was a lucky shot, one in a million. I could have hit Ben instead."

"Then what happened?"

"The other wolf—the one in front of me—screamed. Not howled, not barked. Screamed like a human. Like a woman. I turned back and was going to kill it next, but it was already running. I shot at the thing but it got away."

"And the wolf you did hit?"

"It was the kid, the one I'd been hired to get. The shot knocked him right off the Jeep. When I got to him he was dying. I put a bullet in his head. He turned back to human. Just like he was supposed to."

He was right to do it. A cold, rational part of myself knew that a werewolf who couldn't control himself, who killed indiscriminately, was too dangerous, impossible to control within the legal system. What are you going to do, call the cops and stick him in jail? Strangely enough, that rational part of myself included a little bit of the Wolf, who knew exactly what to do when one of our kind got out of line. Only one thing *to* do. To my human side, to my gut emotional level, it still looked like murder. I couldn't reconcile the two views.

"And Ben?"

"I brought him here. That's the whole story." He drew in a slow breath and let it out with a sigh. "He's not cut out for this shit. He never was."

"Then why did you drag him into it?" My voice was stiff with anger.

For the first time, Cormac looked at me. "He's the only one in the world I trust." He walked to the doorway to the bedroom, leaned on the frame, and stared in.

It wasn't true, that Ben was the only one he trusted. If that were true he wouldn't have brought Ben here. But I didn't say that.

Cormac straightened from the door. "You mind if I crash out on the sofa?"

"Be my guest," I said, trying to smile like a gracious hostess.

"I'll get my bedroll out of the Jeep." He went to the front door and opened it.

Then he stopped. He stared for a long time, holding the knob, not moving.

"What?" I set down my coffee and went to look out the door.

There on the porch lay another dead rabbit, gutted like the first. I wasn't surprised when I looked at the outside of the door and found a cross made of smeared blood, fresh blood covering the stained outlines of the old cross. It hadn't been there when Cormac got here with Ben. They hadn't been here that long, maybe an hour. So this had happened within the hour, and this time I hadn't heard a thing. Of course, I'd been a little preoccupied.

I groaned. "Not again."

Cormac glanced at me. "Again? How many times have you been animal sacrifice central?"

I went outside, smelling the air, staring at the ground, looking for footprints, for anything that showed someone had been here, how this had happened. But the blood and guts might have appeared out of thin air, for all the evidence I saw. I stood on the porch, circling, studying the clearing, the house, everything, which even in the morning light had taken on a sinister cast. The place didn't feel cozy anymore.

"I wanted *Walden* and got *Evil Dead*," I grumbled. I faced Cormac. "This is the second one. You have any idea what it means?"

The scene seemed to pull him out of his recent trauma. He sounded genuinely fascinated when he said, "I don't know. If I had to guess I'd say you've been cursed."

In more ways than I cared to count. I went back inside. "I'm going to call the sheriff."

He moved out to the porch, stepping carefully around the rabbit corpse, and said, "Let me hide my guns someplace first."

Cursed. Right. Cursed didn't begin to describe my life at the moment.

I had to explain Cormac to Sheriff Marks. "He's a friend. Just visiting," I said. Marks gave me that look, the judgmental *none of my business what folks do in the privacy of their own homes* look that left no doubt as to what he *thought* was going on in the privacy of my own home. For his part, Cormac stood on the porch, leaning against the wall of the house, watching the proceedings with an air of detached curiosity. He'd hidden his arsenal—three rifles, four handguns of various shapes and sizes, and a suitcase-sized lock box that held who knew what—under the bed. *My* bed.

Marks and Deputy Ted repeated their search and found just as little as they had the first time.

"Here's what I'll do. I'll post a deputy out here for a couple nights," Marks said, after he'd wrapped up. "I'll also put a call in to somebody I know in the Colorado Springs PD. He's a specialist in satanism and cult behavior. Maybe he'll know if any groups operate in this area."

"If it were satanists, wouldn't the cross be upside down or something?"

His expression of frowning disapproval turned even more disapproving.

"Sheriff, don't you think I'm being targeted because of who I am?" *What* I am, I should have said.

"That's a possibility. We'll have to take all the facts into account."

Suddenly I felt like the bad guy. It was that part of being a victim that made a person ask, what did I do to bring this on myself?

"We'll start our stakeout tonight. Have a better morning, ma'am." Marks and Ted headed back to their car and drove away, leaving me with another mess on my porch.

Cormac nodded toward the departing car. "Small-town cop like him don't know anything about this."

"Do you?"

"It's blood magic."

"Well, yeah. What kind? Who's doing it?"

"Who've you pissed off lately?" He had the gall to smile at me.

I leaned on the porch railing and sighed. "I have no idea."

"We'll figure it out. You got a shovel and garden hose? I'll take care of this."

That was something, anyway. "Thanks."

When I looked in on Ben again, he'd rolled to his side and curled up, pulling the blankets tightly over his shoulder. Color was coming back into his skin, and the scabs on his wounds were healing. I touched his forehead; he still had a fever. He was still shivering.

The room smelled strange. It was filled with the scents of sweat and illness, with Ben's own particular smell that included hints of the clothes he wore, his aftershave and toothpaste. And something else. His smell was changing, something wild and musky creeping into the mundane smells of civilization. I'd always thought of it as fur under the skin—the scent of another lycanthrope. Right here in the room with me. My lycanthropic self, my own Wolf, perked up, shifted within my senses, curious. She wanted the measure of him: *friend, rival, enemy, alpha, same pack, different pack, who?*

Friend. I hoped he was still a friend when he woke up.

I made him drink some water. With Cormac's help I lifted his shoulders, held his head up, and tipped a glass to his mouth. As much spilled out as went in, but his throat moved, and he drank a little. He didn't wake up, but he stirred, squeezing his eyes shut and groaning a little. I shushed him, hoping he stayed asleep. He needed to rest while his body sorted itself out.

Then I made Cormac eat something. He wouldn't tell me when he'd last eaten, when he'd last slept. It might have been days. I made bacon and eggs. I hadn't yet met a meat eater who could resist bacon and eggs. Whatever else he was, Cormac was a meat eater.

After breakfast, he spread his sleeping bag on the sofa and lay down. Broad daylight outside, and he rolled over on his side and fell asleep instantly, his breathing turning deep and regular. I envied that ability to sleep anywhere, anytime.

I sat at my desk, because I didn't have anywhere else to sit, but I didn't turn on the computer. I rubbed my face, hugged my head, and leaned on the table.

I didn't think I could take it anymore. I'd reached my limit. If ever there was a time when turning wolf and running away sounded like a good idea, this was it.

"Norville?"

Startled, I straightened, looked. Cormac wasn't asleep after all. He'd propped himself on one elbow.

"Thank you," he said.

I stared back, meeting his gaze. I saw exhaustion there. Hopelessness. I'd told him Ben would be okay, but I wondered if he'd believed it.

"You're welcome." What else could I say?

He rolled over, putting his back to me, and went to sleep.

chapter 5

I turned on the computer and wrote. Typing whatever came into my head, I wrote about the random shocks of life, the events that brought friends to your doorstep begging for help, even when you felt that your own life had tumbled irrevocably out of control. You did what you had to do, somehow. You kept racing ahead and hoped for the best. I wrote about being at the end of my rope and made a list of the reasons I had to stay human. Chocolate, as always, was near the top of the list. I was in the kitchen eating chocolate chip cookies when Cormac woke up, after dark.

I was looking out the kitchen window, to where Deputy Ted's patrol car was parked at the end of the road, hidden in the trees. I spotted him when he turned on his dome light to eat a sandwich.

Cormac sat up, rubbed his face, then stretched, twisting his back, pulling his arms up. Something cracked. "What're you looking at?"

"Take a look," I said. "You'll like this."

He came to the kitchen area, and I moved aside to give

him room to look out the window. The deputy still had his light on, making his car a glowing beacon among the trees.

Cormac made a derisive grunt. "They're not going to catch anyone if that's how they run a stakeout."

With the cop sitting there, nobody would come within a mile of my place to lay any sort of curse. Nobody smart, anyway. "At least I won't have rabbit guts all over my porch in the morning."

"You're a werewolf, I thought you'd like that sort of thing. Fresh meat, delivered right to your door. Maybe it's a secret admirer."

"I like picking out my own dead meat, thanks."

"I'll remember that."

He crossed his arms, leaned on the counter, and looked at me. I blinked back, trying to think of a clever response. Finally, I offered him the bag I was holding. "Cookie?"

He shook his head at it. "How's Ben?"

"Asleep. How are you?"

"Feeling stupid. I keep thinking of everything I should have done different."

"That's not like you. You're a head down, guns blazing, full steam ahead kind of guy. Not one to dwell in the past."

"You don't know anything about me."

I shrugged, conceding the point. "So what's the story? You know all about my dark past. I don't know anything about yours."

"You're fishing," he said and smirked.

"Can't blame a girl for trying."

"Save it for your show."

Ouch. If only I were doing the show. It occurred to me

to consider how big a favor I would have to do for Cormac before I could talk him into coming on the show for an interview, if taking in him and Ben in their hour of need didn't do it.

Cormac pulled himself from the counter. "You have a bathroom in this place?"

"In the bedroom."

He stalked off to find it. A minute later, the shower started up. At least he'd be clean.

I found my cell phone, dialed the number I wanted, and went outside. The air was cool, energizing. The inside of the house had become stifling. I sat on the porch and put my back against the wall.

A woman answered, "Hello?"

"Hi, Mom."

"Kitty! What a nice surprise. Is everything all right?"

"Why wouldn't it be?"

"Because you never call unless something's happened."

I sighed. She had a point. "I've had kind of a rough couple of days."

"Oh, I'm sorry. What's wrong?"

Between the extracurricular shape-shifting, animal sacrifices on my front porch, my lawyer getting attacked by a werewolf, and a werewolf hunter camping out in my living room, I didn't know where to start. I didn't think I should start.

"A lot of stuff. It's complicated."

"I worry about you being out there all by yourself. Are you sure you don't want to come home for a little while? You've had such a busy year, I think it would be good for you to not have to worry about things like rent."

Strangely enough, rent was one of the few things I wasn't worried about. As much as going back to my parents' and having Mom take care of me for a little while sounded like a good idea, it wasn't an option. Not that Mom would have understood that.

"I'm actually not by myself at the moment," I said, trying to sound positive. "I have a couple of friends staying over."

"That should be fun."

If I would just break down and tell Mom the truth, be straight with her, these conversations would be much less surreal. I'd called her because I needed to hear a friendly voice; I didn't want to tell her all the gory details.

"Yeah, sure. So how are you? How are Dad and Cheryl?"

She relayed the doings of the family since her last call—more of the same, but at least somebody's world was normal—and finished by turning the questions back on me, "How is the writing going?"

"It's fine," I said brightly. If I sounded like everything was okay, maybe it would be, eventually. "I think I've gotten over the writer's block."

"Will you be starting your show again soon? People ask me about it all the time."

I winced. "Maybe. I haven't really thought about it."

"We're so proud of you, Kitty. So many people only ever dream of doing what you've done. It's been so much fun watching your success."

She couldn't have twisted the knife any harder if she'd tried. I was such a success, and here I was flushing it down the toilet. But she really did sound proud, and happy. To think at one point I'd been worried that she'd be scandalized by what I was doing.

I took a deep breath and kept my voice steady. Wouldn't do any good to break down now. "Thanks, Mom. That means a lot."

"When are you finally coming to visit?"

"I'm not sure... you know, Mom, it's been great talking to you, but I really need to get going."

"Oh, but you only just called—"

"I know, I'm really sorry. But I told you I have friends staying, right?"

"Then you'd better get back to it. It's good to hear from you."

"Say hi to Dad for me."

"I will. We love you."

"Love you, too."

I sat on the porch for a long time, the phone sitting in my lap. I was looking for someone to lean on. Cormac and Ben showed up with all this, and I wasn't sure I could handle it. Wolves were supposed to run in packs. I was supposed to have help for something like this. But I didn't have anyone. I went back inside, back to my milk and cookies.

From the bedroom, the shower shut off. Ten minutes or so later, Cormac, hair damp and slicked back, came into the front room. He'd shaved, leaving only his familiar, trademark mustache. He was cinching on his belt and gun holster.

"I'm going to help Rosco out there with his stakeout. Do a little hunting around on my own." The contempt in his voice was plain. He was restless; I hadn't really expected him to stay in bed for twelve hours.

"Be careful."

He gave me a funny look, brows raised. "Really?"

Exasperated, I sighed. "I wouldn't want him to shoot you because he thinks you're the bad guy."

"Who says I'm not?"

Wincing, I rubbed my forehead. "I'm too tired to argue with you about it."

"Get some sleep," he said. "Take the sofa."

"Where'll you sleep?"

"The floor, if I decide I need it. You looked after Ben all day, I'll keep an eye on him tonight. Take the sofa."

This cabin was *not* built for three people who weren't actually all sleeping together.

"Fine." I'd lost a lot of sleep over the last couple of days and was tired. Before I trudged over to the sofa, I faced Cormac. "If Ben wakes up, tell me, okay? He'll be confused, I'll need to talk to him."

"I'll wake you up. Don't worry."

"I can't stop worrying. Sorry."

"Go to sleep, Norville." He raised his hand, started to reach out—for a moment, he seemed about to touch me. I braced for it, my heartbeat speeding up—what was he doing? But he turned around and left the cabin before anything happened.

Slowly, I sat on the sofa, then wrapped myself in the blanket. The cushions were ancient, far too squishy to be comfortable. But it wasn't the floor, so I lay down.

This was a mistake, I thought as I fell asleep. Cormac and I staying in the same house—absolutely a mistake.

I woke up to find Cormac putting a log into the stove. I didn't feel cold. I probably would have let the fire burn out. Outside the window, the sky was pale. It was morning again already. He closed the door to the stove, then sat back on the rug and watched the flames through the tiny grill in front.

I hadn't moved, and he hadn't noticed that I was awake, watching him. Shadows still darkened his eyes, and his hair had dried ruffled. He'd taken off his jacket and boots—and the gun belt. He wore a black T-shirt and jeans. His arms were pale, muscular.

Suddenly he looked over and caught my gaze staring back.

I stilled the fluttering in my stomach and tried not to react. Just stay cool.

"Is 'Rosco' still out there?" I said.

"Yeah. He fell asleep around two A.M. I expect he'll wake up soon and get out of here."

"And no dead animal on my porch?"

"None."

I turned my face into the pillow and giggled. "If it weren't happening to me, this would be downright hilarious."

"I did find this." He held out his hand.

I looked at it first, then gingerly opened my hand to accept it. It was a cross made of barbed wire, a single strand twisted back on itself, about the length of my finger. The steel was smooth, the barbs sharp. Not worn or rusted, which meant this hadn't been sitting outside for very long.

"You think this is from my sacrificial fan club?"

"Could be. If so, the question is Did they leave it on purpose, or did they just drop it? If it's on purpose, then it means something. It's supposed to do something."

"What?"

"I don't know."

I could almost feel malevolence seeping out of the thing. Or maybe the barbs just looked scary. "What am I supposed to do with it?"

"I recommend finding somebody with a forge and have them melt the thing into slag. Just in case."

He thought it was cursed, and he brought the thing into my house? I groaned with frustration. I wanted to throw it, but I set it on the floor instead.

"Why a cross?"

"There's a dozen magic systems that borrow from Christianity. This part of the country, it might be an evangelical sect, or maybe some kind of *curandero*."

"*Curandero*. Mexican folk healer, right?"

"They do all kinds of stuff. Sometimes, they go bad."

"You know a lot about this sort of thing."

"It helps, knowing as much as I can. The people who hire me—they're believers. They have to believe in werewolves and magic to call me in the first place. The symbols may be different, the rituals are different, but they all have one thing in common: they believe in the unbelievable. You know what I'm talking about. You're one of them. One of the believers."

"I only believe because of what I am. I don't know anything about any of it."

"Hell, I don't know anything. This is just scratching the surface. There's a whole world of freaky shit out there."

He was being uncharacteristically chatty. I didn't know if it was stress or sleeplessness. Maybe something about sitting in a tiny cabin in front of a wood-burning stove on a cold morning made people personable.

"How did you find out about the freaky shit? I found out the morning after I was attacked—the whole pack stood there telling me, 'Welcome to the family, have fun.' But who told you?"

He smiled, but the expression was thin and cold. "I don't remember anyone telling me werewolves are real. I've always known. My family—we've been hunting lycanthropes for over a hundred years. My dad taught me."

"How old were you when he died?"

He looked sharply at me. "Who told you he died?"

"Ben."

"Bastard," Cormac muttered.

"That was all he said," I said quickly. "I asked how you two met and if you'd always been so humorless, and he said you had a right to be humorless. I asked why and he told me."

He was staring at me, and I didn't like it. Among wolves, a stare was a challenge. The thought of a challenge from Cormac made the wolf inside me cringe in terror. I couldn't fight Cormac. I looked away, hugging the blanket tightly around me.

"You still talk too much, you know that?" Cormac said.

"I know."

Finally, he said, "I was sixteen. I moved in with Ben and his folks after my dad died. His mother was my dad's sister."

"Then Ben knew, too. He was part of the family history."

"Hard to say. I think Aunt Ellen was just as happy to leave it all behind. Jesus, what am I going to tell her?"

"Nothing," I said wryly. "At least not until the full moon falls on Christmas and Ben has to explain why he's not coming home for the holidays."

"Spoken with the voice of experience."

"Yup. If Ben wasn't in on the werewolf hunting from the start, how did you drag him into it?"

"I didn't drag him—"

"Okay, how did you get him started in it?"

"Why do you want to know all this stuff about me?"

"You're interesting."

Cormac didn't say anything to that, just went back to staring at me with a little too much focus.

I said, "Could you not look at me like that? It's making me nervous."

"But you're interesting."

Oh, my. That clenching feeling in my gut wasn't fear—not this time.

I'd kissed Cormac once. It had been another situation like this. We were sitting and talking, and I let the urge overcome my better judgment. And he kissed back, for about a second, before he marched out of the room, calling me a monster.

Too many incidents like that could give a girl a complex.

He wasn't running away this time.

I swung my legs over the edge of the couch and slipped to the floor. I ended up kneeling in front of him, where he was sitting, close enough to grab. And he still didn't run. In fact, he didn't move at all, like he was waiting for me to come to him. How did wolves do this? Weren't the boys supposed to chase the girls? He wasn't a wolf, though. He wouldn't understand the signals.

Wolf was uncurling, overcoming her anxiety. Yeah, he was scary. Yeah, he was tough. That meant he could protect us. That was enough for her. That, and he smelled like he wanted me. He radiated warmth, and had a tang of sweat that wasn't even visible. A tension held him still as stone. All I had to do was touch him and break him out of his immobility. I raised my hand.

"I—I can smell you." The voice was low and painfully hoarse.

I must have jumped a foot. My heart raced like a jack-hammer and I got ready to run.

Ben stood in the doorway to the bedroom, leaning against the wall. Still shirtless, his skin was pale, damp with sweat, and his hair was tangled. He only half opened his eyes, and he winced with what looked like confusion, like he didn't know where he was.

"I can smell everything," he said, sounding like he had bronchitis. He touched his forehead; his hand was shaking.

"Ben." I rushed to him, intending to take his arm and steer him back to bed. He wasn't well, he shouldn't have been up.

As soon as I touched him, though, he flinched back. He crashed against the wall, his face stiff with terror. "No, you smell—you smell wrong—"

His new instincts identified me as another werewolf—a potential threat.

I turned to call Cormac, but he was already beside Ben, holding his arm, trying to keep him still.

"No, Ben. I'm safe. It's all right. Take a deep breath. Everything's okay." I tried to hold his face still, to make him smell me, to make him recognize that scent as friendly, but he lurched away. He would have fallen if Cormac hadn't been holding him.

I put myself next to him again, intending to help drag him to the bed. This time, Ben leaned closer to me, squint-ing as if trying to focus. His eyesight was changing, too.

"Kitty?"

"Yeah, it's me," I said, relieved that he'd recognized me.

He slumped against me, resting his head on my shoulder, like he wanted to hug me. He found my hand and squeezed it tightly. "I don't remember what happened. I don't remember any of it," he murmured into my shirt.

Except that he remembered that something had happened, and that he should have remembered. A lot of his agitation was probably stress—the anxiety that came from blocking out the trauma.

I held him still for a moment, whispering nonsense comforts at his ear until he stopped shaking. Cormac, looking stiff and awkward, was still propping him upright.

"Come on, Ben. Back to bed." He nodded, and I pulled his arm over my shoulder. Between us, Cormac and I walked him back to the bed. He sank onto it and fell back to sleep almost immediately. He kept hold of my hand. I waited until I was sure he was asleep, his breathing deep and regular, before I coaxed back his fingers and extricated myself from his grip.

Cormac stood at the end of the bed, ran his hands through his hair, and blew out a frustrated sigh. "Is this normal?"

I smoothed back the damp hair from Ben's face. "I don't know, I only know what I went through. I slept through the whole thing. At least, I only remember sleeping through the whole thing. I was hurt a lot worse than he is, though." I'd had my hip mauled and half my leg flayed. Not that I had any scars to prove it.

"Don't lie to me. Is he going to be okay?"

He kept asking me that. "What do I look like, some kind of fortune-teller? I don't know."

"What do you mean you don't know?"

I glared at him, and part of the Wolf stared out of my eyes. I made the challenge and I didn't care if he could read it or not. "His body will be fine. Physically, he's healing. Mentally—that's up to him. We won't know until he wakes up if this is going to drive him crazy or not."

Cormac scrubbed a hand down his face and started pacing. Tension quivered along his whole body; sheer willpower was keeping him from breaking something.

"Ben's tough," he said finally. "This won't drive him crazy. He'll be okay. He'll be fine." He said the words like they were a mantra. Like if he said them enough they'd have to be true.

My glare melted into a look of pity. I wished I could find the right thing to say to calm him down. To convince him that yes, he'd done all he could. Cormac had never been weak. He'd never been this helpless, I'd bet. I wondered if I'd have to worry about him going crazy, too.

Crazier than he already was.

Cormac left the room, and a moment later I heard the front door open and slam shut. I didn't run after him—I didn't dare leave Ben alone. I listened for the Jeep starting up, but it didn't. Cormac wasn't abandoning me to this mess. Maybe he just needed to take a walk.

I brought the laptop into the bedroom, pulled a chair next to the bed, kept watch over Ben, and wrote.

I wouldn't have wished lycanthropy on anyone, much less a friend. Life was hard enough without having something like this to deal with. I'd seen the whole range of how people handled it. In some people, the strength and near-invulnerability went to their heads. They became bullies, reveling in the violence they were capable of.

People who were already close to psychosis tumbled over the edge. One more mental handicap to deal with was too much. Some people became passive, letting it swallow them. And some people adapted. They made adjustments, and they stayed themselves.

I regretted that I didn't know enough about Ben to guess which way he'd go.

My cell phone rang, and I fielded the call from Sheriff Marks.

"The deputy I had on the stakeout didn't see any sign of your perpetrator," he informed me.

"You know he had the interior light on in his car half the time he was out here?" I replied.

Marks was silent for a long time, and picturing the look on his face made me grin. "I'll have a talk with him," he said finally. "I'll try to have someone out there tonight, too. You let me know if you see anything."

"Absolutely, Sheriff," I said.

Hours passed, dusk fell, and Cormac still hadn't returned. I decided not to worry. He was a big boy, he could take care of himself. I certainly wasn't capable of babysitting both him and Ben.

Ben hadn't stirred since the last time he passed out. I had no idea how long he had to stay like this before I had to start worrying. When I did start worrying, who was I supposed to call for help? The werewolf pack that had kicked me out of Denver? The Center for the Study of Paranatural Biology, the government research office that was undergoing reorganization after its former director disappeared—not that I knew anything about that.

I stared at the laptop screen for so long I started to doze off. The words blurred, and even though the straight-backed kitchen chair I sat in wasn't particularly comfortable, I managed to curl up and let my head nod forward.

That was when Ben spoke. "Hi."

He didn't sound delirious or desperate. A little hoarse still, but it was the scratchy voice of someone getting over a cold. He lay on the bed and looked at me. One of his arms rested over the blanket that covered him, his fingers gripping the edge.

I slid out of the chair, set the laptop aside, and moved to the edge of the bed.

"Hey," I said. "How do you feel?"

"Like crap."

I smiled a little. "You should. You've had a crappy week."

He chuckled, then coughed. I almost jumped up and down and started dancing. It was Ben. Ben was back, he hadn't gone crazy.

"You seem awfully happy about my crappy week."

"I'm happy to see you awake. You've been out of it."

"Yeah." He looked away, studying the walls, the ceiling, the blanket covering him. Looking everywhere but at me.

"How much do you remember?" I asked.

He shook his head, meaning that he either didn't remember anything or he wasn't going to tell me. I watched him, feeling anxious and motherly, wanting simultaneously to tuck the blankets in tighter, pat his head, bring him a glass of water, and feed him. I wanted him to relax. I wanted to make everything better, and I didn't have the faintest idea how to do that. So I hovered, perched next to him, on the verge of wringing my hands.

Then he said, his voice flat, "Why did Cormac bring me here?"

"He thought I could help."

"Why didn't he just shoot me?"

As far as I knew, Cormac's guns were still under the bed. *This* bed. Ben didn't have to know that. What if Cormac was wrong, what if Ben did have the guts to shoot himself? What would I have to do to stop him? I couldn't let Ben die. I wouldn't let him—or Cormac—give up.

I spoke quietly, stiff with frustration. "You'll have to ask him."

"Where is he?"

"I don't know. He went out."

His gaze focused on me again, finally. A glimmer of the old Ben showed through. "How long have I been out of it?"

"A couple of days."

"And you two have been stuck here together the whole time?" His face pursed with thoughtfulness. "How's that working out?"

"He hasn't killed me yet."

"He's not going to kill you, Kitty. On the contrary, I think he'd rather—"

I stood suddenly. "Are you hungry? Of course you're hungry, you haven't eaten in two days."

Footsteps pounded up the porch then. Ben looked over to the next room at the same time I did, and his hand clenched on the blanket. Slowly, I went to the front room.

The door slammed open, and Cormac stood there. He carried a rifle.

"You have a freezer, right?" he said.

"Huh?" I blinked, trying to put his question into context. I failed. "Yeah. Why?"

He pointed his thumb over his shoulder to the outside.

I went to the door and looked out. There, in the middle of the clearing in front of the cabin, lay a dead deer. Just flopped there, legs stiff and neck arced back. No antlers. I couldn't see blood, but I could smell it. Still cooling. Freshly killed. My stomach rumbled, and I fiercely ignored it.

"It's a deer," I said stupidly.

"I still have to dress it and put the meat up. Is there room in the freezer?"

"You killed it?"

He gave me a frustrated glare. "Yeah."

"Is it even hunting season?"

"Do you think I care?"

"You shot a deer and just... dragged it here? Carried it? Why?"

"I had to shoot something."

I stared at him. That sounded like me. Rather it sounded like me once a month, on the night of the full moon. "You had to shoot something."

"Yeah." He said the word as a challenge.

So which of us was the monster? At least I had an excuse for my bloodlust.

"Ben's awake," I said. "Awake and lucid, I mean."

In fact, Ben was standing in the doorway, holding a blanket wrapped around his shoulders. His hair was ruffled, stubble covered his jawline, and he appeared wrung-out, but he didn't seem likely to topple over. He and Cormac looked at each other for a moment, and the tension in the room spiked. I couldn't read what passed between them. I had an urge to get out of there. I imagined calling in to my own radio show: *Yeah hi, I'm a werewolf, and I'm stuck in a cabin in the woods with another werewolf and a werewolf hunter...*

"Hey," Cormac said finally. "How are you feeling?"

"I don't know," Ben said. "What's the gun for?"

"Went hunting."

"Any luck?"

"Yeah."

My voice came out bright with false cheerfulness. "Maybe you could cut us up a couple of steaks right now and we could have some dinner."

"That's the plan. If you can stoop to eating meat that someone else picked out," he said. "Oh, and I found another one of these." He tossed something at me.

Startled, I reached for it—then thought better of it and stepped out of the way. Good thing, too, because a piece of barbed wire clattered on the floor. It was bent into the shape of a cross, like the other, which was still lying on the floor by the stove. I kicked the new one in that direction.

Ben moved toward the front door, stepping slowly like he was learning to walk again.

Cormac could change his mind, I thought absently. He gripped the rifle, all he had to do was raise it and fire, and he could kill Ben. Ben didn't seem to notice this, or didn't think it was a danger. Or just didn't care. All his attention was on the front door, on the outside. Cormac let him pass, and Ben went out to the porch.

I went after him.

He stared at the deer. Just stared, clutching the blanket around him and shivering like he was cold, though I didn't think the chill in the air was that sharp.

"I can smell it," he said. "All the way in the bedroom, I could smell it. It smells good. It shouldn't, but it does."

Fresh blood spilled on the ground, hot and rich, seeping out of cooling meat and crunchy, marrow-filled bones—I knew exactly what he was talking about. My mouth would be watering, if I wasn't so nervous.

"It's because you're hungry," I said softly.

"I could eat it right now, couldn't I? If I wanted, I could eat it raw, skin and all—"

"Come inside, Ben. Please. Cormac'll take care of it."

Ben stood so tautly, his whole body rigid, I was afraid that if I touched him he'd snap at me, and I didn't know if his snapping would be figurative or literal. Something animal was waking in him; it lurked just under the surface.

Very gently, I touched his arm. "Come on."

Finally, he looked away from the deer. He turned, and let me guide him inside.

Hours later, Cormac stacked cuts of wrapped venison in the freezer, while I pulled steaks out of the broiler. Turned out everyone here liked them rare. Go figure.

Cormac came in from cleaning up outside and went to the kitchen sink to wash his hands. "Tomorrow I'll find someone to take care of the hide. The rest of it I buried—"

"I don't want to know what you did with the rest of it," I said, giving him a "stop" gesture while I took plates out of the cupboard.

"Come on, it's not like you haven't seen any of it before. In fact, you might have offered some help."

"I don't know anything about dressing a deer for real. I usually just rip into it with my teeth."

Ben sat at the kitchen table, staring blankly at the table-top. Cormac had given him a change of clothes, but he still wrapped himself with the blanket. I tried not to be worried.

He needed time to adjust. That was all. Not having him take part in the banter was weird, though.

The table, an antique made of varnished wood with a couple of matching straight-backed chairs, was small, barely big enough for two people, totally inadequate for three. After I arranged the steaks on plates, Cormac picked up his and stayed put, eating while standing by the counter. I brought the other two plates to the table. I set one, along with a set of utensils, in front of Ben. His gaze shifted, startled out of whatever reverie he'd been in, and tracked the food.

Determined not to hover, I sat down with my own meal. I couldn't help it, though; I watched him closely.

Meat looks different to a werewolf. I didn't used to be much of a meat eater at all. I used to be the kind of person who went to a steakhouse and ordered a salad. But after I was attacked, and I woke up and had a look at my first steak, so rare that it was bleeding all the way through—I could have swallowed the thing whole. I'd wanted to, and the thought had made me ill. It had been so strange, being hungry and nauseous at the same time. I'd almost burst into tears, because I'd realized that I was different, right through to the bones, and that my life would never be the same.

What would Ben do?

After a moment, he picked up the fork and knife and calmly sliced into the meat, and calmly put the bite into his mouth, and calmly chewed and swallowed. Like nothing was wrong.

We might have been having a calm, normal meal. Three normal people eating their normal food—except for the spine-freezing tension that made the silence painful. The scraping of knives on plates made my nerves twinge.

Ben had eaten half his steak when he stopped, resting the fork and knife at the edge of the plate. He remained staring down when he asked, "How long?"

"How long until what?" I said, being willfully stupid. I knew exactly what he was talking about.

He spoke in almost a whisper. "How long until the full moon?"

"Four days," I said, equally subdued.

"Not long."

"No."

"I can't do it," he said, without any emotion. Just an observation of fact.

He was making this hard. I didn't know what else I expected. He'd acquired a chronic disease, not won the lottery. Ben wasn't a stranger to the supernatural. He was coming into this with his eyes wide open. He'd seen a werewolf shape-shift—on video, at least. He knew exactly what would happen to him when the full moon rose.

"Everyone says that," I said, frustration creeping into my voice. "But you can. If I can do it, you can do it."

"Cormac?" Ben said, looking at his cousin.

"No," the hunter said. "I didn't do it then and I won't do it now. Norville's right, that isn't the way."

Ben stared at him a moment, then said, "I swear to God, I never thought I'd hear you say anything like that." Cormac looked away, but Ben continued. "Your father would have done it in a heartbeat. Hell, what if he'd survived? You know he'd have shot himself."

My mind tripped over that one entirely. My mouth, as usual, picked up where intelligent thought failed. "Whoa, wait a minute. Hold on a minute. Cormac—your father. Your father was killed by a werewolf? Is that what he's saying?"

We embarked on a three-way staring contest: Cormac glared at Ben, Ben glared back, and I glared back and forth between them. Nobody said anything until Cormac spoke, his voice cool as granite.

"You know where my guns are. You want it done, do it yourself."

He walked out of the kitchen, to the front door, then out into the night, slamming the door behind him.

Ben stared after him. I was about ready to scream, because he still wasn't saying anything.

"Ben?"

He started eating again, methodically cutting, chewing, swallowing, watching his plate the whole time.

I, on the other hand, had lost my appetite. I pushed my plate away and comforted myself with the knowledge that if Ben was eating, he probably wouldn't kill himself. At least not right this minute.

After supper, Ben went back to bed and passed out again. Still sick, still needing time to mend. Or maybe he was avoiding the situation. I didn't press the issue. In the continued absence of Cormac, I took the sofa. Dealing with Ben had exhausted me. I needed to get some sleep. Or maybe I was just avoiding the situation.

I fervently hoped Cormac wasn't out shooting another deer. My freezer couldn't handle it.

I dreamed of blood.

I stood in a clearing, on a rocky hill in the middle of the forest. I recognized the place; it was near the cabin. When I turned my face up, blood rained from the sky. It poured onto my face, ran across my cheeks, down my neck, matting my fur. I was covered in fur, but I couldn't tell if I was wolf or human. Both, neither. The forest smelled like slaughter. Red crosses marked the trunks of the trees closest to me. Painted in blood. Then the screaming started, like the trees themselves were crying at me: Get out, get out, get out. Leave. Run. But they hemmed me in, the trees moved to stop me, ringing me, blocking my way. I tried to scream back at them, but my voice died, and still the blood rained, and my heart raced.

It only lasted a second. At least, it only felt like a second. It felt like I had just closed my eyes when I woke up. But early sunlight filled the room. It was morning, and Cormac was kneeling by the sofa.

"Norville?"

Quickly I sat up. I looked around for danger—for blood seeping from the walls. I expected to hear screaming. My heart beat fast. But Cormac seemed calm. I didn't see anything unusual.

"How long have you been there?" I said, a bit breathlessly.

"I just got here. I found something, I think you should come take a look."

I nodded, pushed back the blankets, and followed him, after pulling on a coat and sneakers.

The air outside was freezing. I wasn't sure it was just the temperature. After that dream, I expected to find another gutted rabbit on the porch. I expected to see crosses on every tree. I hugged myself and trudged over the forest earth.

Cormac stopped about fifty paces out from the cabin. He pointed down, and it took me a minute to find what he wanted me to see: another barbed-wire cross, sunk in the dirt as if someone had dropped it there.

"And over here," Cormac said, and led me ten paces farther, along a track that paralleled the cabin.

Another cross lay on the ground here. Without prompting from him, I continued on, and after a moment of searching, I found the next one on my own.

I looked back at Cormac in something of a panic.

He said, "There's a circle of them all the way around the house."

The barbed wire had become more than a symbol. The talismans literally fenced me in. They created a barrier of fear.

"Who would do this?" I said. "Why—why would someone do this?"

"I don't know. Do you smell anything?" he asked.

I shook my head. I didn't smell anything unusual, at least. "That's weird, I ought to be able to smell some trace of whoever left these. But it's like the crosses just appeared out of thin air. Is that possible?"

"If these things are more than just a scare tactic, then I suppose anything's possible. I kept watch all night. I should have seen something."

"Were these here before last night?"

"I didn't see any."

I kicked the dirt, stubbing my toe on the ground. I let out a short growl at the pain. "This is driving me crazy," I muttered.

"That's probably the idea," Cormac said.

"Huh. As if I'm not perfectly capable of driving *myself* crazy."

"Is that what you've been doing stuck out here in the woods? Driving yourself crazy?"

It kind of looked that way. I didn't have to admit that,

though. I started picking up the crosses, searching for the next one around the circle, intending to find every single one.

"Kitty—" His tone made him sound reprimanding, like he was about to burst forth with some great wisdom. We both knew it: picking up all the crosses was probably futile. Until we learned who was leaving these things, there'd always be more.

"You should look in on Ben," I said. "After his talk last night, he shouldn't be left alone. Or you could get some sleep. Or something."

He actually took the hint. After a moment's pause, he ambled back to the cabin.

When I finished, I had sixteen barbed-wire crosses pocketed in the corner of my coat. Eighteen when I added them to the two Cormac had brought into the house. I found a plastic grocery bag, put them all in, tied the bag closed, and left it out on the porch. I didn't want those things inside. Cormac's idea of melting them to slag sounded wise.

Inside, Cormac and Ben were sitting opposite each other at the kitchen table, dead quiet. Cormac looked at Ben, and Ben didn't look at anything in particular. I started fixing breakfast, pretending like nothing was wrong, trying not to throw glances at them over my shoulder. It felt like I had interrupted an argument.

"Eggs, anyone? Cereal? I think I've got some sausage that isn't too out-of-date. Frozen venison?" Silence. My own appetite wasn't what it should have been. I settled for a glass of orange juice. Finally, leaning back against the counter, I asked, "Who died?"

Then I wished I hadn't. Ben looked sharply at me, and Cormac crossed his arms with a frustrated sigh. I couldn't read the series of body language. Maybe if I could get them talking, then close my eyes and pretend I was doing the show, I could figure out what was wrong.

"No, really," I said, my voice flat. "Who died?"

Ben stood up. "I'm taking a shower." He stalked back to the bedroom.

That left me with Cormac, who wouldn't look at me. I said, "You going to tell me what I missed, or are we all going to go around not talking to each other for the rest of the day?"

"I'm inclined to say that it's none of your business."

"Yeah, that's why you brought Ben here in the first place, because it's none of my business. Real cute. What's wrong?"

"Ben and I worked it out."

"Worked what out?"

"A compromise."

I wanted to growl. "Will you just tell me why he won't talk to me and you won't look at me?"

Taking that as a challenge, he looked right at me. If I hadn't been against the counter I would have backed up a step, so much anger and frustration burned out of his gaze.

He said, "After the full moon, if he still wants me to do it, I'll do it."

I had to take a moment to parse that, to understand what it meant. And I did. I still had to spell it out. "You'll shoot him. Just like that. The only person in the world you trust, and you'll kill him."

"If he wants me to."

"That isn't fair. That isn't enough time for him to adjust to what's happened to him. He won't be any happier after the full moon than he is now."

"And how long did it take you to become the stable, well-adjusted werewolf you are today?" His tone dripped with sarcasm.

I crossed my arms and pouted. "Very funny."

"It's what we decided."

"Well, you're both a couple of macho dickheads!"

He stood. "Is it still okay if I sleep on the sofa?"

"I ought to make you sleep on the porch!"

He ignored me, just like I expected, and went to the sofa, wrenched off his boots, lay down, and pulled the blanket over his head.

So much for that.

I went to the desk and fired up the laptop. I started a new page and wrote a title at the top: "Ten Ways to Defeat Macho Dickheadism." Then I realized that most of the world's problems stemmed from macho dickheadism, and if I could defeat that I could save the world. It made for a pretty good rant, since Cormac and Ben were both refusing to get yelled at in person.

Ben came out of the bathroom an hour later, slightly damp and wearing jeans and a gray T-shirt that he must have borrowed from Cormac. It gave him this James Dean look. Or that might have been the only partially suppressed snarl he wore. I expected him to say something about me actually sitting at my desk and working. The old Ben would have said something snide and encouraging at the same time.

This new Ben just looked at me, then sank heavily into the kitchen chair.

I watched him. "Did you have breakfast while you and Cormac planned your suicide, or should I fix something?"

His voice was low. "I expected you of all people to have some sympathy."

"No way. I'm a sentimentalist, remember? You're the bitter, cynical one. I just can't believe you'd go down without a fight."

"I've already lost."

I moved to the kitchen table and sat across from him, where Cormac had been. I stared him down. He fidgeted, nervous, and looked away. Ah-ha, wolfish instincts were kicking in. He didn't try to challenge me back. Good.

"This is what I see: I have three days, plus a full moon night, to convince you that life as a werewolf is better than no life at all."

"Kitty, this isn't about you. It isn't any of your business."

"Tell that to Cormac. He's the one who dumped you in my lap."

"I told him off about that already."

"You really think he made a mistake, bringing you here?"

He pursed his lips. "I do. He should have taken care of this back at Shiprock."

Ben had always been there for me. Now, when it was time for him to accept help, he was throwing it back in my face. Well, screw that.

"You know what, Ben? You're wrong. This is my business. You know why?" He gave the ceiling a long-suffering stare. That was okay, the question was rhetorical anyway. "Because I'm adopting you. You're part of my pack, now. That means you're under my protection and I refuse to let you go off and kill yourself."

He blinked at me. "What are you talking about?"

"Wolves run in packs. You're in my pack. And I'm the alpha female. That means you do what I say."

"Or what?"

"Or... or I'll get really pissed off at you."

He seemed to consider for a moment. In a mental panic, I wondered whether I could take him in a fight, if I had to back up my oh-so-brave words. He wasn't yet used to the strength he gained as a werewolf. He was still sick, still finding his feet. I had experience with this sort of thing. The thing was, I didn't want to have to assert my position by fighting him. I wanted to be able to just talk him into it.

Finally, he said, "Why do I have this urge to take you seriously?"

"Because the wolf inside you knows what's best. Trust me, Ben. Please."

"I thought you didn't have a pack."

I smiled. "I do now."

chapter **6**

"Come on, get your coat," I said, grabbing my own and my bag.

"Why?"

"We're going out. Quietly—don't wake up Cormac."

He went to the bedroom and came back with a jacket. He looked sullen, but didn't argue. That scared me a little. Was he really buying into the whole alpha female thing? I thought I'd been bluffing.

"Where are we going?" he finally asked when we were on the road.

"Into town to buy groceries. You guys are eating all my food." That wasn't all; I'd put the bag of barbed-wire crosses in the car. I planned on getting rid of them.

"Why do I have to come along?"

"Because part of being a werewolf is learning how to function in the real world. It's a little freaky at first. McDonald's will never smell the same."

He wrinkled his nose and made a grunt of disgust.

"Also, I'm not going to leave you alone and let you kill yourself just to spite me."

"I made a deal with Cormac. I'll stick it out through the full moon. I won't go back on that."

I sighed. "You're doing it again. You'll stick it out for Cormac, but not for me. I think you just don't like me."

He paused to consider. "You know you're crazy?"

"*I'm* not the one who wants my best friend to shoot me in the head!"

He turned away to stare out the window.

I'd been through what he was going through now. I'd awakened after being attacked by a werewolf, with my whole world turned upside down, and I hadn't wanted to die. I hadn't even thought about it beyond the vague, unserious half urges that came with depression. I had a life and I wanted to keep it, lycanthropy or no. What was wrong with Ben?

Nothing was wrong with Ben. He was right to be afraid, to want to avoid it. This was about me. I was the problem. Ben knew what was coming, because he'd seen what it did to me. I couldn't blame him at all.

I said, "I'm a werewolf—am I so terrible that you'd rather kill yourself than be that?"

"No." He glanced at me, and his look was sad. "You're not terrible at all. You're..." He turned back to the window without finishing.

I'm what? I almost yelled at him to make him finish. But what would that get me? An answer I wasn't sure I wanted to hear. *You're not terrible, you're...* confused.

I pulled into the driveway of Joe and Alice's store and parked. It was midday, but we were the only ones there. Small favors. I'd already gotten out of the car when Ben said, "I'll just wait here."

I put my hands on my hips. "That defeats the whole

point of you coming along. And I need you to help carry groceries."

He lurched out of the car, slouching in his coat like a sullen teenager, his hands shoved in the pockets. I walked across the dirt parking lot, and Ben fell into step beside me. Halfway to the front door, though, he paused and looked up, turning his nose into the faint breeze. His brow furrowed, faintly worried, faintly curious.

I could filter it all out, the hundred smells that I encountered every day: spilled oil, gasoline, asphalt, the garbage Dumpster, drying paint from the shed around the corner, somebody's loose dog, a feral cat, the earth and trees from the edge of the woods. A normal human wouldn't be able to differentiate them at all. Ben was smelling it all for the first time.

"You okay?" I asked.

After a moment, he nodded. Then he said, "What do I smell like to you?"

I shrugged. I'd never tried to describe it before. "Now? You smell like a werewolf. Human with a little bit of fur and wild thrown in."

He nodded, like that sounded familiar—he could smell me now, after all. Then he said, "And before?"

"I always thought you smelled like your trenchcoat."

He made a sound that was almost a chuckle.

"What do I smell like to you?" I said.

He cocked his head for a moment, testing the air, tasting it. He seemed puzzled, like he was still trying to figure out the sensation. "Safe. You smell safe."

We went inside.

Ben hesitated at the door, once again looking around, nose flaring, wearing an expression of uncertainty and also curiosity. I looked, hoping to see Alice, bracing for Joe and his rifle.

Behind the counter, Alice looked up from the magazine she was reading. She smiled. "Hi, Kitty, how are you today?"

"Oh, fine. I have friends visiting. Alice, this is Ben. Ben, Alice."

Alice smiled warmly and extended her hand for shaking. Ben looked stricken for a moment—to the wolf side, it was not the most harmless of gestures. In fact, it looked a little like an attack. I waited to see how he'd react and let out a bit of a sigh when he recovered and took her hand.

"Good to meet you," he said. He wasn't smiling, but he behaved in a straightforward enough manner.

"Let me know if I can help you find anything," she said.

"Actually, I did want to ask you something. Do you know any blacksmiths around here? Someone with a forge who could melt down a bunch of metal for me?"

"Well, sure. Jake Torres is the local farrier, he's got a forge. What kind of metal?"

This was going to be hard to explain without sounding like a loon. But I *was* crazy, according to Ben anyway. Maybe I should just embrace it. "I've got a bunch of pieces of barbed wire that I'd love to see completely destroyed. You think he'd do that for me?"

She creased her brow. "Oh, probably. What kind of pieces?"

"They're in the car, I'll go get them. Ben"—I grabbed a plastic shopping basket from the pile by the door—"here. Find some food. Whatever looks good."

He took the basket, looked at me quizzically, then headed for the shelves.

Feeling like I was finally accomplishing something, I ran to the car, grabbed the bag of crosses, ran back to the store, and dropped the bag on the counter in front of Alice. It landed with a solid, steely *thunk*. She pulled out one of the crosses, studied it, and looked increasingly worried. That made *me* worried.

"Something's wrong," I said. "What is it? You look like you've seen one of these before."

Shaking her head, she dropped the cross back and quickly tied up the bag. "Oh, you know. Folklore, local superstition. Crosses are supposed to be for protection."

"Yeah, well, someone's been dumping them in a circle around my cabin and I don't feel very protected. Friend of mine thinks it's part of a curse. Like someone isn't happy with me being around."

Alice's eyes widened, startled. "That's certainly odd, isn't it?"

"I just want to get rid of them. Melting them down seems the way to go. You think your farrier will do it?"

"Jake stops in here once a week. He's due in a couple of days. I'll ask him myself," she said with a thin smile. She put the bag under the counter. It was out of my hands now.

That was easy. A weight lifted from me. "Thanks, Alice. That'd be great."

I went to check on Ben. He was standing with the still empty basket in front of a shelf full of canned soup, chili, and pasta sauce.

"Nothing sounds good," he said. "I just keep thinking about all that venison in your freezer. Is that normal?"

I patted his arm. "I know what you mean."

We stocked up on the basics—bacon and eggs, bread

and milk. Ben gamely carried the basket for me, and Alice rang up the goods, her demeanor more cheerful than ever. We made it back to the car without incident.

"There," I said as I pulled the car back on the road, "that wasn't so hard."

After some long minutes of driving, Ben said, "I could hear her heartbeat. Smell her blood. It's strange."

I wet my lips, because my mouth had gone dry. Even smelling him, smelling him change into something not quite human, even seeing the bite wounds and knowing intellectually what was happening to him, it didn't really hit me until that moment. Ben was a werewolf. He may not have shape-shifted yet, he may have been infected for less than a week. But there it was.

"It makes them seem like prey," I said, aware that I was talking about people, normal people like Alice, in the third person. Like they were something different than Ben and I. "Like you could hunt them." Like you could almost taste the blood.

"Does that happen every time you meet somebody?" he said.

"Most of the time, yeah," I said softly.

He didn't say a word for the rest of the trip home.

When we entered the house, Cormac was awake, sitting at the kitchen table, cleaning a gun or three. As soon as the front door opened, he stood and turned to us. I'd have said he was in a panic, if I didn't know him better.

"Where'd you go?" he said.

"Shopping?" I said, uncertain. Both Ben and I hefted

filled plastic grocery bags, which we brought to the kitchen. "You want to help unpack?"

He just stood there. "You couldn't have left a note?"

"I didn't think you'd wake up before we got back."

"Don't worry," Ben said. "She looked out for me."

"Should you even be out?" Cormac said accusingly, almost motherly.

I nearly snapped at him, something juvenile like *what's your problem?* Then I realized—I'd never seen Cormac worried before. At least, worried and actually showing it. He was downright stressed out. It was almost chilling.

Ben slumped into the other chair at the kitchen table. "I survived, didn't I?" Cormac scowled and looked away, which prompted Ben to add, "I'm okay, Cormac."

"At least for another three days," I muttered as I shoved food into the fridge. I put the groceries away loudly and angrily, as if that would make me feel better. The guys ignored me.

"You need help with that?" Ben indicated the spread of gun oil and gun parts on the kitchen table. Cormac had put paper towels down first, so I couldn't even get mad at him for messing up the table.

"I'm done." Cormac began cleaning up the mess, packing everything away into a metal toolbox.

Ben watched for a minute, then said, "If you'd just shot me, you wouldn't have to deal with this crap now."

"You are never going to let me live that down, are you?"

"We had a deal—"

Cormac slammed the toolbox on the table, making a wrenching crash. "We were sixteen years old when we made that deal! We were just kids! We didn't have a clue!"

Ben dropped his gaze.

I left the room.

Couldn't go far, of course. A whole five feet to the so-called living room. Still, the space made ignoring them marginally easier. The whole cabin became entrenched in a thick, obvious silence. A moment later, Cormac left out the front door, toolbox and rifles in hand. Then I heard him repacking his Jeep. I half expected the engine to start up, to hear him drive away forever, leaving me to deal with Ben all by myself. But he didn't. Maybe he planned on sleeping out there to avoid any more arguments, but he didn't drive away. Ben went to the bedroom. I sat at my desk, at my computer, pretending to write, and wanted to pull out my hair.

I'd spent a year on the radio telling people how to fix their supernaturally complicated relationship problems. And now I couldn't deal with the one right in front of me.

Ben emerged long enough for supper. More venison steaks. After, he pulled a chair into the living room and sat in front of the stove, just watching the embers burning through the grate, slipping into some kind of fugue state. I couldn't really argue. I'd done the same thing when this had happened to me. As the body changed, perceptions changed, and the world seemed to slow down. You blinked and a whole afternoon went by. The sense of disconnection had lasted for weeks. I'd almost flunked out that semester. If I hadn't been just a year away from finishing, I might have given into that urge to drop out and walk away. Walk into the woods, never to return.

Cormac stayed in the kitchen. They still weren't speaking.

Later, at the appropriate hour, I turned on the radio. Yes, it was that time of the week again. I curled up on the sofa, cell phone in hand.

Ben looked at the radio, brow furrowed. Then, he narrowed his eyes—an expression of dawning comprehension. "What day is it?"

"Saturday," I said.

Immediately he stood, shaking his head. "No, uh-uh, there is no way I am listening to this. I'm not watching you listen to this. I'm out of here. Good night." He went to the bedroom and flopped on the bed.

Cormac came from the kitchen, glancing at the bedroom, and sat on the other end of the sofa. "What's this?"

"The competition," I said.

The sultry voice announced herself.

"Good evening. I am Ariel, Priestess of the Night. Welcome to my show." And again, "Bela Lugosi's Dead." Of all the pretentious...

I muttered at the radio in a manic snit. "Tell us, Ariel, what shall we talk about *this* week?"

Ariel, via the radio, answered. "We've all heard of werewolves," she intoned. "We've seen countless movies. My little brother even dressed up as the Wolf Man for Halloween one year. All this attention has given short shrift to the *other* species. Lions and tigers and bears. And a dozen other documented lycanthropic varieties. *Oh, my.*"

Cormac crossed his arms and leaned back. "You have to wonder if she's got a body to go with that voice."

I *so* wasn't going to tell him about the Web site. I glared at him instead. Then, a niggling voice started scratching at the back of my mind. Scratching, gnawing, aggravating, until I had to ask, "What about my show? You know, before you saw me in person—did my voice ever, you know, make you wonder if I maybe had a body to go with it?"

He looked at me, stricken for a moment. "You're a little different," he said finally.

Oh, God, I'm a hack. An ugly, talentless hack and nobody ever liked me, not once, not ever. I hugged the pillow that was on the sofa and stewed. Cormac rolled his eyes.

Ariel was still talking. "Are you a lycanthrope who is something other than the standard lupine fare? Give me a call, let's chat."

I had the number on speed dial by this time. I punched the call button and waited.

Cormac watched thoughtfully. "What are you doing?"

I ignored him. I got a busy signal the first time, then tried again. And again, until finally, "Hello, you've reached Ariel, Priestess of the Night. What's your name and hometown?"

I had it all planned out this time. "I'm Irene from Tulsa," I said brightly.

"And what do you want to talk about?"

"I'm a were-jaguar. Very rare," I said. "I'm so glad that Ariel's talking about this. I've felt so alone, you know? I'd love a chance to talk."

"All right, Irene. Turn down your radio and hold, please."

I did so, pressing the phone to my ear and tapping my foot happily.

Cormac stared at me. "That's really pathetic."

"Shut up."

Then he had the nerve to take the radio to the next room, to the kitchen table. He hunched before it, listening with the volume turned down low. Couldn't he leave me alone?

I listened in on three calls: the callers claimed to be a were-leopard, a were-fox, and a werewolf who refused to believe that lycanthropes could be anything other than wolves, because, well, *he'd* never met any others *personally*. If he'd called into my show I would have told him off with a rant that would have left him dumbstruck. Something along the lines of: *Okay, you big jerk, let's try out a new word, shall we? Say it along with me: narcissistic...*

By comparison, Ariel was shockingly polite. "Marty, do you consider yourself to be an open-minded person?"

"Well, yeah, I suppose," said Marty the caller.

"Good, that's really good," Ariel purred. "I'd expect a werewolf to be open-minded. You're involved so deeply in the world behind the veil, after all. I'm sure there are lots of things you haven't had personal experience with, yet you believe—like the Pope, or the Queen of England. So exactly why is it that you can't accept the existence of other species of lycanthropes, just because you've never met one?"

Marty hadn't thought this one through. You could always spot the ones who spouted rhetoric with no thought behind it. "Well, you know. All the stories are about were-*wolves*. And the movies—werewolves, all of them. It's the Wolf Man, not the Leopard Man!"

"And what about *Cat People?*"

Hey, that was what I'd have said.

"That's different," Marty said petulantly. "That was, you know, made-up."

Ariel continued. "Stories about shape-shifters are found all over the world, and they're about all kinds of animals.

Whatever's common locally. You really have to accept that there might be something to all these stories, yes?"

"*I've* never heard of these stories."

Wow, I loved how some people were so good at digging their own holes.

"Your culture isn't the only one in the world, Marty. Moving on to the next call, we have Irene from Tulsa, hello."

My turn? Me? I was ready for this. I tried to sound more chipper and ditzy than I had the last time I called. "Hi, Ariel!"

"So, you're a were-jaguar. Can you tell me how exactly that happened? Jaguars aren't exactly native to Tulsa."

"When I was in college I spent a summer volunteering in Brazil for an environmental group, working in the jungle. One time I started back to camp a little late, and, well..." I took a deep, significant breath. "I was attacked."

How could you not sympathize with that story? Oh, yeah, somebody nominate me for an Oscar. I wondered how long it would take her to spot the fake.

"That's an amazing story," Ariel said, clearly impressed. "How have you coped since then?"

"I have good days, I have bad days. It's really hard not having anyone to talk to about it. As far as I know, all the other were-jaguars are in Brazil."

"You ever think about going back and finding someone who might be able to help you?"

"It just never worked out." *I'm so sad, pity me...*

"Well, Irene, if you really want something, there's always a way."

Maybe that was why Ariel bothered me so much: that Pollyanna sunshine attitude. Sometimes, things just didn't work out.

"I want to get married under a full moon. Is there a way for me to get that?"

"Sometimes you have to adjust your wants to be a little more realistic."

"Easy for you to say."

She dodged, yanking control of the conversation back to her. "Tell me why you really haven't been back to Brazil."

I said breezily, "Well, you know, I had to come back home, finish school, then I met this guy, see, and then I broke up with this guy—and you know how it is, one thing then another, and I guess I got distracted."

Ariel wasn't having it. "Irene, are you pulling my leg?"

Damn, she got me. That didn't mean I had to admit it. "Oh, Ariel, why would I do something like that?"

"You tell me."

"Calling you with a fake story about being a were-jaguar would be—oh, I don't know—a delusion based in some psychiatric disorder? A desperate cry for attention?"

"That's what I'm thinking," Ariel said. "Moving on to the next call, Gerald—"

I hung up in disgust. I still hadn't gotten her to say anything stupid. *I* was feeling pretty stupid, but never mind that. My inner two-year-old was enjoying herself.

Cormac was watching me from the kitchen, which made me even more disgruntled. I didn't need an audience. At least not one that was sitting there staring at me.

He said, "You ever think that maybe she's really a vampire or a witch or something, the same way that you're really a werewolf? That she's keeping it under wraps like you did?"

"Right up until you blew my cover, you mean?"

He shrugged noncommittally, as if to say, *Who me?*

"She's a hack," I muttered.

"Then what the hell does that make you?"

"A has-been, evidently." I brushed back my hair and sighed.

He stood and grabbed his coat and gun off the kitchen counter. "You want a pity party, you can have it by yourself."

"I'm not... this isn't... I'm not looking for your pity."

"Good. 'Cause you're not getting any. If you're a has-been it's your own damn fault."

"Where are you going?"

"Guard duty. If I see any gutted rabbits I'll let you know."

Bang, he slammed the front door behind him and that was that.

I let out a frustrated growl, grabbed the blanket, and cocooned myself on the sofa.

I wasn't a has-been. I *wasn't.*

Yet.

chapter 7

I woke, startled, and sat up on the sofa. I hadn't heard anything, nothing specific had jolted me awake, but I felt like someone had slammed a door or fired a gun.

Cormac.

He was asleep in a chair, which he'd pulled over to the living-room window. He'd been keeping watch, just like he'd said. But I never thought he'd fall asleep on guard duty. It just wasn't like him.

Whatever had shocked me awake hadn't affected him. He even snored a little, his chin tipped forward so it almost touched his chest.

Outside, the sky was gray. Light, so it was past dawn, but still overcast, like it was about to snow. I had a queasy, stuffy-headed feeling that told me I hadn't gotten enough sleep.

"Cormac?" I said.

Immediately he sat up and put his hand on the revolver he'd left sitting on my desk. Only after looking around, tensed at the edge of the chair as if waiting for an attack, did he say, "What happened?" He didn't look at me; his attention focused on the window and the door.

"Something woke me up," I said.

"I hadn't meant to fall asleep," he said. "I shouldn't have fallen asleep." His hand clenched on his weapon like it was a security blanket. He didn't pick it up, but I had no doubt he could aim and shoot it in a heartbeat. Speaking of heartbeats, his had sped up. I could hear it, and smell his anxiety. He wasn't used to getting caught off guard. His fear fed mine.

"Something's out there," I whispered.

"You hear something?"

"I don't know." I concentrated, trying yet again to remember what my senses had told me, what exactly had fired my nerves awake.

I smelled blood. It wasn't new blood, fresh blood. It was old, rotten, stinking. And not just a little, but a slaughter-house's worth. A massive amount, and it was everywhere, as if someone had painted the walls with it. No—no—

Get a grip. Keep it together.

"Do you smell something?" I said, my voice cracking. Of course he didn't. Not like this. How could he?

"I assume you mean something out of the ordinary."

"Blood."

"Are you okay?"

I went to the door. *Get out.*

My hand on the knob, I squeezed my eyes shut. There wasn't a voice. I hadn't heard anything. I cracked open the door.

The smell washed over me. I'd never sensed anything like it. The odor was hateful, oppressive, like it was attacking me. Could a smell be evil?

"There's something out there," I said. And it hated me. It had left all those signs that it hated me.

"Move over." Cormac, gun raised, displaced me from in front of the door. "Stay back."

I did, holding my clenched hands to my chest. He opened the door a little wider. His gun arm led the way as he stepped out, the weapon ready to face the lurking danger.

Sheltered behind the door, I watched his face. His expression never changed. It stayed cold, stony—his professional look. Then he froze.

"Jesus Christ," he said, his voice filled with something like awe. He didn't lower his weapon.

I slipped out the door to stand next to him on the porch and looked out.

All around the clearing in front of the house, carcasses hung from the lower branches of trees. Skinless—pink and bloody, wet with a sheen of fat and flesh, the dead animals were hung up by their hind legs, so that their front legs and heads dangled. Their teeth—the sharp teeth of carnivores—were bared, and lidless eyes stared. There must have been a dozen of them. They swayed a little on their ropes, ghosts in the dawn light.

I moved forward, like that would help me see better— like I even wanted to see them better—and leaned against the porch railing. They looked alien and terrible, so that I couldn't identify them at first. Four legs, straight naked tails, slim bodies with round rib cages and narrow hips. Heads with narrow snouts and triangular ears.

They were dogs. Some kind of dogs. Canines. Wolflike.

I made a noise like a sob.

I had to get out of here, but I couldn't, not yet, not until I'd gotten Ben through the full moon. But the walls were closing in. And there weren't even walls out here. The dead eyes all stared at me. *Get out.*

"Kitty?"

"Who hates me this much?" I started crying. Tension, exhaustion, uncertainty—in the space of a few days my whole life had fallen apart, and I didn't know what to do about it. It all just came out.

I stumbled back, away from the mess, and bumped into Cormac. Then I leaned into him. He was close, and I needed a shoulder, so I turned to his. Eyes leaking and nose dripping on his T-shirt, I let it all out, feeling profoundly embarrassed about it even as I did. I didn't care.

He put his arms around me. He held me firmly without squeezing, moving one hand to stroke my hair. For some reason this made me cry harder.

I didn't like being an alpha. For the last couple of days, I'd been pulling out alpha left and right. Now, though, Cormac was willing to take care of me, at least for a little while. I was profoundly grateful.

"We'll figure it out," he said softly. "After tomorrow, we'll work on figuring this out."

Tomorrow. After the full moon. After we got all that sorted out. I held on to him.

Arm around my shoulder, he guided me inside, shut the door, and set his gun on the desk. I stayed close to him. I didn't want him to pull away, and he took the hint. We stood there for a long time; I clung to him, and he kept his arms around me. I felt safer, believing he could actually protect me from the horrors outside.

"You're being very patient with me," I said, murmuring into his T-shirt.

"Hm. It's not every day a woman throws herself into my arms. I have to take advantage of it while I can."

I made a complaining noise. "I didn't throw myself into your arms."

"Whatever you say."

I chuckled in spite of myself. When I tilted my head back, I saw he was smiling.

"You'd better be careful," I said. "You're getting to be downright likable."

I could kiss him. Another two inches closer—standing on my toes—and I could kiss him. His hand shifted on my back, flattening like he was getting ready to hold me steady, like he wanted to kiss me, too. Then the hand moved away. He touched my cheek, smoothed away the tears. He pulled back.

"I'll start some coffee," he said, and went to the kitchen.

Part of me was relieved. All of me was confused. I covered up the confusion with my usual lame bravado. "There, you're doing it again. Being nice."

He ignored me. Cormac, back to normal.

We discussed the situation at the kitchen table over cups of fresh coffee.

"Whoever's doing this doesn't want to kill me," I said.

"But that's some pretty twisted stuff out there. It's all aimed at you, and it's escalating."

"What's next, if I don't listen to it now?"

"Listen to it? What's it saying?"

"Leave. Get out of here. Someone doesn't want me to be here. You'd think they could just write a note."

"Just because they haven't tried to kill you yet doesn't mean they won't. If you don't leave, and if they get desperate enough."

"Could it be that simple? They just want me to leave town?"

"That probably means it's somebody local," he said.

"Shouldn't be too hard to track down somebody local who practices that sort of voodoo."

Ah, the charm of the small town. Everybody knew everybody. We just had to find out which ones were the squirrelly ones. Besides, you know, everybody.

I smiled grimly. "I think I'll give the sheriff a call. Have *him* clean up that mess."

Sheriff Marks was not happy. In a really big way, he was not happy. He only gave the hanging carcasses a cursory glance, wearing a stone-faced tough-guy expression to prove he wasn't grossed out or unduly disturbed.

I sat on the porch steps and watched him survey the clearing—this involved standing in the middle of it, circling, and nodding sagely. He didn't even bring along Deputy Rosco—I mean Ted—to take pictures of my car this time.

Cormac stood nearby, leaning on the railing. Lurking.

I ventured to speak. "We think it might be somebody local trying to scare me off."

Marks turned to me, his frown quivering. "How do I know you didn't do this? That this isn't some practical joke you're playing on me?"

I glared back in shock. "Because I wouldn't do something like this."

"What about him?" He nodded at Cormac. "What did you say your name was?"

"I didn't," Cormac said, and didn't offer.

Marks moved toward him, hands on hips. "Can I see some ID, sir?"

"No," Cormac said. I groaned under my breath.

"Is that so?" Marks said, his attention entirely drawn away from the slaughter around us.

Cormac said, "Unless you're planning to write me a ticket or arrest me for something, I don't have to show you anything."

Marks was actually starting to turn red. I had no doubt he could come up with something—harassing a police officer, loitering with intent to insult—to pin on Cormac, just out of spite.

I stepped between them, distracting them. "Um, could we get back to the dead animals?"

Marks said, "If I'm right, I could have you up on a number of cruelty to animal charges."

"Should I call my lawyer?" My lawyer who was inside, asleep, recovering from a werewolf bite. "Recovering" was my optimism talking.

"I'm just giving you an out, Ms. Norville. A chance to 'fess up."

"I didn't do it."

"I'm still looking for the hidden cameras," he said, peering into the trees.

"Oh, give me a break!"

He jabbed his finger in my direction. "If you think being famous keeps you safe, lets you do whatever the hell you want, you're wrong."

If I'd thought this situation couldn't get any worse, I was obviously mistaken.

"Sheriff, I'm being harassed, and if you're not going to help me, just say it so I can find somebody who will."

"Good luck with that." He started back for his car.

"Hell, I could do a better job than this clown," Cormac said. "At least I can admit when I'm in over my head."

He didn't even try to say it softly, so Marks couldn't hear. No—he raised his voice, so Marks couldn't help but hear.

Marks turned around, glaring. "What did you say?"

Cormac scuffed his boot on the porch and pretended he hadn't heard.

"You'd better watch yourself," Marks said, pointing. "You so much as breathe wrong and I'll get you."

The hunter remained slouching against the railing, as unflappable as ever. He wasn't going to be the one to shoot first in a fight. I wasn't sure Marks knew that.

Marks started back to his car.

"Sheriff, what do I do about them?" I pointed at the dogs. Some of them were swaying gently, as the trees they were tied to creaked in a faint breeze. A garbage bag or a quickly dug hole wasn't going to clean this up.

"Call animal control," he said. The sound of his car door slamming echoed.

I fumed, unable to come up with a word angry enough for what I wanted to hurl after him.

Hearing steps in the house, I turned around. Ben emerged, standing just outside the doorway and staring out. "Holy shit, what's this?"

"Curse," I said.

"Yeah, I guess so."

"I don't suppose anyone's up for breakfast," Cormac said.

"Are you joking?" I said. He smiled. My God, he was joking.

"You two go inside. I'll take care of this."

"Sure you don't need help?" Ben said.

"I'm sure."

Ben hesitated, like he needed convincing. I pulled his arm, guided him inside. He said, "Does this sort of thing happen to you a lot?"

It was starting to seem like it. "I don't know."

"Is it because you're a werewolf or because you're you?"

Now that was an excellent question. I didn't really want to know the answer.

When my phone rang later that day, I almost screamed, because the noise was like claws on a chalkboard. Mom's call.

Cormac hadn't come back yet from taking care of the mess outside. Ben had gone back to bed. I didn't know if he was sleeping.

I curled up on the sofa. "Hi, Mom."

"Hi, Kitty. Are you okay? You sound a little off."

A little off. Ha. "I'm about the same as the last time we talked. Things could be better, but I'm hanging in there." Hanging. I shouldn't have said that. Didn't want to hear about anything having to do with hanging.

"What's wrong? I wish there was something I could do to help. You'll let me know if there's anything I can do—"

"Thanks, Mom. I can't really think of anything. Unless you know something about blood magic?"

She thought for a couple of beats, and I couldn't guess what kind of expression she had. "No, I really don't."

"That's okay."

"Kitty, tell me the truth, are you all right?"

My eyes teared up. I would *not* start crying at Mom. If

I started I wouldn't stop, and then she'd really worry. And she was right to worry, I supposed. I took a deep breath and kept it together.

"I will be." Somehow... "Things are kind of a mess, but I'm working through it."

"You're *sure* there isn't anything I can do?"

"I'm sure."

"Are your friends still with you? Are they helping?"

"Yeah, they are." In fact, if Cormac hadn't been here to take care of the dog thing, I might very well have run screaming and never come back.

"Good. I'm glad. You know I worry about you."

"I know, Mom. I appreciate it, I really do." And I did. It was good to have people looking out for you.

"Well... please call me if you need anything, if there's anything I can do. And don't be afraid to come home if you need to. There's no shame in that."

"Thanks, Mom." Couldn't think of anything else to say. Just... thanks.

chapter 8

Then came the day.

According to the *Farmer's Almanac*, the full moon in January was known as the Wolf Moon. This was the time of year, the deepest part of winter, when people would huddle together in their homes, build up their fires against the cold, listen to the howling of hungry wolves outside, and pray that they were safe. The cold seeped into people's souls as well as their bodies, and their fears multiplied. Summer and safety seemed farthest away.

Maybe being cursed was really only a state of mind.

I decided that I wasn't going to let Ben die. If I had to tie him up with silver to keep him from hurting himself, I'd do it. If tomorrow came and he still wanted Cormac to kill him, I'd stop him. Somehow, I'd stop Cormac. Hide his guns, fight him, something.

Maybe I could knock Cormac out in a hand-to-hand fight—I was stronger than I looked, and maybe he'd forget that. If Cormac had a gun, though, I'd probably die. At least then they'd know how strongly I felt about the issue.

But I was getting ahead of myself. I had to get through today before I could worry about tomorrow.

I woke up at dawn—still on the sofa—but lay there for a long time, curled up and wishing it were all already over. Wolf knew what day it was; a coiling, wriggling feeling made itself known in my gut, and it would get stronger and stronger until nightfall, when it would turn to knives and claws, the creature trying to rip its way out of the weak human shell, until finally it burst forth and forced the Change. In the bedroom, Ben was feeling this for the first time. He wouldn't know what to do with it. He'd need help coping.

I'd meant to check on him, but he emerged first and went to the kitchen, where Cormac was already sitting. I wasn't sure Cormac had ever gone to bed. I stayed very still to try to hear what they said, but the cabin remained quiet.

Finally, I sat up and looked into the kitchen.

Ben sat on one chair, leaning forward to rest his elbows on his knees, and Cormac sat on the other chair, facing him across the table, arms crossed. They might have been like that for hours, staring at each other.

They'd been best friends since they were kids and now they were wondering if this was their last day together. Had Ben told Cormac about the monster waking up inside him?

I had to break this up. I marched into the kitchen and started making noise, pulling out pots and slamming cabinet doors.

"Who wants eggs?" I forced a Mrs. Cleaver smile, but my tone sounded more strained than cheerful.

They didn't even turn, didn't even flinch. At least it would all be over, after tonight. One way or another.

I cooked bacon and eggs, way more than I needed to, but it distracted me. This was going to be a long, long day.

I didn't notice when the anxiety-laden tableau between Ben and Cormac broke. I heard a noise, and turned to see Cormac getting up, going over to put a fresh log in the stove. Ben bowed his head and stared at the floor.

"Food's ready."

Cormac wandered back to the kitchen table and accepted a plate. The eggs had come out scrambled rather than over easy. I didn't much care. I wanted one of them to *say* something.

He smiled a thin, strained thanks. That was all.

"Ben?" Carefully, I prompted him.

He shook his head. "I can't eat. I hardly ate yesterday and I still feel like I'm going to throw up."

"Yeah. It's usually like that. You get used to it."

He glared at me, his lips almost curling into a snarl. "How? How do you *get used* to this?"

"You just do," I snapped back at him.

He started tapping his foot, a rapid, nervous patter.

So that was breakfast.

I don't know how I managed it, but I was thinking ahead today. I grabbed a change of clothes. I wanted to set up a den for tonight, a place to wake up in the morning.

I paused next to Ben, still camped on the kitchen chair, tense as a wire and frowning.

"I'm going to take a walk. You want to come with me?" I asked softly.

"Is that an order?" He spat the words. He was already in pain. He was already having to hold it in. I'd forgotten what it was like when it was all new; I'd had four years of practice holding it in, learning to ignore it. Getting used to it.

I wanted to grab his collar and shake him—growl at him. I grit my teeth and held my temper. "No. I just thought you might like to take a walk. Do you have a change of clothes I could take? Sweatpants and a T-shirt or something."

He looked at me, eyes narrowed, as he considered this—and then realized what I was really going to do on my walk. He grimaced, like he was holding back a scream, or a sob. I had a sudden urge to hug him, but I didn't. If I even tried to touch him, he might hit the ceiling, he was so tightly wound. That was what I'd have done.

Then, without a word he pulled out a duffel bag from next to the sofa, rummaged in it for a moment, and found the clothes.

I was at the front door when Cormac said, "If you're looking for company—"

"Actually, no offense, but I don't want you to know where I'm going. I don't want to wake up tomorrow morning staring down one of your guns."

"You think I'd shoot you in your sleep? Either one of you?" he said angrily. Clearly, I'd offended him.

I wanted to scream. I looked away. "I don't know. I just don't know."

"If I really wanted to do that, I'd track you. You know I could."

I left.

I was torn between wanting to hurry back in case Ben decided to do something rash while I was gone, and taking my time to avoid the situation at the house. I found my usual den and stashed the stuff. Then I sat there for a long time, tucked in the hollow, reveling in the peaceful scent of it. It smelled like me, like fur and warmth, and it felt safe. I wondered what it would feel like with two people in it.

Then I was ashamed to realize I was looking forward to finding out. I was looking forward to having a friend along for the run tonight.

God, I'd be lucky if either Ben or Cormac were still friends after tonight. I laced my fingers in my hair and made fists, as if trying to pull the craziness out of my head. Ben was going through hell; I was not going to look on it as a good thing.

I must have stayed there an hour before I decided to wander back to the house. I dreaded what I'd find when I got there. So help me God if Cormac was cleaning his guns—

He wasn't. He was in the kitchen reading my copy of *Walden.*

I must have stood there staring at him, because he glanced up and said, "What are you looking at?"

I shrugged. "I guess I'd halfway decided you didn't know how to read."

Ben, stretched out on the sofa pretending to sleep, snorted a chuckle.

Ah, the boy retained a sense of humor. Maybe there was hope.

"How are you doing?" I said to him, gently.

"Don't patronize me."

"I'm not—" But what I'd meant and what it sounded like to him could certainly be two different things. I wanted to kick the sofa, knock him out of it. "You're making this way more difficult than it needs to be."

He sat up suddenly; I thought he was going to lunge at me. I even took a step back.

He almost shouted. "You know how to make it easy? You want to tell me how to make it easier? 'Cause I'd sure love to hear about it. You keep talking about getting used to it, so if you know any tricks, now would be a great time to share!"

We glared at each other, eye to eye. My Wolf thought he was going to start a fight right here and wanted to growl. I closed my eyes and took a deep breath, to keep her in check. Let the human side deal with this. I just had to tell him to calm down. Had to be patronizing again.

Cormac interrupted. "Maybe I oughta shoot you both, put you both out of your misery."

Why did that make me want to laugh? Hysterical, psychotic laughter, yes. But still. If it wasn't so serious, it would have been funny.

I was looking at Ben when I said, "Who says we're miserable?"

Something sparked. He thought it was funny, too. At least part of him thought part of it was funny. He looked away, but not before I saw the smile flicker on his lips and disappear.

I pulled the chair from the desk and sat. I was in front of my laptop, not facing him. I'd planned on pretending I was working.

"Broccoli," I said after a moment. He looked at me. "I think about broccoli. And Bach. I think about things that are as far away from the Wolf as I can. Anything that keeps me human and makes the Wolf go away."

"Does it actually work?"

"Usually. Sometimes. You ought to make Cormac give you the book. To distract yourself."

"Don't tell me that's the only book you have in the house."

I huffed. "What kind of English major do you take me for?"

I dug through the box of books and CDs I'd brought and set him up with a copy of Jack London. Which probably wasn't the best choice, but oh well. The philistine had scoffed at Virginia Woolf. Maybe he'd thought I was trying to be funny.

I managed to write something that afternoon. I wasn't sure how coherent it was. I didn't have the patience to read back over it. Time enough for that tomorrow.

I wrote for so long that I didn't notice when darkness fell outside.

"Kitty." The word came out sharp and filled with pain.

Ben gripped the arm of the sofa; the fabric had started to rip under his hand. His fingers were growing claws. He was staring at his hands like they were alien to him.

I rushed over and knelt before him. I put my hands on his cheeks and turned his face, made him look away from the scene of horror to look at me instead. His eyes grew wide, filled with shock.

He said with a kind of rough laugh, "It really hurts."

"I know, I know." I hushed him, brushing his hair back from his face, which was starting to drip with sweat. "Ben, do you trust me? Please say you trust me."

He nodded. He squeezed his eyes shut and nodded. "I trust you."

"I'll take care of you," I said. "I'm not going to leave you. Okay? You'll be all right. Just get through this and you'll be all right. We're going to go outside now, okay?"

He slipped forward off the couch to fall into my arms, pressing his face to my shoulder and groaning. For a moment, I worried that he'd try to hold me with those hands turning into claws, but no, he'd pulled his arms in close and had gone almost fetal. Tears slipped from my eyes, stinging my cheeks. I hated this. I hated seeing him like this.

"What can I do?" Cormac stood by, hands clenched into fists, watching us with an expression I'd never seen on him before. Helplessness, maybe?

"Stay out of the way," I said. "Stay inside and lock the door."

"Cormac—" Ben's voice wasn't his own anymore. His jaw was clenched, his breath coming in gasps, and his words were thick. "Watch, I want you to see. Kitty, he has to watch."

I helped him stand, putting my arm around his back and hauling up. "Ben, I need you to walk outside with me. Stand up."

Somehow, he lurched to his feet, leaning hard against me.

Cormac started toward us. "Let me help—"

"No!" I said harshly. Growling, even. "He's got claws, he might scratch you. Just get out of the way."

Cormac stepped aside and opened the door for us.

Outside, the forest was silver and filled with crisp, deep shadows. Full moon night, bright and beckoning. The cold air sent a charge through my body.

I could feel Ben's body rippling under my arm, like slimy things moved under the skin. It would have been nausea-inducing, if I hadn't felt this happen to my own body. He was locked up with the pain; I half dragged him off the porch to the clearing in front of the cabin. We weren't going to get any farther than that. I let him drop to the ground, where he curled up on his side. Thick stubble covered his arms.

I took his moment of immobility to unfasten the button and zipper of his jeans. It took too long; my hands were shaking. But I had to get his clothes off before they tangled him up. That would only add to the pain and confusion. Taking both waistbands—jeans and underwear—at once, I pulled down as far as I could, then grabbed the hem of his T-shirt and pulled up, forcing it over his head.

"Come on, Ben, help me out here," I muttered. My own Wolf was bucking inside me—*It's time, it's time!*—she had a pack now, and we were all supposed to Change together to go running. I locked her away, clamped down on the writhing beast, and ignored it. I had to get Ben through this. His whole body was covered in fuzz—I could almost see the fur growing.

He groaned again, through grinding teeth and clenched jaw. He was doing his damnedest not to scream. I helped him straighten his arms to get the shirt off.

Once again, I took his face in my hands. The bones were stretching under my touch.

"Ben, don't fight it. I know you want to, but you can't stop it, and the more you fight it the worse it is. Look at me!" He'd squeezed his eyes shut, but they snapped open again and his gaze locked on mine. His eyes were amber. "Let it go. You have to let it go."

"It" was humanity. He had to let go of the body he'd had his whole life. It wasn't easy. It was all he'd ever known. And it was slipping away as sure as the sky turned above us and the full moon rose.

Finally, the scream that had been growing in him burst loose. The full-lunged note of agony echoed around us and into the sky. When the breath left him, he sounded a whine—a wolf's whine. He broke away from me and fell forward, hugging his belly, chest heaving with every gasp.

I stayed with him, got up behind him, hugged him

from behind, my cheek pressed to his fur-covered back, and held him as tightly as I could so he would know I was here. He had to know he wasn't alone. My best friend T.J. had held me like this, my first time. The fear might have driven me crazy, otherwise.

He Changed.

His back arced with a powerful seizure, but I held on. Then his bones slipped, stretched, melted, re-formed. It happened slowly. Maybe it always did, the first time. I couldn't say I really remembered. I remembered the wide sweep of events and emotion from when it happened to me, not the details like this. It seemed to take forever, and I was too frightened to cry. What if he didn't come back together again?

Then the movement stopped, the groaning stopped. I was lying on the ground, my arms around a large, sleek wolf, who was stretched out and gasping for breath, whining with every heave of his chest as if he were dying. But he wasn't, only exhausted. I ran my fingers through his thick, luxurious fur. He was dark gray, flecked with a rust color that ran to cream on his nose and belly. Large ears lay flat against his head, and he had a long, thick snout. He was damp with sweat—human sweat matted into lupine fur.

I brushed my face along his neck and whispered by his ear, "You're all right, you're going to be fine. Just rest now. Just rest." Meaningless comforts, spoken through tears. He flicked his ears at the sound, shifted his head, looked at me. I swore I saw Ben in those eyes, looking at me as if saying, *Are you serious? You call this all right?*

I almost laughed, but the sound choked in my throat and came out as a whimper. He licked my chin—a wolfish gesture that said, *I won't make trouble, I trust you, I'm in your hands.*

Now, finally, it was time to join him. I could feel Wolf burning along every nerve. I pulled off my T-shirt.

"Kitty."

Startled, I looked behind me. Cormac leaned on the porch railing, backlit by the still open front door. He'd watched the whole thing. He saw what Ben was, now.

I couldn't see him well enough to read his expression, to guess what he was thinking. Not sure I wanted to.

"Look after him," Cormac said.

I answered him, my voice rough, thick with tears and failing. "I will. I promise. Now go inside and lock the door."

He went. Closed the door. Ben's wolf and I were left in shining moonlight. Quickly now, I peeled off my sweatpants. Let it come quickly, flowing like water, slipping from one form to the other. I kept an eye on Ben—he raised his wolf's head and watched me—until my vision blurred and I had to shut my eyes—

*O*pens *her eyes to the moonlit world.*

The scent of another fills her first breath. She recognizes him, knows him—she's claimed him as pack, which makes them family, and they'll run together, free this night.

He lies stretched out, unmoving, and gives a faint whine. He's weak, he's scared. She bows, stretches, yips at him—she has to show him that he's free, that this is good. Still he won't move, so she nips at him, snapping at his hind legs and haunches, telling him to get up, he has to get up. He flinches, then finally lurches to his feet, to get away from her teeth. He looks back at her, ears flat and tail between his legs.

He's just a pup, brand-new, and she'll have to teach him everything.

Bumping his flank with her shoulder, she urges him on, gets him to walk. His steps are hesitant—he's never walked on four legs before, he starts slowly. She runs ahead, circles back, bumps him again. As they pace into the woods of her territory, his steps become more sure. He starts to trot, his head low, his tail drooping. She can't contain her joy—she could run circles around him all night. She tries to get him to chase her. She tries to chase him, but he only looks at her in confusion. She has to teach him how to play, bowing and yipping—life isn't all about food and territory.

She shows him how to run. And how to hunt. She kills a rabbit and shares it with him, shows him the taste of blood. The eating comes naturally. She doesn't have to teach him how to devour the flesh and break the bones with his jaws. He does so eagerly, then licks the blood that has smeared on her muzzle.

He'll kill the next one, on another night.

They run, and she shows him the shape of their territory. He tires quickly though—his first night on four legs, she understands. She leads him home, to the place where they can bed down, curl up together, tails tucked close, and bury their noses in each other's fur so they fall asleep with the smell of pack and safety in their minds.

She hasn't felt so safe in a long, long time. She'll keep her packmate close, to preserve the safety. He is hers, and she'll look after him forever.

chapter **9**

The thing was, Ben was part of my pack before this ever happened to him.

I might have been alone, a werewolf on my own, but I had people I could call. People who would help me if I showed up on their doorstep in the middle of the night. Ben was near the top of that list. Yes, he was my lawyer and I sort of paid him to be there for me. But he'd handled the supernatural craziness in my life without blinking, and as far as I was concerned that went above and beyond the call of duty. He could have dumped me as a client anytime he wanted, and he didn't. I could count on him, and that made him pack.

I didn't sleep well, waking before dawn. I was nervous— I wanted to make sure I woke up before Ben did. I had to look after him.

As the sun rose, I watched him. I curled on my side, pillowing my head on my bent arm, just a breath away from him—close enough to touch. Even in sleep, his face was lined, tense with worry. He'd had an exhausting night; the evidence of it remained etched in his expression. Shifted back to human, he lay on his back, one arm resting on his stomach, the other crooked up, the hand curled by his shoulder. One of his legs was bent, the foot tucked under the opposite knee.

His build was average. He didn't work out, but he wasn't soft; it was like he'd been thin as a wire when he was a kid, and was only just now filling out to a normal size. He had a stripe of hair running down his sternum. The hair on his head, still damp with sweat, stuck out, mussed and wild. I held back an urge to brush my fingers through it, smoothing it back. I didn't want to startle him.

The bite wounds on his arm and shoulder were completely healed, as if they'd never existed.

Almost, I dozed back to sleep myself, waiting for him to come around. Then, his slow, steady breathing changed. His lungs filled deep, like a bellows. His eyes flashed open, and his whole body jerked, as if every muscle flinched at once.

He gasped, a cutoff sound of terror, and tried to get up, tried to crawl back as if he could escape whatever it was that had scared him. His limbs gave out, and he didn't go anywhere.

I lunged over and grabbed his shoulders, pushing him to the ground. I had to lean my whole weight on him—that average build was powerful.

"Ben! Quiet, you're okay, you're okay, Ben. Please calm down."

He stilled quickly enough, but I kept hushing him until he lay flat again, his eyes closed, panting for breath. I knelt by him, keeping my hands on his chest, keeping him quiet, and watching his face for any reaction.

After a moment his breathing slowed. He brought a

Carrie Vaughn

hand to his face, covered his eyes, then dragged it across his forehead. "I remember," he said in a tired, sticky voice. "I remember the smells. Running. Blood—" His voice strained, cracked.

"Shh." I lay next to him so I could bring my face close to his, brush his hair back, breathe in his scent, let him smell me, let him know that smell meant safety. "We're safe, Ben. It's okay."

"Kitty—" He said my name with a gasp of desperation, then clung to me, gripping my arm and shoulder, kneading the skin and muscle painfully. I bore it, hugging him back as well as I could. He was so warm in the freezing winter air; holding each other warmed us.

I kissed the hairline by his ear and said, "You're back. Two arms, two legs, human skin. You're back. You feel it?"

He nodded, which gave me hope because it meant he was listening.

"Wolf is gone, it's not going to come back for another month. You get to be yourself until then. It's okay, it's okay." I kept repeating it.

He relaxed. I could feel the tension leave him under my touch. He eased back against the ground instead of holding himself rigid from it. His death grip on me lessened until it was simple holding, and it was okay if he didn't let go. I didn't want him to. I didn't want him to withdraw, lock himself inside himself where I couldn't talk to him.

"Two arms, two legs," he said finally, wearily. Then he smoothed back my sweaty and tangled hair, the way I'd been brushing his. "Opposable thumbs."

I giggled, bowing my face to his shoulder. He was back.

"How do you feel?" I asked. He kept his arms around me, like he was still clinging for safety, and I snuggled into his embrace. Wolves touched for comfort. We both needed it.

After a long moment he said, "Strange. Broken. But coming back together. Like I can feel the pieces closing up." I tilted my head, trying to look at him. I saw his jaw, the slope of cheek, half an eye. "But I remember... it felt good. It felt free. Didn't it?" His face shifted into a wince. "I wasn't expecting that."

"Yeah," I said, and kissed his closest body part, his shoulder. Then I propped myself on my elbow, touched his face, and turned it to me, making him look at me. I held his gaze. "You're doing just fine, Ben. You believe me?" *You're going to live. You're not going to make Cormac shoot you.*

He nodded, and I kissed his forehead. I was trying to make him feel safe, to make him feel wanted, so he wouldn't leave.

"You're doing just fine," I repeated softly.

"That's because I have a determined teacher," he said, giving me a thin smile.

I kissed his lips. They were right there. It seemed so natural. His smile fell—then he kissed me back. And again, long enough this time that I lost my breath. Then we both froze for a moment.

My skin flushed, my whole body growing warm—*it* knew what it wanted to do, anyway. I stole a glance down Ben's torso—and yes, *his* body knew what it wanted to do, too.

Ben's hazel-colored eyes—green, mud, gold, all mixed together—flickered, trying to hold my gaze again. I looked away, human enough to be chagrined.

I said, "I should have mentioned, the lycanthropy

thing, it sort of throws gasoline on the libido. You know—whoosh, fire, out of control."

He kept staring at me, until I couldn't keep looking away.

He said, with an unreadable curl on his lips, "I'm sure it has nothing to do with the fact that I'm lying here naked with a beautiful woman, who is also naked."

Blink. Double blink. My heart may have even stopped for a moment. "Did you just call me beautiful?"

He touched my cheek, my neck, sending an electric rush along my skin, then buried his hand in my hair. "Yeah."

That was it. I was gone.

I moved, sliding one leg over his stomach, slipping on top of him until I straddled him. I kept close, my chest against his, my breath on his cheek. His arms held me tight, hands sliding down my back, clenching, and we kissed, deeply, tasting each other, sharing our heat. We touched, nuzzled; I moved my lips along his jaw, to his ear. My eyes were closed, my mind gone. Mostly gone.

"I hadn't planned on this, honest," I murmured.

He said, his voice thick with sarcasm, "Gee, thanks."

"That's not what I meant," I said, smiling. "I feel like I'm taking advantage of you."

He made what sounded to my ears like a groan of contentment. "You just want me to like being a werewolf. That's what this is about."

I pulled away, just for a moment. "You don't have to like it. You just have to survive it."

His gaze focused, met mine. "All right."

I kissed him, and kissed, shivering to try to get closer to him—we already lay skin to skin along the length of our bodies. One of his hands clasped the back of my neck, the other worked its way to my backside, locking me close to him. His touch burned in the cold winter air.

He managed one more bit of commentary, his voice low and rough, "Kitty, just so you know, you can take advantage of me anytime you want."

So I did.

He lay curled in my arms, and I reveled in the scent of him—sweaty, warm, musky. All my mornings alone I had woken anxious and discontented. Now, here with him—I had a pack again, and all felt right with the world.

It was the lycanthropy, I told myself. I never would have slept with Ben if it hadn't been for the lycanthropy. Not that I regretted it.

But still.

The sun was almost above the trees. However much I wanted to stay here all day, we had to go back. Back to the world.

Ben was the one who said, "I guess we ought to get back before Cormac comes looking for us."

The bounty hunter would do it, too. Track us down. I wasn't entirely confident what he would do when he found us. I dug out the clothes I'd stashed and split them between us. We dressed, helped each other to our feet, and set off for the cabin.

In my pack back in Denver, the alpha male, Carl, had made sleeping around a habit. If lycanthropy was to the libido what gasoline was to fire, Carl took full advantage of it. Shape-shifting was foreplay to him, and as head of the pack he had his own harem. At his call, every one of us would roll over on our backs, showing him our bellies like good submissive wolves. My Wolf had loved it: the attention, the affection, the sex. The abuse—verbal and occasionally otherwise—that he heaped along with the attention hardly mattered. At least until I couldn't take it anymore. Carl was still in Denver. That was why I couldn't go back.

I didn't want to be like that. If I had to be the alpha of our little pack of two, I didn't want to be that kind of alpha. I didn't want to screw around just because I could.

Or had it happened because I liked him? I did like him. But would I have ever slept with him, if we hadn't been naked in the woods and smelling like wolves? Would it have ever even been an issue?

Had that been Ben holding me tightly and kissing me eagerly, or his wolf?

Did it even matter?

These things were so much clearer to the Wolf side: You like him? He's naked? He's interested? Then go for it! Only the human side was worried about people's feelings getting hurt.

He walked a couple steps behind me—that submissive wolf thing again. His head was bent, and he looked tired, with shadows under his eyes. But he didn't seem angry, frightened, tense, or any of the other things I might have expected to see in a newly minted werewolf. He caught me watching him, and I smiled, trying to be encouraging. He smiled back.

"What are you going to tell Cormac?"

"Don't shoot?" He winced and shook his head. "You were right, I was wrong? I don't know. I'm confused. I don't want to die. I never did. You know that, right?"

I slowed my steps until we were walking side by side. A couple of barefooted nature freaks out for a morning stroll in the dead of winter. I wasn't cold; I could still feel his arms around me. "You were pretty determined there for a while."

"I was scared," he said. After a moment, he added, "Does it get easier? Less confusing? Less like there's an extra voice in your head telling you what to do?"

I had to shake my head. "No. It just gets confusing in different ways."

Then, almost suddenly, the trees thinned and the clearing in front of the cabin opened before us. The sun was shining full on the porch. Cormac stood there, leaning on the railing. A rifle was propped next to him. Ready and waiting.

I stopped; Ben stopped next to me. My instinct said to run, but Cormac had already seen us. He didn't move, he just looked out at us, waiting for us to do something.

Cormac had had plenty of chances to shoot me dead and hadn't yet. I didn't think he'd start now. I hoped he wouldn't start now. I walked toward the front door like nothing was wrong. Ben followed, slowly, falling behind. Cormac watched him, not me.

"Morning," I said, waving a little as I came within earshot. I tried to sound cheerful, but it came out wary.

"Well?"

Climbing the stairs, I crossed my arms and continued my campaign of strained brightness. "Well, it's a nice day. Lots of sun. Everything's fine."

By then Ben reached the porch stairs. Cormac's glare was challenging, but he wouldn't know that. Ben hesitated—I could almost see him start to wilt, growing defensive.

"Ben?" I said. He shifted his gaze to me, and the confrontation was broken.

"You okay?" Cormac said to him.

After a moment he said, "Yeah. Just fine." He sounded resigned rather than convinced.

"No more talk about shooting you, then."

"No."

I didn't know what Cormac expected. Maybe he'd spent all night working himself up to kill his cousin in cold blood, and now it seemed like he didn't quite believe that Ben had opted out. His expression was neutral, unreadable, as usual.

"What happened?" he said.

Ben bowed his head, hiding a smile. "It's hard to explain."

"You look like you had a pretty good time," Cormac said.

"Maybe I did." Ben stared at him. He actually did look pretty good, considering: tired, but relaxed. Not freaked out, like Cormac might have expected. Ben looked better than he had in days, since Cormac brought him here.

For my part, my face felt like I was blushing fire-engine-red. Yup, human Kitty was back. Wolf never blushed.

Cormac stared, like he could see through Ben, study him with x-ray vision. Cormac was the kind of guy who didn't like being out of control, who didn't like not knowing everything. Ben had traveled somewhere he couldn't go. He wanted to know what had happened to his cousin over the last twelve hours—that was all. But Ben couldn't tell him. He couldn't explain it—I couldn't explain it. That reality was part of the Wolf, inhuman and unspeakable.

Ben slumped under the pressure of his gaze. Shoulders

hunched, he went into the cabin and slammed the door. Leaving Cormac and me on the porch.

I wanted to tell Cormac to leave Ben alone. He couldn't possibly understand, no matter how much he stared at Ben. Before I could think of a way to say this to him without him getting pissed off at me, he spoke.

"You were right about him changing his mind. I really wasn't sure he would. But you knew."

Actually, I'd hoped. I let Cormac think otherwise. "I've been through it myself. I knew he'd feel differently."

"You knew he'd like being a werewolf."

"That's not a good way to describe it."

"What happened out there?"

Surely he'd figured it out. Or his imagination had. I didn't know why he wanted me to spell it out for him. "That's not any of your business."

I turned to go inside.

"Kitty—" He grabbed my wrist.

I froze before I hit him. It was only instinct, my pulling back with fingers bent like outstretched claws. He saw it; we stood like that in a tableau. So many unasked questions played in his gaze.

He brought Ben here so I could help him, keep him alive. Not shack up with him. None of us had expected that. And now Cormac actually looked hurt, some pain-filled anguish touching his features. If Cormac had wanted things to happen differently between us, why couldn't he just come out and say it? He'd had his chance. I'd given him plenty of chances. I couldn't go backward.

"Cormac, I'm sorry." I brushed myself out of his grasp and went into the house.

My usual routine after a full moon: I came home, took

a shower, and crawled into bed for a couple hours of more comfortable sleep. Then I woke up and had some coffee. No breakfast because I wasn't hungry. Wolf usually had had plenty to eat during the night.

Ben had already started the coffee. The scent filled the house, and I had to admit it smelled wonderful. Soothing, like I could curl up on the sofa and forget about the guys in my house. I didn't want to leave them alone long enough to take a shower. Like I still thought Cormac might draw a bead on Ben with that rifle. Easy to forget that Cormac was the one who'd brought Ben here because he *didn't* want to shoot him.

I was too wired to sleep. I'd already spent the extra time napping back in the woods with Ben. That man had screwed up my entire schedule. Though if I thought about it, what I really wanted to do was crawl back into bed with *him*—

I went to the kitchen and poured myself a cup of coffee. Ben, sitting at the table with his own cup, didn't say anything. Whatever he said, I was sure it would make me snap at him. I didn't want to do that. I gave him what I hoped was a reassuring smile.

Cormac joined us a minute later, after I heard the door to the Jeep open and close. He didn't have the rifle with him, so I assumed he put it away. Good. He sat across from Ben. I leaned back against the counter.

Here we were, back in the kitchen, glaring at tabletops and not saying anything.

I couldn't stand long silences. That probably came from working in radio. "So, kids. Any questions? We all squared away?"

"I don't know that I'd go that far," Ben said, chuckling

softly. He shrugged his hands in a gesture of helplessness. "What do I do now? If I'm really going to live with this, what do I do?"

I said, "You're a lawyer. Go back and... lawyer. What would you be doing if this hadn't happened?"

"It's not that simple," he said. "It can't possibly be that simple."

He was right, of course.

"You take it one day at a time, Ben. Some days are easier than others. But you just have to work through it."

He scowled. "Don't talk to me like I'm one of the losers on your show."

That stung like a kick in the gut. My callers weren't losers—they were my audience. My *fans*. I wanted to defend them. But yeah, they had problems. A guy like Ben? He didn't have problems. He was a tough guy.

"Then stop acting like a loser," I said.

"That's rich, coming from someone who ran off to the woods with her tail between her legs—"

I took a step toward him, teeth bared in a silent growl, my hands clenched into fists. He flinched back in a sudden panic, jerking the chair off its front legs. We stared at each other for a moment—I dared him to take me. I dared him to say what he was thinking.

He looked down. Then he pulled his hands through his hair and leaned his elbows on the table. "What the hell's happening to me?" he muttered.

I turned away. I knew what was happening to him, but how did I explain it all? A whole new set of body language and emotions—I'd been living with them for years now. I took them for granted.

"Right, you two are even freaking me out," Cormac said,

hands raised in a gesture of surrender. He stood. "I'm taking a walk."

"Cormac." Ben reached across the table, stopping him for a moment. The tableau held until Ben took a breath and said, "I'm sorry. I'm sorry for saddling you with this."

The hunter looked away, and his face tensed, pursing into an expression I couldn't read. Some emotion was there, that he was trying desperately to hide.

"No," he said. "I'm the one who got you into this mess. I'm sorry."

As he had so many times before during the past week, he walked out the door. Taking a walk. It was how he coped with the long, awkward silences.

Ben's arm still lay draped across the table, and he sighed, almost bowing his head to its surface. "I knew he was going to do that. I knew he was going to blame himself."

I went to Ben—slowly this time, nonthreateningly. He glanced sideways at me, warily, but didn't flinch. I touched his shoulder, held my hand there. Didn't say anything for once, but I smiled when he leaned into the touch.

Miracle of miracles, Ben listened to me. He went back to work. Borrowed my phone to check his voice mail, used my computer and Internet connection to check his e-mail, replied to a couple of panicked messages from clients. He had his own practice, small enough for one person to run but enough to make a living, fully in keeping with his independent character. Evidently, he'd decided that if he was going to live, he'd better get back to work. Werewolves still had to pay the rent. The human half did, anyway.

We had venison for dinner again. That stuff never got old. Though I was beginning to think I should invest in a grill, so we didn't have to keep sticking them under the broiler. Cormac ate leaning up against the counter, Ben and I sat at the table. The meal felt almost normal. Nobody was staring at anybody, nobody asked to get shot, and Cormac had put his guns away.

We talked about my evil stalker.

"How long's this been going on?" Ben asked.

"About ten days. The first one happened right before you got here," I said. "Okay, so whoever has it in for me knows what I am. Why didn't something happen last night? Why didn't they go after the wolf half?"

"They're scared," Ben said. "You're strongest at the full moon. They're not going to want to confront that."

Cormac said, "He's right. Full moon's the worst night to go after a werewolf. You wait until the morning after. Get 'em while they're sleeping it off." He smiled.

Even Ben shook his head at that one. "You just got a whole hell of a lot creepier."

"Me? I haven't changed a bit." He gave Ben a hard look.

I wasn't going to let that topic go any further than it already had. "They didn't come after me this morning. They were scared enough to stay inside last night, but didn't know to come looking for me this morning."

"They don't know what they're doing." Ben looked to Cormac for confirmation.

The hunter tapped the flat of his steak knife thoughtfully against his opposite hand. "If they'd wanted to kill you all it would take was a sniper sitting up on the road. Deputy Rosco could do it. They're just trying to scare you into leaving."

"So who is 'they'? Or he, or she, or it?" I said.

Ben continued the brainstorming. "Someone who doesn't want to kill you and doesn't know what they're doing."

"Amateurs," Cormac said. "Amateurs practicing some kind of fucked up blood magic. This is going to turn around and bite somebody on the ass."

"Hello?" I raised a hand. "I'm feeling pretty ass-bitten right here."

"But you're still here. Whatever spell it is your fan club thinks they're casting isn't working. You can't work the kind of magic that calls for hanging skinned dogs up in trees without paying some price. They've either got to give up soon, or escalate. I'd hate to see where that could go."

"You have any contacts who might know something about this?" Ben asked.

"I might. I'll make a call." He retrieved his cell phone from his duffel bag and went outside.

All I wanted was for the torture of small animals outside my house to stop, the book to be finished, and Ben to be okay.

I could check on at least one of those. "How are you doing?"

He thought for a moment, then shrugged. "All right, I think. I'm not feeling much of anything. It's a whole lot better than yesterday, though."

"Good," I said, inordinately pleased.

Ben and I were washing dishes when Cormac came back in. He didn't say anything about how his call went, and we didn't ask. If he didn't tell us, asking him wouldn't get him to talk.

It was strange, how I was getting used to having him around. Maybe the three of us still had a chance of coming to some sort of equilibrium. Some arrangement where Ben didn't lose his best friend, I didn't lose my new wolf pack, and Cormac could hold on to the only people who anchored him to the world. Or maybe that was wishful thinking.

Later, I found Ben changing the sheets on the bed. He'd found the clean set in the closet, and was stripping off the ones he'd sweated, tossed, and turned on over the last week.

"I thought I'd get it ready for you," he explained as I leaned in the doorway. "I've kept you out of it long enough."

This was going to be more awkward than I thought. We weren't wolves tonight, and the lycanthropy wasn't lighting any fires. Any acknowledged fires, at least.

"Where'll you sleep?" I asked.

Cormac answered, "The sofa. I'll take the floor."

"I can take the floor," Ben said. Cormac was already pulling out his bedroll and spreading it out by the desk. "We can draw straws."

"Do I get to draw straws?" I said.

"No," they said, in unison.

My, what gentlemen. I smirked.

Ben ended up on the sofa. Cormac was very hard to argue with.

Eventually, the lights went out and the house fell quiet.

I hadn't gotten any sleep the night before. Being in my own bed again, I should have been out for the count. But I lay there, staring at the darkened ceiling, wondering why I couldn't sleep. I had too much on my mind, I decided.

Then the floorboards leading into the bedroom creaked, very faintly. I propped myself on an elbow. The figure edging inside the room was in shadow, a silhouette only. I took a breath through my nose, smelling—

It was Ben.

"I can't sleep," he whispered. He stepped toward the bed, slouching a little—sheepish, if I didn't know him better. "I keep fidgeting. It feels... weird. Being alone. I was wondering: could I... I mean with you—" He gestured toward the bed, shoulders tensed, and looked away.

He was a new wolf. A pup. A kid having nightmares. I'd been the same way.

I pushed back the covers and scooted to one side of the bed.

Letting out a sigh, he climbed in beside me, curling up on his side as I pulled the covers over us both. I put my arms around him, he settled close, and that was all. In moments, he was asleep, his chest rising and falling regularly. He was exhausted, but he'd needed to feel safe before he could sleep.

God help anybody who felt safer with me looking after him. I could barely take care of myself. But what else could I do? I held him and settled in to sleep. Tried not to worry.

As I faded, sinking into a half-asleep state, I glimpsed another shadow at the doorway. A figure looked in briefly, then moved away. Then I heard the front door open and close, and faintly, like a buzzing in a distant dream, the Jeep's engine started up, and tires crunched on the gravel drive.

He's gone, my dream self thought, and there wasn't anything I could do about it.

chapter 10

He's gone," Ben said, leaning over the kitchen sink and looking out the window to the clearing where Cormac's Jeep was no longer parked.

Cormac had cleared out his bedroll, his duffel bag, his guns. After sharing the space with him for a week, the house seemed empty without him and his things. He'd packed everything up and driven off in the middle of the night. It was how he often made his exits.

This time, though, the bastard had left me to figure out this curse business on my own. I'd been counting on his help.

"Why?" Ben said.

"You know him better than I do. You know what he's like." I sat at the table, feet up on the seat of my chair, hugging my knees. "Did he have someplace he needed to be? Maybe he's following up on his contact, about the blood magic."

Ben shook his head. "Three's a crowd. That's what he was thinking. That's why he left."

"But..." And I couldn't think of anything more to say. If Cormac had felt that way, he should have said something.

He should have told me. Why couldn't he ever just come out and say it? "Should we go after him? Should we call him?" I had his number stored on my cell phone. I'd entered it in when I first got the phone, a short time after I met him. He was the kind of person you could call in an emergency.

Again, Ben shook his head. "If he'd wanted us to contact him, he'd have left a note."

"It's not a matter of what he wants, it's a matter of what's good for him. He's not going to go do something crazy to get himself hurt, is he?"

Ben arched a brow wryly. "Any more so than he usually does?"

He had a point.

"What's the plan now?" I said. "Cormac left us with that curse. I'd just as soon let the curse win and get out of here."

Ben continued looking out into the forest. He seemed peaceful, if sad. The calm was holding. "One more day. Give me one more day to pull myself together. I don't think I'm ready for civilization yet."

I couldn't argue with that. I'd give him all the time I could. "You got it."

So. That started our first day without Cormac.

I worked at the computer. I'd tried to pull off a modern-day *Walden,* but I'd failed to live up to Thoreau's ideals. The real problem was that I didn't have a pond. It was Walden *Pond.* I needed a large body of water for effective contemplation.

But really, what would Thoreau have done if a friend had shown up with a werewolf bite and begged for his help? Which made me wonder if maybe there was a more sinister reason Thoreau went off to live by himself in the woods, and he dressed the whole experience up in all this rhetoric about simple living to cover it up. Werewolves were not exactly part of the accepted canon of American literature. What *would* Thoreau have done?

A WWTD? bumper sticker would take too much explaining. And really, he'd have probably lectured the poor guy about how his dissolute lifestyle had gotten him into the situation.

I wasn't Thoreau. Wasn't ever going to be Thoreau. Screw it. I wrote pages about the glories of mass consumerism offered by the height of modern civilization. All the reasons *not* to run off to the woods and deny yourself a few basic indulgences in life.

That night, without a word spoken about it, Ben and I slipped into bed together and snuggled under the covers for warmth. No making out, no sex, not so much as a kiss, and that was fine. We were pack, and we needed to be together.

We should have left town that day.

Something happened, woke me up. I could barely feel it as it pressed against the air, making its own little wind with its passage. A predator, stalking *me*.

No. This was my place, my territory. I didn't have to take this. I wasn't going to run and let it win. Just *no*.

I slipped out of bed and stomped out to the porch, in the dark of night, no visible moon or stars or anything.

"Kitty?" Ben said, from the bedroom.

Leaning on the railing, I smelled the air. Trees, hills, and *something*. Something wrong. Couldn't see anything in the forest, but it was here. Whatever hated me was here.

"Come out!" I screamed. I ran into the clearing, turned

around, searched, and still didn't see anything. "I want to see you! Let me see you, you coward!"

This was stupid. Whoever laid that curse on this place wasn't going to come out in the open. If they'd wanted to face me, they'd never have snuck around gutting rabbits on my porch in the first place. All I'd do with my screaming and thrashing around was chase it off.

But that feeling was still there. That weight, that hint that something wasn't just watching me. It had trapped me. It had marked my territory as its own, and was now smothering me rather than letting me run.

Maybe this wasn't the curse. Maybe this was something else. Cormac said it might escalate, but escalate to what?

Something like eyes glowed, making a shape in the darkness.

My imagination. There wasn't really anything out there. But I went into the trees, stepping lightly. Think of wolf paws, pads barely touching earth, moving easily as air. My stride grew longer. I could jog like this for hours without losing my breath.

"Kitty!" Ben pounded down the porch steps, but I didn't turn around. If something was out there, if this thing was after me, I'd find it.

There, movement. That same shadow, large but low to the ground. Lurking. My pulse sped up, beating hot. This was what I should have been doing all along, turning the tables, hunting the hunter. Counterintuitively, I slowed, waiting to see what it would do, giving it a chance to leap this way or that. Once it moved, all I had to do was pounce and pin it with my claws.

Two red eyes, glaring, caught me. The gaze fixed on me, and I couldn't move.

I had good eyesight—a wolf's eyes. But I couldn't make out the form the eyes belonged to. Even when it moved closer, I only saw shadow. I heard a low noise, like a growl, so low it shook the ground under me.

All my instincts screamed for me to run. Get out. This wasn't right, this wasn't real. But I couldn't move.

Something grabbed my arm and yanked me from behind. I stayed on my feet, but I might as well have flipped head over heels, the way my vision swam and the world shifted.

"Kitty!"

My senses started working again, and I smelled friend. Pack. Ben.

"Did you see it?" I said, gasping for air, clinging to his arm.

"No, nothing. You ran out of the house like you were in some kind of trance."

And he followed, out of trust, out of loyalty. I pulled myself close to him. I kept looking out, scanning the trees, the spaces between them, looking for red eyes and a shadow. I saw skeletal branches against a sky made indistinct with clouds, earth rising up the hill, and patches of snow.

Both of our breaths fogged in the cold, releasing billowing clouds that quickly faded. Nothing else moved. We might have been the only living things out here. I shivered. Once I stopped running, the cold hit me like a wall, chilling my skin from toe to scalp. I was only wearing sweats and a T-shirt and went barefoot.

Ben blazed with warmth; I wrapped myself up with him. He was smart—he'd grabbed a coat. We stood, holding each other.

"What is it?" he asked. "What did you see?"

"Eyes," I said, my voice shaking. "I saw eyes."

"Something's here? What?"

"I don't know." My voice whined. Worse, I didn't know what would have happened if Ben hadn't come for me. If he hadn't shaken me loose from that thing's gaze. I made it a simple observation. "You came after me."

"I didn't want to be alone."

I hugged him tightly, still shaken, speechless. With my arm around him, I urged him forward, starting back for the cabin. "Let's go."

I'd traveled much farther than I thought. I couldn't have been following the shadow for more than a couple of minutes. But the cabin was over a mile away. I hadn't noticed the time passing. We followed the scent of smoke from the stove back home.

"It had red eyes," I said, but only when I could see the light in the windows.

"Like the thing Cormac saw," he said.

Yeah. Just like it.

That was it. This was war. I didn't need Cormac's help stopping this. I was a clever girl. I'd figure it out.

I hunted for it that day. Searched for tracks, smelled for a scent. I followed the tracks I'd made, the path I'd cut through the woods, ranging out from it on both sides. It had to be there, it had to have left some sign.

None of my enemies here had ever left a trail before. Why should they start now?

I walked for miles and lost track of time. Once again, Ben came for me, calling my name, following my scent, probably, whether he knew he was doing it or not.

When he finally caught up, he said, "Any luck?"

I had to say no, and it didn't make any sense. I should have found something.

He said, "I take it we're not leaving tomorrow."

"No. No, I have to figure this out. I can figure this out. It's not going to beat me." I was still searching the woods, my vision blurring I was staring so hard into the trees. Every one of them might have hidden something.

"It's after noon," Ben said. "At least come back and eat something. I fixed some lunch."

"Let me guess—venison."

He donned his familiar, half-smirking grin. How long had it been since I'd seen it?

"No. Sandwiches. Would you believe Cormac took most of the meat with him?"

Yes. Yes I would. "He uses it for bait, doesn't he?"

"You really want me to answer that?"

"No, I don't."

I worked while we ate, going online to search whatever relevant came to mind: barbed-wire cross, blood curses, animal sacrifice. Red eyes. Red-eyed monsters, to try to filter out all the medical pages and photography advice I got with that search. I found a lot of sites that skirted around the topics. A lot of people out there made jewelry that was supposed to look like barbed wire but wasn't nearly vicious enough to be the real thing. A lot of sites bragged, but few had any kind of authority.

As usual, the people who really knew about this stuff didn't talk about it, and certainly didn't blog about it.

I found one thing, though. A long shot, but an interesting one. The Walsenburg Public Library's electronic card catalog was online. Their three titles on the occult were checked out.

I called them up. A woman answered.

"Hi," I said cheerfully. "I'm interested in a couple of books you have, but the catalog says they're checked out."

"If they've been checked out for more than two weeks I can put a recall on them—"

"No, that's okay. I was actually wondering if you could tell me who checked them out."

Her demeanor instantly chilled. "I'm sorry, I really can't give you that information."

I clearly should have known better than to ask. In retrospect, her answer didn't surprise me. I tried again anyway. "Not even a hint?"

"I'm sorry. Do you want me to try that recall?"

"No, thanks. That's okay." I hung up. I wasn't interested in the books. I wanted to know who in the county was studying the occult. What amateur had maybe gotten a little too good at this sort of thing.

Again, we slept curled up together, looking for basic comfort. Rather, I tried to sleep, but spent more time staring at the ceiling, waiting for that moment of pressure, of fear, the sure knowledge that something unknown and terrifying was out there stalking me. The feeling had changed from when it was dead rabbits on my porch. This new force didn't just want me to leave—it wanted me dead. It made me think there was nothing I could do but freeze and wait for it to strike me.

Nothing had been slaughtered on my porch in days. The barbed-wire crosses had disappeared. Did that mean the curse was gone, or had it turned into something else?

I waited, but nothing happened that night. A breeze whispered through winter pines, and that was all. I thought I was going to break from listening, and waiting.

The next morning, Ben chopped wood for the stove. He was getting his strength back, looking for things to do. Normal, closer to normal. I watched him out the window, from my desk. He knew how to use an ax, swinging smoothly and easily, quickly splitting logs and building up the pile next to the porch. For some reason this surprised me, like I assumed that a lawyer couldn't also know anything about manual labor. It occurred to me that I knew as little about Ben's background as I knew about Cormac's. Ben had definitely spent some time in his past splitting logs.

He paused often to look around, turn his nose to the air, presumably smelling the whole range of scents he'd never known before. It took time sorting them out.

At one point he stopped and tensed. I could actually see his shoulders bunch up. He stared toward the road. Then he set the ax by the woodpile and backed toward the front door.

I went to meet him, my own nerves quivering. That thing that was hunting us . . .

"Someone's coming," he said, just as the sheriff's car came over the dirt road and into the clearing. Side by side, we watched the car creep to a stop.

Ben's whole body seemed to tremble with anxiety. He stared at Sheriff Marks getting out of the car.

I touched his arm. "Calm down."

Ben winced, tilting his head with a confused expression. "Why do I feel like growling at him?"

I smiled and patted him on the shoulder. "He's invading our territory. And he doesn't smell like a real nice person, either. Just try to act normal."

He shook his head. "This is crazy."

"How you doing, Sheriff Marks?" I called out nicely.

"Not so good, Ms. Norville. I've got a problem."

My stomach turned over. Why was the first thought that popped into my head, *What has Cormac done?*

"Sorry to hear that. Can I help?"

"I hope so." He stopped at the base of the porch and took a good, slow look at Ben. I could almost see his little mind ticking off the points on a formal police description: hair, height, build, race, and general suspiciousness. Ben crossed his arms and stared back. Finally Marks said, "Who's this?"

"This is Ben. He's a friend."

Marks smirked. "Another one? How many friends you shacking up with out here?"

Right, now I wanted to growl at him. "You said there was something I could help you with?"

Marks jerked his thumb over his shoulder to point at the car. "You mind taking a little ride with me?"

I did mind. I minded a lot. "Why? I'm not being arrested—"

"Oh, no," Marks said. "Not yet."

"How about I follow you in my car?" I said, admiring how steady my voice sounded. Something was very wrong. It was Cormac. It had to be Cormac. I wasn't going to say the name until Marks did, though.

But Marks was staring hard at me. Like it was me he was after. He had no idea what his glare was doing to Wolf. I had to look away. That fight or flight thing was kicking at me.

"I don't know. I'd hate for you to run off," Marks said.

What in God's name had happened? "I'm not going to run off. All my stuff is here. And why are you worried about me running off?"

"You'll see. Let's get going. Take your car, but I'm keeping an eye on you."

"Of course." I went to find my keys and backpack.

"Can I come with you?" Ben said.

I relaxed a little. It would be good to have a friend at my back. "Sure. You're my lawyer. I have this creepy feeling I might need my lawyer."

I drove behind Marks's car as close as I could without actually tailgating, so that I wouldn't give him the slightest idea that I was "running off." I watched him through his rear window as he checked his rearview mirror every five seconds.

Ben frowned. "It's a werewolf thing. Something happened, and he thinks a werewolf did it."

"Yeah. Maybe he's just trying to get back at me for all those times I called him about the dead rabbits. Maybe this is some practical joke. I'll end up on the first werewolf reality TV show. Wouldn't that be a hoot?" I muttered.

After a few miles we turned off the highway onto a wide dirt road, then after several more miles made another turn onto a narrow dirt road, then onto a driveway. A carved wood sign posted in front of a barbed-wire fence announced the Baker Ranch. A quarter of a mile along, Marks pulled off onto the verge behind a pickup truck, and I pulled in behind him. Dry, yellowed grass cracked under the tires.

An older man wearing a denim jacket, jeans, and cowboy boots leaned against a weathered fence post. Marks went to him, and they shook hands. The man looked over at us, still in the car. I expected to see the determined suspicion in him that I saw on Marks's face. But he looked at us with curiosity.

I got out of the car and went to join them. Ben followed.

Marks made introductions. "Ms. Norville, this is Chad Baker. Chad, Kitty Norville."

"Miss Norville." Baker offered his hand, and we shook.

"Call me Kitty. This is Ben O'Farrell." More hand-shaking all around. I looked at Marks and waited for him to tell me why we were all here.

"Why don't we all go take a look at the problem, shall we?" Marks said, smiling, and gestured across the field on the other side of the fence.

Baker slipped a loop of wire off the top of the nearest fence post, pulling back the top strand of barbed wire. The tension made it coil back on itself. We could all climb over the bottom part of the fence without too much effort.

We walked across the field, up a rise that overlooked a depression that was hidden from the road. Marks and Baker stood aside and let us look.

Six dead cows lay sprawled before me. They weren't just dead. They'd been gutted, torn to pieces, throats ripped out, guts spilled, tongues lolling. The grass and dirt around them had turned to sticky mud, so much blood had poured out of them. They hadn't even had time to run, it looked like. They'd all dropped where they stood. The air smelled of rotten meat, of blood and waste.

One werewolf couldn't have done this. It would have taken a whole pack.

Or something lurking in the dark, gazing out with red eyes.

"You want to tell me what happened here?" Marks said

in a tone that suggested he already knew exactly what had happened.

I swallowed. What could I say? What did he want me to say? "Ah... it looks like some cows were killed."

"Massacred, more like," Marks said. Chad Baker's expression didn't change. I assumed they were his cows. He was taking this very calmly.

"What do you want me to tell you, Sheriff? What do you think I know?" I spoke softly, unable to muster any more righteous sarcasm.

"I think you know exactly what I think."

"What, you think I can read minds?" I was just being cagey. He was right, I knew: I was Kitty, the famous were-wolf, who moved into his jurisdiction and then this happened. I told him, "You think I did this."

"Well?" he said.

"I assure you, I'm not in any way, shape, or form capable of this. No single wolf, lycanthropic or otherwise, is capable of this."

"That's what I told him," Baker said, flickering a smile. My heart instantly went out to him.

"Thank you," I said. "I don't think I could bring down one cow on my own, much less a whole herd."

"*Something* did this," Marks said unhelpfully.

"We couldn't find any prints," Baker said. "My dogs didn't hear a thing, and they'll set up a racket at the drop of a hat. It's like something dropped on them out of the sky."

"A werewolf isn't a normal wolf," Marks said, unable to let it go. "God knows what the hell you're capable of."

I took a deep breath, quelling the nausea brought on by the stench of death—not even Wolf could stomach this mess. I filtered out the smells I knew, looking for the one

I was afraid I'd find: the musky human/lupine mix that meant werewolves had been here.

I didn't smell it.

"This wasn't werewolves," I murmured. What was weird, though: I didn't smell *anything* outside of what I expected. No predator, no intruder. Nothing that wasn't already here; no hint of what had *been* here. Just like around my cabin, when I chased after that intruder. Like Baker said, it was as if something dropped on them out of the sky.

"Kitty." Low and strained, Ben's voice grated like sandpaper.

He stared at the scene with unmistakable hunger. And revulsion, the two sides of him, wolf and human, battling over what emotion he should feel. His wolf might very well look on this as a feast and claw its way to the surface. The smell of blood—so thick on the air—was like an invitation, and he wasn't used to dealing with it. He clenched his hands. Sweat had broken out on his hairline. He was losing it.

I grabbed his arm and turned him away.

He squeezed his eyes shut, and his breaths came quick. I whispered, "Keep it together, okay? Don't think of the blood, think about something else. Keep it locked up inside, all curled up and harmless."

He started to turn around, to look back over his shoulder at the slaughter. Hand on his cheek, I made him look back at me. I held his face and pulled his head down closer to me. We touched foreheads, and I kept talking until I felt him nod, until I knew he heard me.

His breathing slowed, and some of the tension sagged out of him. Only then did I let go. "Take a walk if you need to," I said. "Walk back to the car and don't think about it, okay?"

"Okay," he said. Without looking up, he started back for the car, hunched in and unhappy looking.

"Weak stomach?" Baker asked.

"Something like that," I said. "Is there anything else I need to see here, or can we go back to the cars?"

We climbed back over the fence, and Baker replaced the top strand of wire. Ben was leaning on the hood of my car, arms crossed and head bowed. I wished Marks had given me some kind of warning, so I wouldn't have had to bring Ben into that. He wasn't ready to deal with that.

"We're having a hard time explaining what happened out there, Ms. Norville. Werewolves, though. That's a pretty interesting explanation," Marks said.

"Yeah, but it's wrong," I said. "I didn't do it. I don't know what did." I didn't tell him about the thing I saw outside my cabin. That thing I thought I saw. If I couldn't describe it, what was the point?

Marks clearly didn't believe me. He might as well have been holding a pair of handcuffs. Baker's expression was maddeningly neutral. Like he was happy to put it all in Marks's hands and get back to the business of ranching. Western reserve to the extreme.

"Look," I started, growing flustered. "It's easy enough to prove I didn't do it. Get somebody out here to take some samples, find the bite marks and get some saliva, test it. I'll give you a sample to compare—"

"You don't have to do that," Ben said, looking up. "Let him get a warrant first."

Marks glanced at him. "Who did you say you were?"

"Benjamin O'Farrell. Attorney-at-law."

The sheriff didn't like that answer. He frowned. "Well ain't that something."

Ben sticking up for me settled me down. He was right; I didn't have to defend myself here. They had no proof. I said, "You think about trying the UFO people? I hear they have a bead on this sort of thing." Anything could have done this.

"This isn't a joke. This is a man's livelihood." Marks gave Baker a nod.

"I'm not joking. Can we go now?"

Scowling, he went to the door of his car. "Don't think about leaving town. Either one of you."

Whatever. I opened my own car door and started to climb in.

Baker called out, "If you come up with any ideas about what happened here, you'll let me know?"

I nodded. My only idea at the moment was that this whole town was cursed.

As soon as I left the driveway leading out of Baker's ranch, Ben said, "Do you have your phone?"

"It's in my bag." I gestured to the floor of the backseat.

Ben found it, then dialed a number.

He must have gotten voice mail. "Cormac, it's me. There's been some cattle killed up here. Matches the MO of those flocks killed at Shiprock. Your rogue wolf may have found its way out here. I don't know where you've gone, but you might want to get back."

He lowered the phone and switched it off.

I glanced at him, though I wanted to stare. I still had to drive.

"Rogue wolf," I said. "The one he wasn't able to kill back in New Mexico?" I remembered he'd mentioned the sheep that had been killed. That there'd been two werewolves, and he'd only shot the one. "Why didn't you say anything back there?"

"Because I couldn't." Ben's voice was tight, almost angry. "Because that smell hit me and—and I wasn't in my head anymore. Something else was. I couldn't talk, I couldn't even think."

My own anger drained out of me. "It's the wolf. Certain smells, sometimes tastes, or if you're scared or angry, all of that makes it stronger. Calls it up. You have to work extra hard to keep it locked away. If I'd known what we were going to see I would have warned you. Or kept you away."

"I hate it," he said, glaring out the side window. "I hate losing control like that."

This was Ben, who stood in courtrooms telling off judges, who stared down cops, who didn't pull punches. Probably couldn't stand the idea of something else inside him running the show. I reached over, found his hand, and held it. I half expected him to pull away, but he didn't. He squeezed back and kept staring out the window.

We returned to the cabin, but I didn't go inside. I went out, into the trees, the direction I'd run the other night, chasing that thing. That nightmare. If I hadn't just seen that slaughtered herd, I might have been able to convince myself that shadow had been a figment of my imagination.

Ben followed reluctantly. "Where are you going?"

"I've got to figure out what did that."

"Clear your name?"

It wasn't that. Marks couldn't prove I'd done it, however much he wanted to. Rather, I'd gotten this feeling that things would only get worse until I stood up and did something. I was tired of waiting, cornered and shivering in the dark. That might have been okay for a lone wolf, but I had a pack to protect now.

Running away wasn't an option because what if this thing up and followed me?

Ben said, "You think this is the thing you saw the other night?"

"I'm still not sure I saw anything."

"And you think it's the same thing Cormac was hunting."

"What if it followed him here?" Whatever had been here, the signs were two days old now. Harder to find—and I hadn't found anything in the first place. But if it was the same thing, I had a second point of contact now. I headed overland, as the crow flies or wolf runs, in the direction of the Baker ranch. "I'll look around. I can cover this whole area between here and the ranch. You should stay here."

"No. You're not leaving me out of this. I'll come with you. I'll help."

"Ben—"

"I don't want to hear any more of that alpha wolf bullshit. Just let me help, please."

I could have gotten angry and stood my ground on principle. That would have been the alpha thing to do. Alphas didn't let new wolves argue with them. But it was just the two of us. I didn't have anything to prove. Maybe we'd be better off together.

"Look for anything out of place. Any sign, any feeling."

"Anything that smells like those cattle," he said, his voice low.

"Yeah."

Together, we hunted. I let a bit of that Wolf-sense bleed into my human self. Smell, sound, senses—the least movement of a squirrel became profound, I looked sharply at every rustling branch. Daylight wasn't the time to be doing this. Too many distractions. Whatever had made that carnage had done so at night. This was a nighttime kind of evil.

I watched Ben, worried that he might let too much of his wolf out, wondering if he might lose control and shift. Mostly, he seemed introspective, looking around like the world was new, or like he was waking up after a dream. He was right to want to come along, I realized. Being out here, learning to look at the world again, was better than him staying holed up at home.

We rounded the hill at the edge of the Baker ranch, overlooking his land. A backhoe was dumping the last of the carcasses onto a truck, to be hauled away.

We'd found no sign of the creature, and somehow I wasn't surprised. We turned around and went home.

That afternoon, I went online again, checking the usual weird Web sites and forums that might have the sort of data—or at worst, rumors and anecdotes—I wanted. I searched for livestock mutilations, particularly in the Southwest U.S. Sure enough, the hits I found included an inordinate number of UFOlogist sites. Kind of annoying. I tried to avoid knee-jerk skepticism, since lately I'd been forced to reassess a lot of my assumptions. About, like, the existence of werewolves for example. But I wasn't quite willing to believe that a vastly superior extraterrestrial intelligence would travel all the way to Earth just to turn a few cows inside out.

But I found something. It wasn't aliens, it wasn't werewolves. On a few sites people talked about a sort of haunting. Not by the dead, but by a kind of evil. It left death and destruction in its wake. It originated in the Native American tribes of the Southwest, particularly the Navajo and Zuni. They talked about witches laying curses that killed entire families, destroyed livelihoods, haunted entire communities. And about skinwalkers: witches who had the power to change themselves into animals. Like lycanthropes. They had red eyes.

Nobody seemed to want to talk about them in detail. Knowing too much about them drew suspicion onto oneself. In some places, a person could be excused for killing someone who was suspected of being a skinwalker. Like lycanthropes, again.

Again I avoided knee-jerk skepticism. In my experience, accusations of evilness often stemmed from the fears of the accuser rather than the real nature of the accused.

What attacked Ben in New Mexico was a werewolf, plain and simple. We had the proof of that in Ben himself. But there'd been two of them.

I grilled Ben about what he knew.

"Not much," he said. "Cormac picked up this contract for the werewolf, but he got down there and found signs that there were two of them. So he called me. I saw some of the sheep they'd killed. Completely ripped open, like the cattle today." He paused, closing his eyes and taking a deep breath. The memory had triggered a reaction, caused his wolf to prick his ears. Ben collected himself and continued. "I only caught a glimpse of it, right before I was attacked. It was a wolf, it looked like a wolf. Something was wrong, Cormac was letting it walk right up to him. He could have shot the thing from ten paces off. I started to shout, then..." He shook his head. Then he was attacked, and that was that. He'd been watching Cormac, and not what came after him.

"Cormac said you saved him. You got a shot off and that broke some kind of spell."

"I don't know. I don't remember it too clearly. Anything could have happened, I suppose. I do know there was something messed up going on."

"And now it's moved here. I really hate my life right now."

"Join the club," he said. Then, more thoughtfully, "I grew up on a cattle ranch. Dead cattle—it's serious. Every one of them is a piece of the rancher's income. It's a big business. Marks will go after it until he figures it out."

"Well, as long as he's after me, he isn't going to figure it out." Marks didn't know about Ben; I figured we'd keep it that way. Nobody had to know about Ben.

"You suppose there's a connection with what's been going on here, with your dead rabbits and dogs?"

I shook my head. "Those were organized. Ritual killings. That today—was just slaughter." Like we needed another curse around here.

I almost wished they were connected, so we'd only have one problem to solve.

That night, we lay sprawled in bed, like a couple of dogs in front of the fireplace. He pillowed his head on my stomach, nestling in the space formed by my bent legs. I held one of his hands, while resting the other on his increasingly shaggy head of hair. We didn't look at each other, but stared into space, not ready for sleep.

He was still shaken by the day's adventure. Not quite comfortable in his skin. I knew the feeling. I let him talk as much as he wanted.

He said, "It feels like a parasite. Like there's this thing inside me and all it wants to do is suck the life out of me then crawl out of my empty skin."

Now there was a lovely image. "I never looked at it that way. To me it's always kind of felt like this voice, it's looking at everything over my shoulder and it always has an opinion. It's like an evil Jiminy Cricket."

He chuckled. "Jiminy Cricket with claws. I like it."

"It digs into your skin like a kitten with those needley little things." I giggled. Silly was better than scary.

Ben winced. "Ugh, those things *are* evil. You ever want to see something fun, throw a kitten down somebody's shirt. Watch them squirm trying to avoid getting clawed while not hurting the kitten."

Now I winced. I could almost feel those little claws scratching on my stomach. "You sound like you've done it before."

"Or had it done."

I couldn't help it. I giggled again, because I could see it: him and Cormac as kids, cousins fooling around at the family reunion, and I just knew who would have thrown a kitten down whose shirt. Oh, the humanity.

Wearing a wry smile, he looked at me. His voice turned thoughtful. "I don't think I'd have made it this far without you. Cormac did the right thing, bringing me here."

"That's nice of you to finally admit it."

"When this happened to you, did you get through it alone or did someone help you?"

"Hmm, I had a whole pack. A dozen or so other

werewolves, and half of them wanted to help and half of them were worried I'd be competition. But there was someone in the middle of all that. T.J. looked out for me. The first time I Changed, he held me. I tried to be there for you the same way. But T.J.—he was special. He was very Zen about the whole thing most of the time. He used to tell me not to look at the Wolf as the enemy, but to learn to use it as a strength. You take those strengths into your-self and become more than the sum of the parts." Always, this was easier said than done. But I could still hear T.J.'s voice telling me these things. Reminding me.

"Where is he now?"

To think, I had just been about to congratulate myself that I'd spent a whole minute talking about T.J. without cry-ing. I spoke softly, to keep my voice from cracking, because I was supposed to be the strong one. "Dead. I called out the alpha male of our pack, and T.J. swooped in to back me up. We lost. He died protecting me. That's why I had to leave Denver."

"I hear that happens a lot, in werewolf packs."

"Maybe. I don't really know. There's a lot of different kinds of packs out there."

"I'd just as soon keep this one to you and me."

"Afraid of a little healthy competition?" I said wryly.

"Of course. I'd hate to have to share you with anyone."

"Or is it that you'd hate to have to fight to keep me to yourself?"

He shifted so he was looking at me. I looked back, down the length of my body. "You know, I think I would. If I had to." The playful tone went out of his voice.

My whole body flushed. Suddenly we weren't two friends snuggled together for comfort. He was male, I was female, and there were sparks. The weight of him leaning against me sent warm ripples through my gut.

"Is that you talking—you the human, I mean. Or is it the wolf?" I said.

He hesitated, then said, "It's all the same thing. Isn't it?"

Helplessly, I nodded.

He moved again, propping himself on an elbow so he leaned over me. Tentatively, he touched the waistband of my sweatpants. I didn't say anything. In fact, I pulled my arms away, tucking my hands under my head, so I wouldn't be tempted to stop him.

He pushed up the hem of my tank top, tugged down on my sweatpants, exposing a stretch of naked skin across my belly. He kissed this, working his way across, gently and carefully, like he wanted to be sure to touch every spot. Warmth flushed along my skin everywhere he touched. He eased the edge of my pants down farther, until he was kissing the curve of my hip, using his tongue, tasting me. My heart was beating hard, my breaths coming deep. I closed my eyes and squirmed with pleasure.

It was all I could do to keep from grabbing him, ripping off his clothes, and pulling him into me. He started this, so I let him work, reveling in the focused intensity of his attention. He kept at it until I gasped, a sudden jolt of sensation startling even me.

Then I grabbed him and ripped all his clothes off.

After that, we acted like we were on some kind of honeymoon. We'd start out washing dishes and end up making out over the sink, pawing each other with soapy hands.

The bed got a workout. The sofa got a workout. The floor got a workout. The kitchen table—after one attempt we decided it wasn't stable enough to withstand a workout.

I got a heck of a workout. I was *sore.*

It distracted us from our problems, from the curse, from the slaughter, from the threats that had taken up residence in my dreams. The reason Ben gave me for not sleeping was a much better one than lying awake waiting for doom to strike.

Then there was the nagging little voice that kept telling me it wasn't Ben, it was the wolf inside of him that had inspired this heroic passion. He wouldn't be here if he weren't a werewolf. Circumstance had brought us together, but I was enough of a romantic to want to be in love.

Neither one of us brought up the subject.

Over the next several days, two more herds of cattle were attacked. A dozen cows in all were slaughtered, torn to pieces. Each time, Marks called me up, wanting to know where I'd been the night before, what I'd been doing, and did I have witnesses who could verify that. Not really, seeing as how Ben and I were each other's alibi. Each time, Ben and I went out and searched the area, looking for something out of place, unnatural. Something that turned the world dark, and glared out with red eyes. But it must have been avoiding us.

I tried calling Cormac again, more than once. Voice mail picked up every time without ringing, so he was out of range or his phone was off. He didn't have a message, just let the automated voice carry on. I tried not to worry. Cormac was fine, he could take care of himself.

The second time Marks called I accused him of racial profiling—the only reason he suspected me was the fact that I was the only known lycanthrope in the region. He replied that he had applied for that warrant to collect a DNA sample from me.

I finished that phone conversation to see Ben sitting on the sofa holding his forehead like it ached and shaking his head slowly.

Ben and I were on the sofa, undressed, snuggled together under a blanket, basking in the warmth of the stove and drinking morning coffee. Didn't do much talking in favor of reveling in the simple animal comforts.

A tickling in the back of my mind disturbed the comfort. I lifted my head, felt myself tilting it—like a dog perking its ears up. And yes, I did hear something, very faint. Leaves rustling. Footsteps.

Ben tensed up against me. "What's wrong?"

"Somebody's outside. Wait here."

I slipped off the sofa and into the bedroom to find some jeans and a sweater to throw on.

It couldn't have been my mad dog–flaying curse meister, or the red-eyed thing. I'd never heard anybody actually moving around the house like this. Maybe it was some hiker who'd gotten lost. I could point them back to the road and be done with it.

Unfortunately, my life was never that simple, and dread gnawed at my chest.

I wished Cormac were here with a couple of his guns.

I went down the porch steps and looked around. Lifting my chin, I breathed deep. Didn't smell anything odd, but that didn't mean anything. Whoever it was could just be in the wrong place.

Something called through the trees, a low, echoing hoot. An owl, incongruous in the morning light. I couldn't see it, but it made me feel like something watched me.

Listening hard, looking into the trees, I started to walk around the house. Then I heard a crunching of dried leaves. Up the hill toward the road.

Knowing where to look now, I saw him. A short man, maybe forty, probably latino, his round face tanned to rust, wrinkles fanning from the corners of his eyes. His long black hair was tied in a ponytail. He wore a thick army-style canvas jacket, jeans, and cowboy boots. He wandered among the trees, hands on his hips like this was property he was planning on buying.

This was *my* territory. I walked toward him, stomping to make noise of my own, until he looked at me. He didn't seem surprised to see me standing in front of him.

I glared. "Can I help you with something?"

He glanced at me, not seeming at all startled or concerned.

"There was something here—" He pointed to the ground, drawing a line in the air that arced halfway around him. "In a circle all the way around the house. It's all kind of blurry now. But it's like someone was trying to build a fence or something."

He gestured right to where the ring of barbed-wire crosses had lain on the ground.

"There's been a lot of blood spilled here, too. All kinds. This place is pretty messed up, spiritually speaking."

I stared. My jaw might even have dropped open.

"Who are you?" I managed to demand without shrieking.

"Sorry. Name's Tony. Tony Rivera. Cormac asked me

to come out and have a look. I haven't had the time until now."

Simultaneously, the situation became more clear and more confused. This guy knew Cormac *how?* "He said he called someone, but didn't say anything about you."

"That surprise you? Is he here?"

"No." Though he'd probably expected to still be here when he'd called.

"You must be Kitty." He approached me slowly, obliquely, swinging a bit to the side—not directly toward me—and keeping his gaze off center, looking out and around, to the ground and the trees, everywhere but directly at me.

He was speaking wolf. Using wolf body language, at least. Giving me space and letting me take a good look at him. The gesture startled me into thinking well of him. I tilted my chin, breathed deeply—he wasn't a lycanthrope. He smelled absolutely human, normal and a little earthy, like he spent a lot of time outside.

"Hi," I said, able to smile nicely while he stood in front of me. Before I realized I was speaking, I asked, "How'd you learn to do that?"

"I pay attention. So, what seems to be the problem out here?"

"You the witch doctor?"

"Something like that."

I gestured over my shoulder. "You want to come in for coffee while we talk?"

"Sure, thanks."

Ben, clever boy that he was, was dressed and waiting in the doorway when Tony and I reached the cabin.

Tony saw him and waved. "Hi, Ben. Cormac said you were here."

Ben's eyes widened. "Tony?" Tony just smiled, and Ben shook his head. "Should have known."

I said, "So, ah, I guess you two know each other."

"He's my lawyer," Tony said.

Small world and all that. I looked at Ben. He shrugged. "Guess I'm everybody's lawyer. Cormac didn't say it was you he'd called."

Tony glanced at me with a sparkle in his eyes. "Cormac likes his secrets, doesn't he?"

"I'm going to get some coffee." I went into the house.

I turned around with a fresh mug of coffee for Tony to find him and Ben studying each other. Ben wilted under the scrutiny, bowing his head and slouching, and I suppressed an urge to jump between them in an effort to protect him.

Tony said, "When did that happen?"

That. The lycanthropy. Tony could tell just by looking.

"Couple weeks ago, I guess. I was out on a job with Cormac."

"I'm sorry. That's rough." He pointed at me. "So you didn't—you're not the one who turned him, are you?"

"Do you think Cormac would have let me live if I'd done it?"

An uncomfortable silence fell. Tony took the mug I offered him, but didn't drink.

Tony wasn't here about werewolves, or about Ben. Cormac had called him here for the curse.

"Cormac thought you might know something about what's been going on. He thought it was some kind of curse."

"Yeah, he told me some of it. You still have any of the stuff? The crosses or the animals?"

I shook my head and tried not to feel guilty about getting rid of the bag of crosses.

He said, "That's too bad. I might have been able to lead you right to whoever's doing this."

"Yeah, well you try living with a dozen skinned dogs hanging outside your house."

"Fair enough. You know anything about who might be doing this?"

"We decided it has to be someone local, since they seem to want me to get out. Cormac thinks whoever it is doesn't know what they're doing. It's been pretty messy, and it isn't working." In a low, grumbly voice I added, "Much."

Ben said, "Can you really tell who's doing this just by looking at the mess?"

Tony shrugged. "Sometimes. Sometimes there's spiritual fingerprints. Even when two different people work the same spell, each of them leaves their own stamp on it. Their own personality. If the person is local, it might be as simple as driving around looking for that same stamp. If someone's trying to put a curse on you, you can bet they've cast spells around their own place for protection."

"Magic spells," I couldn't help but mutter. "Huh."

"You don't believe?" Tony said.

"Look at me, you can tell what I am. I have to believe in pretty much anything these days. It doesn't make believing easy. Magic sounds like so much fun when you're a kid, until you realize how complicated it makes everything. Because you know what? It makes no sense. It makes no sense that throwing a bunch of barbed-wire crosses around my house should scare the pants off me." My voice rose in volume. This whole situation had made me incredibly cranky.

"Except it does make sense, because finding a bunch of plastic Mickey Mouses around your house probably wouldn't have scared you so much, right?" Tony said, donning a half smile that creased his brown face.

My own smile answered his. "I don't know. That'd be pretty weird. I always thought Mickey Mouse was kind of creepy."

"Tony." Ben sat in the kitchen chair, leaning forward on his knees, an idea lighting his eyes. "You can spot the type of magic of something by looking at it. Sense it. Whatever. There's something else that's been happening around here. Probably not connected to what's been happening at the house, but who knows. You mind taking a look while you're out here?"

"What is it?" Tony asked.

"Messy," Ben said.

I tried to catch Ben's gaze, to silently ask him what he was doing. He was talking about the cattle mutilations, about the second werewolf that he and Cormac had tracked in New Mexico. What did he think Tony could tell about it?

Tony frowned thoughtfully. "What do you think it is?"

"I'd rather not say. Let you take a look at it without me giving you ideas."

"Sure. I'm game."

Ben looked at me. "How about it? Where was the last one, out by county line road?"

Marks wouldn't tell me exactly where it was. He'd sort of acted like he assumed I already knew. But he'd indicated that general direction.

"What do you think he's going to find?"

"Just curious," Ben said. "You keep saying this isn't a werewolf. I'd like to hear what Tony has to say about it."

With a complaining sigh, I went to find my car keys. "Ben, you're going to have to start trusting your nose." I looked at Tony. "It isn't a werewolf."

"Now I'm curious," he said.

"Whatever it is, I want to know so it doesn't blindside us like it did the last time," Ben said.

Which made it sound like there was going to be a next time. Why was I not surprised?

chapter 11

The county line road turned off from the state highway a few miles outside town. It was two narrow lanes, paved, no discernible shoulder. Barbed-wire fences lined yellowed pastures on both sides. We all kept our eyes open, peering out the windows for anything unusual, any break in the consistent rangeland.

Tony spotted it, pointing. "There."

I slowed down and pulled onto the grass on the side of the road. To the left, on the other side of a slope of grassland, someone had parked a backhoe. The ordinary piece of equipment seemed ominous somehow, lurking out here by itself. The operator didn't seem to be around. Gone to lunch, maybe.

The three of us crossed the road and picked our way over the barbed wire. Walking toward the backhoe—and whatever work it was here for—felt like the last time, when Marks had brought us to see the slaughtered herd. This marching inexorably toward some unnamed horror. I didn't want to see what lay over that slope. And yet I kept walking.

Finally, we crested the slope and looked down to what lay beyond.

The backhoe's work was done. A mound of newly turned earth lay over a recently covered ditch, a hole some twenty feet to a side. The evidence was buried, cleaned away.

I could see where the dead cattle had lain, though: the swathes of crushed grass, the dark stains of blood on the earth. Anybody could tell that *something* had happened here.

Tony stood with his arms crossed, regarding the scene, his brows furrowed. "Werewolves didn't do this."

"How do you even know what happened?" Ben said.

"Something died here," Tony said matter-of-factly. "Messy, like you said. But more. Evil. Can't you feel it?"

"I don't know. What am I supposed to be feeling?"

I knew what Tony was talking about. Werewolves weren't inherently evil. They came in all varieties. They were individuals, exhibiting a whole range of behaviors and individual intentions. But this—some miasma rose from the earth itself, seeping under my skin, raising the hair on my arms. It felt like something in the trees was watching me, but I looked and smelled the air, and couldn't find anything.

"Evil," I echoed. "It feels evil. All it wants to do is destroy."

Ben spoke with a clenched jaw. "I've been feeling that crawling under my skin ever since that son of a bitch bit me. How am I supposed to tell the difference?"

He could smell the blood, and the scent prodded his wolf, like poking a hornet's nest with a stick. But he didn't recognize it. Couldn't separate his own hunger from the wrongness that permeated the earth here. His shoulders and arms were tense, like he was bracing against something.

His face held an expression of horror, but I couldn't tell if the expression was turned out to the scene before us, or inward, to himself.

I went to him. Didn't look at him, but gripped his hand and leaned my face against his shoulder.

"Practice, Ben. Patience."

He turned slightly, rubbing his cheek against my head, and I thought he might say something. I thought he might talk it out until this made some kind of sense. Instead, he abruptly broke away from me and stalked back to the road.

Tony watched him leave. "How's he doing really?"

"Oh, just fine," I answered lightly. "That's the scary part."

I couldn't imagine what Ben would be like if he were handling this *really* badly.

Side by side, Tony and I followed Ben back to the road. I tried to pin Tony down, studying him out of the corner of my eye. Despite the weirdness of the area, despite having spent most of the morning with a couple of werewolves, he didn't seem tense at all. He kept his head up, his gaze out, looking around at the trees, the top of the hills, the sky, watching everything just in case something interesting chanced by.

I didn't make him nervous, and that was refreshing.

"Did Ben tell you where he'd seen this before?" Tony asked.

"That job in New Mexico," I said. "The one that blindsided him and Cormac. They kept thinking there were two werewolves, but the evidence didn't add up."

"So one werewolf, and one something else? That narrows it down."

I couldn't help it; I laughed. Tony smiled in reply.

"One more question," he said. "Cormac said he'd meet me here. What happened?"

That one was a little harder to answer, because I wasn't sure myself. The tension had gotten thick. Then it had twisted, gone weird somehow. When we either couldn't stop glaring at each other, or couldn't look each other in the eye, something had to break.

I hadn't realized I'd let my hesitation stretch into a long silence until Tony answered for me.

"Ah—you and Cormac, and then you and Ben—"

"There was never a me and Cormac," I said.

"Oh. Okay."

He didn't sound convinced, and I declined to argue the point further. The lady doth protest too much, and all that.

Another car was parked on the shoulder, right behind mine. I recognized it; I'd seen it all too often the last week or so. Sheriff Marks's patrol car. His arms crossed, Marks leaned on the hood of his car, staring down Ben, who leaned on the back of mine, staring back.

"Who's that?" Tony asked as we made our way over the barbed-wire fence. Marks turned to watch our progress, his expression even more hooded and suspicious than ever.

"Sheriff Avery Marks. The local stalwart defender of truth, justice, and the American way."

"Hm, one of those."

"Norville," Marks called. He'd dropped the "Ms." I knew I was in trouble now. "May I ask what you're doing trespassing on Len Ford's land? Trying to clean up a little mess?"

I couldn't quite think of a response that wouldn't get me arrested on the spot. If he'd been five minutes later he wouldn't have seen us, and it wouldn't have been an issue. His timing was impeccable.

A bit too impeccable. "Have you been following me?" I said.

I didn't think it possible, but his frown deepened. "I have the right to keep a suspect under surveillance."

Ben straightened, pushing off from the car. "Your 'surveillance' is coming awfully close to harassment, Sheriff."

"You going to sue me?"

Ben only raised his brow. Marks didn't recognize the *try me* look, but I did.

Oh, this was going to get ugly.

Tony butted in, shouldering past me and in front of Marks like he really was breaking up a fight. "Hello, Sheriff Marks? I'm Tony Rivera. I'm afraid this is my fault, I asked Kitty to show me around. She said some weird stuff's been happening and I wanted to check it out."

He held out his hand, an obvious peacemaking gesture, but Marks took his time reaching out to it. Finally, though, they clasped hands. They held on for a long moment, locked in one of those macho *who's going to wince first* gripping matches.

Finally, they let go. Tony's face had gone funny, and it took me a moment to figure out what it was. He was frowning. He hadn't frowned once all morning.

He looked at me. "He's the one. One of them, anyway."

"One of them, what?" I said, perplexed, at nearly the same time Marks said, "One of who?"

Then my eyes widened as I realized what Tony was talking about: what he'd come here to look for, the curse, my house—Marks was the one.

"*You?*" I drew the word out into an accusation and glared at Marks. He didn't seem like the type to hang skinned dogs from trees. I'd have expected him to just shoot me. I'd never have pegged him as someone who knew *anything* about magic, even if what he knew was wrong. He was just so... boneheaded.

"What the hell are you people talking about?"

Tony said, "Anyone ever tell you that when you lay a curse, you better do it right or it's going to come back and smack you?"

If Tony was wrong and Marks didn't have anything to do with it, I'd have expected denials. I'd have expected more of the sheriff's blowhard posturing, maybe even threats. Instead, the fury left him for a moment, leaving his face slack and disbelieving.

His protest was too little, too late. "I don't know what you're talking about," he said in a low voice.

Tony ignored him, and glanced between Ben and me. "Remember what I said about spirits having fingerprints? Everybody's soul has its own little flavor. It follows them around, touches everything they do. This guy's stamp is all over your place."

"I called him out there a couple of times, to check things out. That could be why," I said.

"No. Too strong for that," Tony said. "This has malice in it."

Marks seemed to wake out of a daze. His defenses slammed into place, and the look of puckered rage returned. "You're accusing me of being the one who pinned those dead rabbits to her porch, and all that other garbage? What a load of crap. I don't believe this hocus-pocus nonsense."

I said, "But you believe I'm a werewolf—a monster that could do something like slaughter a herd of cattle. You can't have it both ways, Sheriff. Believe one and not the other." I'd learned that quickly enough.

"Okay, I won't say I don't believe it. Somebody's done something out at your place, I won't deny that. But I wouldn't know the first thing about *cursing* someone."

"Maybe you were just following directions," Tony said.

Again, that blank look while he organized his defense. "That doesn't even make sense."

I said, "Sheriff, you don't like me. You've made no secret of that. You don't like what I am, you don't like that I'm in your town. Maybe you're not the only one. And maybe you didn't do it, but I'm betting you backed who-ever did."

The three of us—Tony, Ben, and me—surrounded him, pinning him against his car almost. If Marks had reached for his gun, I wouldn't have been surprised. To his credit, he didn't. He appeared stricken, though. Frozen almost, like he expected us to pounce.

I said, "I haven't hurt anyone. I didn't kill those cattle. I don't deserve what's been done to me, and I just want it to stop. That's all."

His lips pursed, his expression hardening. We weren't going to get anything out of him. In his mind, he'd drawn some kind of line in the dirt. I stood on one side, he stood on the other, and because of that we'd never come to an understanding. I might as well pack my bags and leave.

Tony reached out to him. He moved quickly. Marks and I held each other's gazes so strongly I didn't even notice it until Tony held Marks's collar. Marks only had time to flinch before Tony had pulled out a pendant on a hemp cord that had been tucked under the sheriff's shirt.

Tony held the pendant flat in his hand, displaying it: a flint arrowhead of gray stone, tied to the cord.

"Zuni charm," Tony said. "Defense against werewolves. He knows all about this magic."

Was *that* why I wanted to growl at Marks every time I saw him?

Marks snatched the arrowhead away from Tony, closing his hand around it. He took a step back, bumping against the hood of his car. His armor had slipped; now, he seemed uncertain.

"It wasn't my idea," he said finally.

The air seemed to lighten around us. At last, he'd said something that sounded like truth.

"Whose was it? I'm not out for revenge, Marks. I just want to know why."

"We wanted you to leave. We're a quiet community. We didn't want any trouble."

"I wasn't going to bring any trouble! I just wanted to be left alone."

"But you brought trouble. That's trouble." He pointed out to the backhoe across the pasture.

I shouted. I didn't mean to. It just came out. "You pinned rabbits to my porch before any of those cows died! You assumed I'd do something before anything even happened! You heard what he said about a curse coming back to smack you—you brought this on yourself! And then you had the gall to pretend to investigate, when you knew all along who was doing it—"

"Kitty, maybe a little more calm," Ben said softly. I must have been really worked up if Ben was having to settle me down. My whole back and shoulders felt tight as springs.

When Marks spoke, his voice had changed. He sounded suddenly tired, defeated. "We—we knew it wasn't working right. You should have just left. Quietly, without a word. We wanted it to be quiet."

"Well, you screwed up big time, didn't you?" I said.

"Can you blame us for trying?" he said roughly.

"Uh, yeah. Hello, I *am* blaming you."

"We all know what you are! A—a monster! We don't want that in our town! Nobody would!"

"You know, I don't think I'm the monster here, really."

Thankfully, Tony interceded. "Sheriff, I think I can help clean this all up. We can remove the curse, and remove the consequences of it." He pointed a thumb over his shoulder at the site of the slaughter. "But the person who planned it, who worked the spell, needs to agree to it."

He nodded. "All right. Okay. It's Alice. She planned it."

"Alice?" My jaw dropped, truly astonished. "But she's always been so nice to me. Why—"

"Because she's nice to everybody, at least in person," Marks said. "I don't think she could be mean to somebody to their face if you held a gun to her head."

Tony looked at me. "Should we go talk to Alice, then?"

I still couldn't believe it. Sweet, friendly Alice. Alice who kept healing crystals on her cash register and hung good luck charms on her front door.

Then again, maybe she did know something about planting curses.

"Right, then. Off we go." To Marks I said, "You want to come along? Back us up?"

"To break this thing right, everyone involved should be there," Tony said. He had an authority about him, from the gentle way he spoke to the way he'd grabbed Marks's arrowhead charm. Marks had let it go; it lay on top of his uniform shirt now, exposed.

The sheriff hesitated, then said, curtly, "I'll meet you there." He turned to yank open his car door. He revved the engine when he started it, and barely gave us time to get out of the way before he lurched the car into reverse, then spun in a U-turn, kicking up gravel all the way.

"I don't believe it," I said, on general principle.

"She didn't really seem the type," Ben said.

Tony said, "Those are the ones you really have to watch out for. The real mean *brujas?* Always the little old lady down the street. The one who feeds cats off her back porch."

"Every neighborhood has one of those," I said.

"Makes you wonder, don't it?" Tony grinned.

Sighing, I marched to the driver's side of my car. "Let's go and get this over with."

Marks was already at the convenience store when we pulled into the parking lot. That meant he'd had time to warn her, to prep and get their stories straight. That made me mad. The whole town was against me, and the worst part was I shouldn't have been surprised. I was the monster, they carried the torches and pitchforks, and nothing would change that. Human nature being what it was.

At least I had backup this time.

I didn't wait for Ben and Tony, though. I wanted to break up their little witches' coven, and I wanted to do it now. While they were still getting out of the car, I stalked to the door of the store. Slammed it open. Sure enough, Marks and Alice were in conference, leaning over the counter by the cash register. They looked at me, shocked, though they should have expected me. Joe, standing behind Alice, quickly ducked for his rifle. I should have kept my distance, but I wasn't thinking too straight.

I went right toward them, closing the gap in a few long strides, and I must have had murder in my eyes because they both flinched back. That inspired me; let them think I wanted to rip their throats out.

I slammed my hand on the counter, making them jump, at the moment Joe cocked and leveled his rifle, mere inches from my skull. I could smell it, cold and oily.

The bell on the door rang as it opened again. "Kitty!" Ben called, at the same time Tony said, "No, wait." I imagined Tony held him back from rushing to my rescue. I couldn't look away. I only had eyes for Alice.

"So," I said, filled with fake cheerfulness. "Did you really give those crosses to Jake to melt them down, or did you keep them so you could dump them back around my place?"

Bug-eyed and stricken, she stared back at me. Almost, she trembled, and a scent of fear-laden sweat broke out on her skin. She looked like prey. Like a rabbit caught in Wolf's sight.

What a great feeling. I had the power; I was the badass. If I so much as raised a finger, she'd probably scream.

Then, she knelt. Slowly, she disappeared behind the counter, and when she stood again, she held the bag of crosses I'd given her. They chimed when she set them on the counter.

This was one of those times when I hated being right.

"God*damn* it, Alice. I *liked* you! Why'd you have to turn out to be such a bitch?"

The overly polite woman, the one who couldn't be

mean to anyone's face, took command. "You don't have to be so angry," she said, with a righteous tilt to her chin.

I wasn't finished. "If you hate me enough to kill small animals over it, don't turn around and pretend to be nice to me. Honestly, I prefer Joe here with his gun pointed at me. At least I know where I stand with him!"

Joe blinked at me over the stock of his rifle, like he was unable to process the rather backhanded compliment.

Marks said, "Joe, why don't you put that thing away." Joe obeyed and slowly lowered the weapon.

"I don't hate you," Alice said softly. "I just don't want you to live here." Her thin-lipped grimace was almost apologetic.

I didn't even know where to start. Maybe she wanted me to sympathize. Maybe she wanted me to feel sorry for her. Instead, the rage flared even higher. I had to pause a moment, take a breath, and think happy vegetarian thoughts before I growled for real. What had I told Ben about holding it in taking practice? I was getting a lot of practice right now.

Finally, I said, "Guess what? You don't get to tell me where to live."

She looked away.

Tony stepped up then, sweeping away the tension with his presence. "You know what you did wrong, don't you?" He addressed Alice.

"Who are you?" she asked.

"Tony. You know what you did wrong?"

She shook her head, hesitant, still full of that befuddled rabbit look.

"The cross on the doorway," Tony said, gesturing back to where Alice had hung a cross above the door. "The barrier of crosses. They're supposed to prevent evil from crossing, yes? Keep evil contained, keep it from intruding." He waited for her to nod, to acknowledge what he said. "Kitty's not evil. I've only known her half a day and I know that."

He said "evil" and I almost heard "dangerous." As in, "She's not dangerous. She's harmless." I had an inexplicable urge to argue, but Tony kept talking.

"She may have danger and darkness in her nature, but so do we all. That isn't evil. Evil is seeking out the darkness, seeking out the pain of others."

I glanced back at Ben, to make sure he'd heard. That was what I'd been trying to tell him. He looked at me, gave a tiny smile. Yes, he'd heard.

"Is it true what Sheriff Marks said, that our spell caused what's been happening to the cattle?"

"Your spell called out to evil. You may have drawn it here, yes."

She rubbed her face—wiping away sudden tears, springing from reddening eyes. "I'm so sorry. I thought I knew what I was doing, I was sure I knew—I have to fix it. How do I fix it?"

"Apologizing is always a good start," Tony said.

Alice looked at me, and for a moment I did feel sorry for her. She obviously felt so badly, and so tortured when the true consequences of what she'd done sunk in, I didn't want to be angry at her anymore. The words—*Oh, it's all right, just as long as she never does it again*—were on the tip of my tongue.

But the Wolf in me shifted testily. And you know, she was right. Alice wasn't going to get off that easily. I waited for the apology.

"I'm sorry, Kitty," she said. "I'm sorry for all the trouble."

You'd better be . . . "Thank you," I said instead.

"I think I can help clean all this up," Tony said. "There's a ritual I know, it'll clear away the curse. Heal some of the bad feelings. Will you all help?"

He looked at each of us, and we all nodded. Even Joe.

"Good," he said. "Be at Kitty's cabin at twilight, about five o'clock. We'll get this taken care of. Oh—and I'll take those. Thanks." Smiling amiably, he grabbed the bag of crosses off the counter.

We left the store, Tony bringing up the rear, almost like he was herding us. Or keeping me from lingering and doing something stupid. Within minutes, we were in the car and back on the road.

"Cormac wanted me to have those melted down," I said, nodding at the bag of crosses in his lap.

"That'd work, but I was just going to hold them under running water."

"You mean that's all we had to do?" I shook my head. The more I learned . . .

He said, "I'm curious where Alice learned her magic. If she was raised in some kind of tradition—healer or witchcraft or something—or if she got those spells out of a book somewhere. That's the trouble with you white people, you read something out of a book, you think you understand it. This kind of magic, though—you really have to live with it to know it."

That reminded me of learning a language, how really learning it requires living it, speaking with native speakers, growing up with it—total immersion. Repeating vocabulary words in high school wasn't going to cut it.

I said, "I can assure you, everything I know about the supernatural I've lived with personally." That didn't mean I understood any of it.

Tony laughed. "I believe you."

From the backseat, Ben said, "You really think what they did caused what happened to the cattle? What about what we saw in New Mexico?"

"Maybe what Alice and them did drew it here," Tony said.

"Or did it follow Cormac?" I said.

That left us with an ominous silence. Because it made sense. There'd been two of them. Cormac killed one, and the other followed him, seeking revenge. Only Cormac wasn't here anymore. So it went wild, killing, like it had before.

If that was the case, Tony's cleansing spell wouldn't help. We needed Cormac back. If for no other reason than to warn him.

chapter **12**

Twilight settled over the forest, clear and stark. The sky turned the beautiful deep blue of prize sapphires. The first star shone like a diamond against it. That clean, organic pine forest smell permeated everything.

Ben and I sat on the front porch and waited, watching Tony make preparations. He'd parked his truck at a national forest trailhead a few miles up the road, and moved it to my driveway during the afternoon. He pulled a box of supplies out of the back and got to work. First, he leaned a broom against the porch railing, then placed unlit white votive candles along the porch and around the clearing. Moving around the clearing to the four quarters of the compass, he drew something out of the leather pouch he carried and threw it into the air. A fine powder left his hands, and the smell of home cooking in a well-kept kitchen hit me. Dried herbs. Sage, oregano. I felt better.

"You think this'll work?" Ben said.

"I've learned to keep an open mind. I've seen something like this work before. So, yeah. I think it will."

"You look better already."

I felt a smile light my face. "What can I say? The man inspires confidence."

"Do you know in some regions it's traditional to pay a *curandero* in silver?"

I blinked, then frowned, suddenly worried. Would the ironies of my life never end? "Well, that's unfortunate. He knows I don't let silver get within miles of me if I can help it, right?"

Grinning, Ben leaned back against the wall. "Maybe he'll take a check."

I reveled in the moment of peace. Ben was getting his sense of humor back.

The sound of a driving car hummed up the road, then crunched onto the driveway that led to the clearing. Marks's patrol car, a pale ghost in the twilight, moved into sight, then pulled in behind Tony's pickup.

Wary, I stood. Ben stood with me. I felt that same sense of foreboding and invasion I had every time Marks had come here. I understood it, now: the spite he brought with him, his part in the curse that had been cast. Now, though, I felt something else: like a wall stood between us, a defensive barrier. This time, I had protection.

Sheriff Marks, Alice, and Joe got out of the car, and Tony walked out to meet them. They all shook hands, like they'd come for some kind of dinner party.

"Sheriff, Joe, I'm going to have to ask you to leave your guns in the car," Tony said.

"Like hell," Marks said, as expected.

"This is supposed to be a peacemaking. Kind of misses the point if you bring guns."

It was asking a lot, telling men like that they couldn't

bring their guns. The whole thing might have come to a screeching halt right there.

Alice said, "Please. I really want this to work. I want to make this right."

They listened to her, and Tony led them into the clearing.

"Everyone ready to get started?" he said. No one gave a particularly enthusiastic affirmation, but no one said no, either. Tony went around and started lighting candles. Golden circles of light flared from them, warm spots in the night. They wrecked my night vision; I couldn't see anything past the clearing now.

"Gather in a circle. Blood has been spilled here, in malice. There must be atonement for that."

The others did so, then looked to me. I hesitated—they needed atonement, and as the wronged party here I had the power to forgive, or not. In Tony's ritual, as I saw it taking shape, that gave me control.

But it wouldn't do any of us any good if I withheld that forgiveness out of spite. This ritual seemed to be less about magic than it was a mechanism for reconciliation. Get us all in one place, make us willing to talk it out. The actions themselves were as important as the result.

I stepped off the porch and into the clearing. Ben followed me.

Nervously, we looked at one another, because nobody but Tony knew what would happen next. Alice seemed sad but resigned, her face pulled into a deep frown, her eyes staring. Marks's frown was different, suspicious. He kept looking over his shoulder. Joe simply stood, stoic as ever.

Tony snuck up behind me. I flinched, startled, because I hadn't heard him. I'd been too distracted by the strange mood settling over the area—a kind of suspended, timeless feeling, like the air itself had frozen.

"Sorry," he said, smiling, and handed me something. A tightly bound bundle of some kind of dried plant. Sage, it smelled like, about as long as my hand and as thick as my thumb. He went to each of us in the circle, until everyone had a bundle.

I assumed he'd tell us what to do with it. I tried not to feel too silly just holding it. Alice clutched hers in both hands, held it to her chest, near to her heart, and closed her eyes.

Then Tony picked up the broom and began sweeping the dirt in front of the porch. Slowly, he made his way around the circle, clockwise.

An owl called. This wasn't a calm, random hooting, the low-pitched, hollow whisper I'd heard the first time Tony came to the cabin. This was rushed, urgent—a note of warning, rapid and increasing in pitch. Branches rustled—there was no sound of wings, but the owl's cry next sounded from the roof of the cabin, above where Tony stood. I still couldn't see the bird. It hid itself well in the shadows, or my eyes weren't working right.

Tony looked around, searching for something.

Something wasn't right. I'd have sworn I hadn't heard anything, hadn't noticed any scent on the air, but the smell of herbs and candles might have covered up anything else. Still, an all-too-familiar tingling wracked my spine. A sense of invasion. My sense of territory being violated.

It was out there. Tense to the point of shivering, I looked out, trying to see into the trees, beyond the light of the candles.

"What is it?" Ben breathed. He'd moved—we'd both moved, until we stood apart from the others, back to back, looking out, ready for danger. I hadn't noticed it because it had happened so smoothly, instinctively, unbidden. Even our little pack circled in the face of whatever danger lurked out there.

This was driving me crazy. It was like the mornings I'd found the rabbits and dogs all over again. If something was out to get me, why couldn't it just show itself, let me face it down?

Ben grabbed my hand and nodded over to a spot north of the circle. The sky had deepened almost to black now, and the trees were lost in darkness.

Red eyes stared back. Points of glowing embers, about the height of a tall wolf. I wasn't imagining it.

"Was that the thing you saw in New Mexico?" I whispered.

"I never got a good look at it." His voice trembled, just a little.

The others looked out to where we stared.

"Jesus—" I thought that was Joe.

"Nobody move," Tony said, his calm slipping a little.

"It's not a wolf," I said. "It doesn't smell like wolf."

"It smells like death," Ben said, and he was right. The embers went out for just a moment—blinking. The eyes blinked at us.

"Oh, God—" Alice said, her voice gone high, like a little girl's.

Tony said, "Alice, stay where you are, don't run!"

Too late. She backed up, her footsteps scraping clumsily on the ground. Then she turned, arms flailing, and raced. Not to the cars, not to the house, either of which offered safety. She ran blindly into the darkness, guided only by panic.

That was exactly what the monster wanted.

"No!" Tony called.

"Joe, get your rifle!" Marks shouted.

The wolf shot out of the darkness like a rocket.

My senses collided. It wasn't a wolf. It didn't smell right, it didn't look right, nothing about this was right. But it had four legs, a long snout, a sleek body with a tail stuck straight back like a rudder. Its coat shone coal-black, and its eyes glared red. Angrily red.

I intercepted it.

It raced straight for Alice, latching on to her terror and marking her as prey. Movement attracted notice. I knew the feeling. I didn't think about it—I just knew that I could stand up to the monster better than Alice could.

I crashed into it from the side, tackling its flank, wrapping my arms around it, pulling it down. I wasn't human—I had this thing inside me that let me move faster than I ever thought I could, that made me stronger than I should have been. My Wolf was a match for it.

But the wrongness of it was overwhelming. As soon as I touched it, a numbness wracked my limbs, poured into my body. It made me want to curl into a ball, fetal, and scream until the world turned right again. My vision went gray.

We rolled together in the dirt. The black wolf snarled and twisted back on itself, snapping at the sudden anchor that had brought it down. Teeth closed on my arm, jaws clamping down hard, ripping into my skin. Better me than Alice. I was already a lycanthrope. I could take it.

I gasped, and my Wolf writhed, growling in pain and anger. Again, a sense of wrongness—the attack didn't just happen on the surface of my body, but crawled inside it, trying to eat through me from the inside. I'd never felt anything like it. My body slipped a little—she wanted to

Change, she could fight better as a wolf, she wanted out so she could protect herself.

Claws, I needed claws to tear. But I couldn't move. I expected my hands to thicken, my arms to melt. I wanted to feel my nails grow thick, hard as knives, and break through that monster's skin.

But I didn't.

I usually resisted the Wolf, kept her leashed tight. This time, now, when I wanted to feel her, wanted her to break free and save me—nothing happened. I froze with astonishment. With fear, while the monster grabbed hold of me.

"Kitty!" Ben shouted.

I prayed he stayed back. I wanted him out of this. I didn't want him to have to fight like this.

In something of a panic I slashed, as if I had claws. My fingers raked rough, oily, ugly fur, causing no damage. The thing slammed me onto my back—and made a noise that almost sounded like laughter. My head cracked against the ground, and I saw stars. It pinned me, thick paws on my chest, claws digging in. Its breath smelled of carrion, of sickness. Plague and death. I thrashed in pure animal panic, kicked, got my hands up, took hold of its throat, and pushed. *Get off... get the hell off me...*

Its jaws opened over my throat, and its sickly breath gusted over me. I melted, my strength ebbing.

"Kitty, get back!"

I kicked its ribs, and its hold broke. I twisted to slip from under its weight, obeying the voice instantly because I trusted it, because it belonged to a man who'd watched my back before. Cormac. As fast as I could, I rolled away from the black wolf.

In the same moment, a shot echoed, then another, and

another. They were close, thunder in my ears, rattling my brain.

The wolf cried out—a human scream. Too human, a woman in pain.

The creature lay still before me. I swore I could see motes of dust settling around us, where we'd been fighting.

I couldn't think at all. I felt like I'd been locked in darkness and the prison door just blew open, and now my body floated through the opening. Now, Wolf wanted to run. On my knees, I bent over double, clutching my stomach, trying to pull my body back into myself. Trying to make myself human again. Skin, not fur. I wanted hands and fingers, not paws and claws. Keep it together, keep the line between us drawn. *Please, please...*

My Wolf crept back to her lair, growling low the whole time, not believing the danger was over, not believing I could take care of us. *Please...*

I took a deep breath, and my body stopped slipping. I flexed my hands, which were hands again.

"Stay back. Give her space. She might still shift." Cormac was speaking.

I kept my eyes closed, stayed crouched over for another moment, taking advantage of the moment of space and silence he made for me.

I want you to take care of me, I wanted to say to him. *I wish you were a wolf and could be my alpha.*

"I'm okay," I said, though my voice was weak and uncertain. I looked up. Cormac stood just a few feet away, looking the worse for wear, a few days' worth of beard covering his jaw. He held a rifle in both hands, ready to fire again if he had to. Briefly, his gaze shifted from the body of the monster to me. His look was searching, asking. *Are you all right?* I tried to pour gratitude back to him. *Yes, because of you.* I smiled. "You came back."

"I got your messages."

"Was this the second wolf you'd been tracking?"

"Yeah."

Ben stood beside me, close enough to touch, but he held back, his body fairly quivering with anxiety. He seemed to need reassurance as much as I did. I reached for him, and he grabbed my hand and knelt beside me.

"You okay?" he said.

"I'll heal." My whole body ached, pain stabbing along every limb. I wouldn't know how badly the wolf had torn me up until I got into some light and looked.

"The wolf," Cormac said. "It's not changing back."

When a werewolf died in its wolf form, the body shifted back to human—returned to its original state. Cormac had put at least three bullets in it, and I knew he used silver. The thing lay in a widening pool of blood. It had to be dead. It even looked dead, a pile of dull fur rather than a glowing, rippling creature.

But it wasn't changing back. It had never smelled like a werewolf.

I crept forward. Wrong, this was all wrong, and my flesh crawled. I wanted to go inside and lock the door. But I had to know.

Cormac said, "Kitty, don't—"

I touched its neck. It felt cold and strangely pliant under my touch. Its chest was shattered, multiple flowering wounds on its back bleeding into one another. Cormac's bullets had found their marks. I ran my hand down its flank.

Fur. It was only fur.

I lifted back the head, and the fur and skin came off. Lifted right off, like it was a cloak. I pulled it all the way back and moved it aside. It was a tanned wolf hide, that was all.

A young woman lay before me, naked, sprawled on her side, exit wounds ripped in her chest. Her sleek black hair was long, tangled around her, matted with blood. Despite being marred by blood and destroyed flesh, her body seemed young, lean, and powerful.

"What the hell," Ben murmured, on behalf of us all, it seemed.

"*Dios,*" Tony said.

He was on the other side of the clearing, with Marks, Joe, and Alice. They'd grabbed her before she'd gone too far. Joe held her around the middle, supporting her, because she seemed about to fall to her knees. Marks had had time to retrieve his handgun from his car, and he stood over them protectively.

Tony moved toward us, in something of an astonished daze. When he reached the body, he knelt, put out his hand, and seemed about to touch the woman's hair. Instead, he drew back and crossed himself.

"*Dios,*" he said again. "I've heard of this but never thought to see it in my life."

"She's not a lycanthrope," I said.

"No. She's a skinwalker."

I'd read the stories, but wasn't sure I'd believed them. Everything started out as just stories. Even seeing the evidence lying before me, I didn't want to believe.

Then, as if belatedly responding to Tony's near-touch, she moved. Her head tilted a little, her lips pressed like she wanted to speak, and her eyes shifted under closed lids. Something in her still lived—something inside that ruined chest survived.

"Oh my God, she's not—" I only started to say it.

Cormac's rifle fired again, exploding close by like a crack of thunder in my ears.

At almost the same instant, the woman's face disappeared.

Instinctively, my arm went up to cover my face. I fell back, but not quickly enough to avoid the spray of blood and bits that fanned out from her head and over my jeans, my arm—everywhere. Across from me Tony sprawled away from her in much the same way, arm protecting his face, spatters of blood on his clothing. I looked back at the woman under the wolf skin. Half her head, where Cormac's bullet hit, was now a jagged, pulped mess.

Nothing moved now, except blood dripping from the wound.

Cormac looked down at her over his rifle, finger tight on the trigger, like he still expected her to leap up and attack. He was ready for her to move again. I couldn't tell what appalled and frightened me more: his lack of hesitation in finishing her off, or the lack of emotion in his eyes over doing it.

I gagged, pressed my face against my arm, and managed to not throw up.

Marks aimed his gun at Cormac and approached him warningly.

Cormac's finger remained on the trigger of his rifle. He could shoot back in a fraction of a second. Marks had to know that. He had to know better than to start a shoot-out with the hunter. But for some reason it wouldn't have surprised me if he did anyway.

"Would both of you put your guns down!" I shouted. My ears still rang from the shot. Everything sounded muffled.

Cormac did, slowly. Marks didn't. But he did relax enough to glance away from Cormac and to the woman's body.

The sheriff said, "Who is she?"

"How should I know?" Cormac answered roughly.

Ben said, "You might check missing person reports out of Shiprock." He'd taken my hand again, and I leaned into him.

"But you knew she was going to be here," Marks said to the bounty hunter.

"I've been tracking it, yeah."

Marks said, "I'm going to have to arrest you. A formality, you understand." But the look on his face said, *Got you.* He wore a thin smile.

Surely that was a joke. Cormac had saved my life. Then he'd... I didn't want to think about that. The look on his face, the woman's head vanishing in a spray of blood. But Marks didn't like either one of us. He didn't care about me—he had a dead woman and her killer standing there with the gun still smoking.

Cormac leveled that cold stare, unreadable and unsettling, at the sheriff. Beside me, Ben tensed. He didn't know what Cormac was going to do, either. The bounty hunter was going to spook Marks at this rate. Cormac was like some kind of animal himself, and Marks wasn't going to wait around to let him pounce.

Cormac put his left hand around the barrel of the rifle and dropped the gun to his side. "I kind of expected that."

Now, Marks approached him without hesitation. Still with his gun up and ready. I wanted to smack the guy. The sheriff held out his hand; Cormac handed him the rifle.

Marks holstered his handgun, tucked Cormac's rifle under his arm, and pulled out the handcuffs. Cormac handled it like he'd done this before.

"Don't talk until I get there," Ben said.

"Yeah, I know the drill." Handcuffed now, he went with Marks to his patrol car without argument.

"Joe, Alice, watch the body. Don't let anyone touch anything until the coroner gets here. Nobody leave until I get your statements," Marks said. The two were clinging to each other. Quick glances told that they'd heard him, but they didn't move.

I felt like I'd landed in a bad episode of some prime-time police show. Dead body, unlikely circumstances, too much drama.

"You want to go inside and get cleaned up?" Ben said.

I supposed I ought to. I felt like I'd been through a shredder. "Yeah. Should you go with Cormac?"

He looked after the pair, uncertain, his lips pressed together. "As soon as you're okay."

He helped me to my feet. My shoulders were stiff, and blood covered the front of my shirt. Another T-shirt ruined.

Tony had withdrawn, holding himself apart, hands folded in front of him. The candles had all gone out. I hadn't noticed how dark the clearing had become.

"That thing cut you," he said. "You're cursed. You're both cursed." He nodded after Cormac.

"Story of my life," I said. "Any recommendations?"

"A man can only meddle so much. Sometimes you just have to let things run their course."

That was the sort of thing people said when they had no idea what to do next. "Thanks," I muttered.

"I don't think you understand. That magic, the trade one must make to become a skinwalker—it's terrible. It's supposed to be too terrible to think about. But she did it, clearly. She sacrificed someone in her own family to work the blood magic." He held himself stiffly, the horror clear in his manner.

"I'm already a werewolf," I said. "So what are these cuts going to turn me into?"

Tony shrugged. "God knows. I tell you, though, this isn't over."

Well, no silver for him. I knew better than to ask how much worse this could get.

I started toward the cabin, wincing. I had to lean on Ben, because my whole body felt like glass on the verge of shattering.

Joe's words startled me because he spoke so seldom. "I can't believe you're all right. I thought you were dead. You ought to be dead after that."

"If I wasn't a werewolf, I would be dead." I still couldn't see how bad it was. My whole front was dark and shining with blood.

So much for the ritual of peacemaking. This situation had ramped up to a whole new level of surreal and frightening. I probably should have just left town. None of this would have happened.

I didn't want everyone to leave feeling like this.

"Do you guys want to come inside for some coffee? Or I might have some tea somewhere." Or a bottle of whiskey.

Joe and Alice exchanged a glance. Alice nodded, and the two of them approached.

"You, too," I said to Tony. "If you can stand being so close to someone who's as badly cursed as I am."

Tony hesitated for such a long time I thought he was going to refuse. That I was so tainted he really couldn't stand being near me, even though he'd declared me "not evil" earlier that day. I couldn't believe this was still the same day.

Then he said, "I have some tea. It should help. It helps to drink it when you've had a fright."

It certainly couldn't hurt. I hoped.

"Okay," I said, and he went to his truck.

The others gathered in the kitchen. Ben took me to the bathroom.

"Jesus, look at you," he said when he turned on the light.

I whimpered. I didn't want to look. I turned away from the mirror.

"Should we take you to a hospital or something?"

"No, it'll be okay. I've had worse." Brave words.

We had to cut away my shirt and bra. My chest and shoulders had a dozen puncture wounds where the skin-walker had dug in her claws again and again. My right arm was shredded. This was where she'd bitten and worried, and dozens of slashes and tooth marks streaked the flesh. I stood over the sink while Ben sponged me off. The blood had spattered on my face and hair as well. I'd have to stay in the shower for a week to get clean.

"I should have done something," Ben murmured. "I should have helped."

"I'm glad you didn't. We'd both have ended up like this. That thing—I was frozen. I couldn't move, I couldn't do anything. Just like Cormac said." Just like those cows. They couldn't run, they couldn't struggle. She'd slaughtered them at her leisure.

"When does this rapid healing start?"

"It should have started already." All the wounds still oozed and hurt like hell.

He shook his head absently, dabbing away fresh blood. "You have a first-aid kit? I think we're going to have to tape some of this up. You have something you can wear?"

"I think there's a button-up shirt in the closet. I ought to be able to get that on without crying." I was still propped up against the sink, afraid to move because I knew it would hurt.

Ben regarded me a moment, and then had the gall to smile. "For someone who says she doesn't like to get mixed up in the middle of things, you sure have a way of getting mixed up in the middle of things." He kissed my lips and left on his errand. That made me feel better. Heck, it was almost like I'd planned it: Ben was doing great now that he had someone else to worry about. I'd have to keep that in mind.

He came back with a flannel shirt, and I sent him back for something else. I didn't want to think about bits of flannel mixed with cuts scabbing over.

By the time we emerged back into the kitchen, Alice, Joe, and Tony were chatting. If not happily, at least cordially. Like they might actually come out of this as friends. Tony was pouring hot water from a kettle into mugs. His tea smelled rich, warm, soothing—just like he promised. I identified chamomile twined in with scents I didn't recognize.

Tony said, "You just don't seem like the kind of person who'd be into animal sacrifice."

"Well... I'm not. It was all roadkill Joe and Avery picked up. We added blood from the butcher shop to make it look fresh. The only thing I did, really, was fix it so nobody saw or heard them placing the things."

Of all the... Before I could say something snotty, Tony continued. "That explains a lot. It didn't work, she didn't leave, because you weren't willing to make the sacrifice yourself, to spill the blood. You weren't willing to take that onto yourself to get what you wanted."

Softly, she said, "Not like that girl out there."

After a moment of silence, I took the opportunity to bust in on the group. "I spend all that money in your store, and you still didn't want me sticking around?"

Alice's face puckered like she was going to start crying and I regretted my cattiness. She really hadn't known what she was doing, had she?

"Oh, Kitty, I was just scared. We all were. We didn't know. You hear stories, and you think the worst. We were just trying to keep the town safe, surely you can understand that."

"So... the last couple full moons. Did you notice anything different? Could you tell that a werewolf was living in the neighborhood?" A law-abiding werewolf who made very, very sure that she didn't cause trouble.

"No, I didn't notice."

Joe said, "That's because we spent the night locked in the house with all the lights on."

"And the days I shape-shifted that *weren't* on the full moon—you didn't notice then, did you?"

They both looked at me. Alice said, "You turn into a wolf on other days, too?"

Even Ben looked at me sharply. I wasn't supposed to shape-shift on other nights. He knew I wasn't supposed to do that. Now what kind of role model was I?

"Whenever I want."

"I didn't know that," Alice said softly.

Tony straightened from where he'd parked by the counter. "Hey, Alice, you want to help me with something?"

"What?"

"That thing out there left a lot of bad feeling in the air. No reason we can't try to clean it up a little, even if things didn't go the way we planned."

"But the coroner, shouldn't we wait—"

"This won't bother them. We won't have to touch anything."

She brightened. Tony had offered a chance for redemption, and she seemed eager to take it. "All right."

The two left the cabin, and Tony flashed me a smile on the way out.

Joe busily rinsed out mugs.

I started toward him. "Don't worry about that, I can get it."

Ben interceded. "No, you sit down and start healing." He pointed at me until I sank into a kitchen chair. Funny—I hadn't noticed I was dizzy until I sat down and the room stopped trembling. Ben put a mug of something steaming in front of me, then went to help Joe.

Clutching the mug in both hands and sipping carefully, I watched Ben and Joe washing coffee and tea accoutrements at the sink, side by side. Joe, who wouldn't let me, the werewolf, into his store without holding a gun on me, stood next to another werewolf and didn't even know it.

Over the next half hour, Sheriff Marks's backup arrived, including a coroner's van and a few deputies to take statements. While they worked, Tony and Alice walked around the clearing, each waving a smoking bundle of plant matter—some kind of incense. Some kind of blessing, or cleansing. I didn't know if it would work. Alice seemed to feel better, at any rate. At least it worked for someone.

One of the deputies took Joe and Alice home. The cops had taken statements from everyone, and Tony was the next to leave. Before that, he found me, sitting on the porch steps to watch the proceedings.

He sat next to me.

"Here. Take this." He reached over his neck and pulled something from under his shirt: a small leather pouch on a long cord. Before I even had time to lean away in surprise, he put the cord over my head, so I was wearing the pouch around my neck. "It's protected me through the years. It may help protect you."

I put my hand over it. Small enough to fit inside my fist, the brown leather was soft. Stuffed inside was something crunchy and fibrous. Dried herbs, maybe.

"May?" I said.

He shrugged, like we were talking about the weather. "I do what I can."

"Well. Thanks for trying."

"If I had known that's what we were dealing with, I might have been able to do more." He nodded to where the coroner's people were loading the body onto a wheeled stretcher. Some forensics officers wrapped the wolf skin in a plastic bag and carried it away.

"Any advice for what to do next?" I said.

"Let it end here. Don't go asking any more questions. Don't look for any more trouble."

I hid a smile. Good advice, to be sure. Not sure it was

the right advice. I had way too many questions, and this hadn't ended because Cormac was still sitting in the back of Marks's car, wearing handcuffs.

"Ben told me about the silver," I said. "I don't usually keep that sort of thing around, but we could probably pay you with some of Cormac's bullets." I'd pay Cormac back later. He'd understand.

"This one's on the house," he said. Then, as unobtrusively as he'd arrived, he disappeared into his truck and away.

Finally, after the coroner's crew and deputies were gone, the sheriff left with Cormac riding in the backseat, leaving the clearing suddenly empty and quiet. Ben and I stood on the porch, watching the chaos disperse. The night wasn't over for us; we had to get in my car and go spring Cormac.

"I don't know if I can do this," Ben said, watching the cars leave.

"Do what?"

"Sit there and argue with those clowns. Not without... something happening. Losing my temper. You know."

"You've done it before, haven't you?" They'd both acted like this was routine. Which was kind of scary.

"Lost my temper? Sure." He smiled a little. "Or do you mean representing Cormac? You keep saying you and I are a pack and we have to look out for each other. I feel like Cormac is part of my pack. I have to protect him. The wolf side would do anything to protect him." He flexed his hands, like he could already feel that anger, that determination, waking up inside him.

I touched his hand, to bring him back to himself. He let out a nervous breath.

"I'll go with you," I said.

Looking away, he nodded. "I was hoping you would."

I hadn't ever considered not going.

The truth was, the thought of him leaving me here, of being alone after all that, made me ill. Between that and the queasy, injured feeling that still lingered after the fight, I wanted to throw up. I wasn't okay at all, and I wasn't going to sit around waiting for the next curse to arrive.

chapter 13

We took my car, and in forty minutes arrived at the sheriff's department and county jail in Walsenburg. Marks had booked Cormac by the time we got into the building, and the hunter was ensconced in a back room, out of sight.

Marks glared at us over the front desk. "He's already asking for his lawyer. You want to get back here so we can take his statement?"

Ben was tense. I knew him well enough by now that I could tell without touching him.

"You'll be fine," I said. "Just breathe slow and think about keeping it in. Stay calm."

"Easier said than done."

"Yup." I tried to make my smile encouraging.

He straightened his shoulders and stalked forward like a man preparing to go into battle.

I'd seen him talk down cops before. I'd seen him face a panel of senators and hold them off. In those cases he'd had this hawk's stare, the fierce-eyed glare of a hunter that had always instilled confidence in me, because he was always on my side.

The hawk was gone. I should have seen it, but it wasn't there. Instead, he looked like he'd been cornered.

I watched him go, wringing my hands on his behalf. Then all I could do was wait in the lobby on a hard plastic chair, leafing through copies of news magazines a month out of date. I wanted to climb the walls. The place was clean, not terribly old or worn out. But it smelled of sweat and fatigue. It was not a good place. People ended up here when they'd hit bottom, or were about to hit bottom.

My wounds still itched. They should have been almost healed. Cursed, Tony had said. I hadn't realized how much I took the quick healing for granted. Then again, if I didn't have rapid healing, I wouldn't go around intercepting attacking wolves.

I watched the clock. Hours later, after midnight, Ben came back to the lobby. He was pale, ill-looking, and sweat dampened his hair. He looked like he'd run a race, not talked with the cops. I stood and met him.

He smelled musky, animal, like his wolf was rising to the surface. I took hold of his hand. "Keep it together, Ben. Take a deep breath."

He did, and it shuddered when he let it out. "I don't know what Cormac did earlier, but Marks has it in for him. He already called the prosecutor. They want to file charges. Six eyewitnesses saw Cormac save your life, and they want to press charges. They won't set bail until the advisement hearing tomorrow. And I just sat there and *stared* at them."

"How does this usually work? You make it sound like this isn't the way things normally go for you guys."

"Usually I have plenty of evidence that Cormac had a good reason for doing whatever he did, and the charges don't even get filed. But we have a couple of problems this time. Somebody around here wants to make a reputation for themselves."

"Marks?"

"Marks and George Espinoza, a very earnest prosecutor who's probably never encountered anything more serious than trespassing." His tone was harsh.

"And?" There was an "and" in there.

"She was already dying when he killed her. It was excessive force, even for Cormac. That's the argument Espinoza's going to use."

This was going to be about splitting hairs. Cormac did what he had to—I could convince myself of that. A hundred horror movie climaxes said he did the right thing.

But how would a judge see it?

"How's Cormac?"

"Stoic. He's Cormac. There's something else. They've ID'd the body. The skinwalker. Miriam Wilson. She's the twin sister of John Wilson, the werewolf that Cormac shot. The one that got me. A missing person report on her was filed three months ago."

As if we needed the situation to be any more complicated. I tried to imagine a state of affairs where a brother and sister would become the things they were, and wreak the havoc they had.

"Brother and sister? One of them a werewolf and one of them a skinwalker. What's the story behind that?"

"I wish I knew."

"And her family reported her disappearance to the police, but they hired Cormac to hunt down the brother?"

He shrugged. "We don't know that it was her family that filed the report. I'm guessing they didn't send Cormac after her because she wasn't a werewolf. We don't know if they knew what she was. We don't know anything. Christ, I'm going to have to go buy a suit. I left all my clothes in my car back in Farmington. I can't go to court without a suit." He was currently wearing his coat over jeans and a T-shirt, like he'd been wearing for the last week.

"We'll go buy you a suit in the morning. Is there anything else you need to do? Can we get out of here?" I wanted to get him out of this place, with its unhappy smells and atmosphere of confrontation.

"Yeah, let's go."

That started a very long night. Ben used my laptop and spent hours looking through online legal libraries for precedents and arguments that would spring Cormac. He scratched out notes on a notepad. I watched, lying on the sofa, wondering how I could help. He grew more agitated by the minute.

"Ben, come to bed. Get some sleep."

"I can't. Too much to do. All my work is back in my car, I have too much to review, I have to catch up." He glared at the screen with a frantic intensity.

"How much are you going to be able to help him if you're falling asleep in the courtroom?"

He took his hands away from the keyboard and bowed his head. I could see the fatigue radiating off him. When he came to the sofa, I sat up, made room for him, and pulled him into an embrace. My body was healing, finally, but still sore. I didn't complain. He needed me to comfort him, however much I wanted someone to comfort me. We stayed like that a long time, his head pillowed on my shoulder, until the tension started to seep out of him. I got him out of his clothes, into bed, and held him close, curled up in my arms, until he finally fell asleep. He never fully relaxed.

The next morning, we went to buy a suit. We weren't going to find anything fancy in Walsenburg. This put Ben even further out of sorts. But we managed, somehow.

He changed clothes in the car on the way to the Huerfano County Courthouse, where Cormac's first hearing was scheduled to take place. The suit didn't fit quite right, it didn't make as slick a picture as he might have wanted. I brushed his hair back with my fingers, straightened his tie, smoothed his lapels. Like I was sending him to the prom or something.

Ben looked like I was sending him to an execution. He was still holding himself tense, shoulders stiff, like the raised hackles on a nervous wolf.

"You going to be okay?"

"Yeah. Yeah, sure. This is just a formality. The judge will look over his statement, the witness statements, and throw out the case. That's all there is to it."

He headed into the building alone to meet with Cormac before the hearing. I made my way to the courtroom. In other circumstances I might have admired the hundred-year-old building, made of functional gray stone and topped by a simple decorated tower. They built them to last in those days.

I didn't know what I expected—some kind of dramatic, busy scene like in a courtroom drama on TV. But the place was almost empty. Marks stood off to one side. A couple of people in business suits conversed quietly. Fluorescent lights glared. The whole place gave the impression of dull bureaucracy. I sat in the first row behind the defense side. I was sure this would be educational if I weren't so nervous on Ben and Cormac's behalf.

Without any preamble, a couple of bailiffs guided Cormac into the courtroom. He'd had a chance to shave, which made him look slightly less psychotic than he had last night. A point in his favor, and that was probably part of the strategy. It was a shock, though, to see him in an orange prison jumpsuit, short-sleeved, baggy, unflattering. It gave me a terrible sense of foreboding.

Ben followed, and both of them positioned themselves behind one of the podiums before the bench.

The whole procedure followed in a kind of haze. The judge, Heller, a middle-aged woman, brown hair pulled into a bun, wearing a no-nonsense expression, came into the room and took her place. Ben and Cormac remained standing before her. Across from them, one of the business suits, a surprisingly young man—no older than Ben and Cormac—shuffled papers on the desk in front of him. George Espinoza, the prosecutor. His suit was neat, his dark hair slicked back, his expression viperish. A crusader. No wonder Ben was worried.

The prosecutor read the facts—and just the facts, ma'am. The time and place of Cormac's arrest, the nature of the crime, the probable cause. The charge: murder. Not just murder, but first-degree murder. That was serious, way too serious.

Espinoza explained: "The accused was heard to say that he had tracked the victim, had in fact been focused on her for quite some time with the intent to kill her. He was seen in the area of Shiprock, New Mexico—the victim's hometown—on several dates over the last month. He was, in fact, lying in wait for the victim's appearance. This presents a clear display of deliberation, meeting the requirement for a charge of first-degree murder."

Cormac had been tracking her. He had meant to kill her. Which made the whole thing murky. I was glad I wasn't the lawyer.

This wasn't a TV show. Nobody shouted, nobody slammed their fists on the tables, nobody rushed in from the back with the crucial piece of information that would free the defendant, or pound the final nail in the prosecution's case.

They might have been lecturing on economic theory, as calmly and analytically as everyone spoke. It made it hard to concentrate on the words.

The judge spoke: "Mr. Espinoza has requested that Mr. Bennett—" Cormac Bennett. I'd never heard his last name before. Even such a small detail as that made the scene surreal. It was like Cormac should have been beyond something as mundane as a last name. "—be held without bail, on the basis of his past associations and the belief that he is a flight risk."

Ben argued: "Your Honor, my client has dealt with law enforcement agencies in several jurisdictions, and has always been cooperative. He's never once given the indication that he's a flight risk."

"Perhaps his past association with the Mountain Patriot Brigade hasn't been an issue until now. It is the experience and opinion of this court that members of such right-wing paramilitary organizations are, in fact, flight risks."

Again, the world shifted, becoming even more surreal, if that was possible. I'd heard of the Mountain Patriot Brigade: it was one of those militia groups, right-wing fanatics who ran around with guns and preached the downfall of the government. When they weren't actually blowing things up.

That didn't sound like Cormac at all. Not the Cormac I knew. Well, except for the running around with guns part. The number of backstories I didn't know was getting frustrating.

Ben's hesitation before responding was maddening. Hesitation meant uncertainty. Meant a weak position. Maybe even guilt. Which made me wonder: Where had Cormac learned about guns? Where had he become such a great shot?

Ben said, "Your Honor, Mr. Bennett's association with that group ended over a decade ago. It hasn't been an issue because it isn't relevant."

"Mr. O'Farrell, I've granted the prosecution's request that Mr. Bennett be held without bail."

"Your Honor, I'd like to lodge a protest. You've got his record—he's never jumped bail."

"And don't you think it's just a little odd how often your client has been arrested and had to post bail? Don't you ever get tired of standing with your client at these hearings?"

"Frankly, that's not your concern."

"Careful, Mr. O'Farrell."

"Your Honor, I'd like to move that the case against my client be dismissed. Miriam Wilson's attack was so brutal, lives were at risk. Katherine Norville's attempt to stop her without lethal force resulted in great injury to herself. My client was well within his right to use force against her under Title eighteen dash one dash seven-oh-four of the Colorado Criminal Code."

Espinoza countered: "The law protecting the right to use deadly force in cases of defense does not apply in this case. On the contrary, the accused was in fact lying in wait for the victim's appearance." That was wrong. I almost stood up and said something. I had to bite my tongue. The prosecutor continued. "Your Honor, the victim was a twenty-year-old woman weighing a hundred and twenty pounds. Her ability to inflict lethal damage with her bare hands is questionable. Moreover, the evidence suggests she was highly mentally disturbed during the incident." He consulted a page of notes. "She was wearing a wolf skin at the time and it has been suggested that she believed that she was a wolf. I find it hard to believe that in such a mental state, judging by her physical attributes, she was at all a danger to anyone. Especially when she already had three bullet wounds in her chest. The victim was already incapacitated when the defendant fired the final, killing shot. In that moment this stopped being a case of defense and became a murder."

And nothing about any of that was false. She had been wearing a wolf skin. That it actually turned her into a wolf—suggesting that would sound ludicrous in this setting. And maybe she'd been fatally wounded. Maybe she wouldn't have lashed out with her skin/walker magic. But Cormac hadn't know that.

Ben offered another volley. "Seeing that a psychological evaluation of the victim is impossible, I would like to offer evidence and precedent that such a mental illness would in fact make her a danger to those around her, even while injured."

Heller asked a question. "The witness who was involved in the physical confrontation with the victim—how extensive are her injuries?"

A moment of silence weighed heavily on the room. How extensive were my injuries? They weren't, not anymore.

I had a few scabs, where the worst of the scratches had healed, a few pink marks. In a couple more days even those would disappear. But if I hadn't been a lycanthrope I'd be in the hospital. If I hadn't been a lycanthrope, we could say, *Look, this is what Cormac saved us from, this is why he shouldn't be in jail.* But we didn't have that.

In lieu of an answer, Heller continued. "Was Ms. Norville even examined by a doctor after the confrontation?"

"No, Your Honor," Ben said softly. I should have let him take me to a hospital. He'd wanted to take me to a hospital. We could have at least taken pictures of what the wounds looked like.

None of us thought we'd be here arguing it in court. That we'd need the evidence.

"Then the violence of the victim's attack has perhaps been exaggerated?"

I should have just let Miriam Wilson kill me. That would have gotten Cormac off the hook. Made everyone's lives a whole lot easier. Nice defeatist thinking there.

Ben's voice changed, falling in pitch, becoming tight with anger. "You have the witness statements, Your Honor. At the time, they all feared for Ms. Norville's life. That's the scene my client encountered, and that's what should be taken into account. The only reason there's even a question is because Sheriff Marks has a grudge against him. This court is biased." He landed his fist on the table. From behind him, I could see his breathing quicken, his ribs expanding under the cheap suit jacket.

Heller shook her head, preparing to close out the hearing. "I am not inclined to dismiss this case on the basis of the evidence you've presented, Mr. O'Farrell."

Hissing a breath, Ben bent double almost, leaning on

the table in front of him, bowing his head. The pose was familiar—it's what I did when the Wolf fought inside me, when she was close to the surface and trying to break out.

I stood quickly; leaning forward as far as I could, I was able to touch Ben's back. It was stiff as a board, in pain. Cormac gripped Ben's arm with his bound hands. *Please, not here,* I begged silently. *Feel my touch, stay human, keep it together.* I tried to see his hands—that was where it usually happened first. The claws—did he have claws or fingers?

"Mr. O'Farrell, are you all right?" Judge Heller frowned with concern.

Everyone in the courtroom stared at us. I didn't care. I kept my hand pressed against his back, hoping he'd respond. Cormac and I both watched him intently, waiting.

Finally, he straightened. Creaking almost, like he had to stack each vertebra into place. His face was pale, and his neck sweating.

"I'm fine," he said, though his voice was still rough, like a growl. "Sorry for the interruption. I'm fine." He smoothed his suit and shook himself out of the spell. Slowly, Cormac and I sat back in our places.

My heart was racing. I couldn't help but feel like we'd had a close call. He shouldn't have been doing this, he shouldn't have had to face the stress of a courtroom in his condition. He was still just a pup.

Heller resumed. "Both parties should consult in order to agree on a time for a preliminary hearing, at which time the defendant will enter his plea to the charges filed."

Then, almost abruptly, anticlimactically, it was over. And Cormac wasn't leaving with us. Held without bail.

The courtroom rustled with activity. Bailiffs approached to take charge of Cormac, who looked over his shoulder at me. "Keep an eye on him. Don't let him out of your sight," he said in a low voice. I nodded quickly and watched them lead him away. He knew how close it had been, too.

Marks glared at us across the room, but didn't stick around for a confrontation.

Espinoza approached Ben, who still looked like he was about to pass out. I could hear his heart racing. I was ready to jump up and leap to his side, if he showed the slightest indication that he needed help—if he was about to break down. He held it together, though. He didn't look good, but he stayed upright, kept breathing.

I didn't like George Espinoza, even though I knew that wasn't fair. I didn't know him, I'd never spoken to him. But I saw him as a threat. He was attacking my people. My pack. I kept wanting to slip in between him and Ben and growl at him. But I had to just step aside and let things happen.

They talked in low voices. Ben did a lot of nodding. The bailiff hustled them out of the room then to make way for the next hearing. I trailed behind, trying to eavesdrop. I heard a couple of phrases. "Give me a week," and "plea bargain."

I approached Ben only after Espinoza left the lobby outside the courtroom. He stood stiffly, hugging a file folder that stood in for his briefcase. He carried himself rigidly—angry, and trying to hold it in. He was used to being able to channel his anger in the courtroom. Using it to strengthen his arguments. Now, the wolf wouldn't let him do that.

I put my hand on his shoulder. "Let's get out of here."

He let me guide him out of the building, leaning on me until we were outside.

Out in the sun I was able to ask him, "How close did you get in there? How close to Changing?"

He shook his head absently. "I don't know. I felt like I could have breathed wrong and it all would have come loose. I felt it push against the inside of my skin. I just don't know." He closed his eyes and took a deep, trembling breath. "I'm losing it."

"No, you're not. You're fine, you kept it together."

"Not me," he said. "I don't care about me. I'm talking about the case."

"It can't be that bad. Can it?" He was the lawyer. Who was I to second-guess him?

"Any rational person looks at the evidence and comes to exactly the conclusion Espinoza presented. If I stand up there and say, no she wasn't just wearing a wolf skin, she'd actually become a wolf, I sound insane. When it comes to believing the eyewitness reports of a few people who were in the dark and scared out of their skulls, or the hard evidence of the coroner's report, it isn't much of a contest. And she was incapacitated when Cormac killed her. He wasn't defending anyone at that point."

"We didn't know that, not for sure. Marks was there— why doesn't he tell them? He's a cop, wouldn't his testimony hold any more weight?"

"He's signed off on Espinoza's version."

Of course he would. "That's not fair. You'd think after everything he did to me he could at least stand up for Cormac."

"Except he's decided that she wasn't that dangerous, and Cormac overreacted. The coroner's report makes more sense than skinwalkers, so that's what he's sticking to. That's what's going to hold up in court. Not the ghost stories."

I wanted to shake Ben. Tell him to snap out of it and get his confidence back. He had to save Cormac, and he wasn't going to do it talking like that.

Ben said, "He shouldn't have shot her there at the end. That was a mistake."

"I know."

And that was what we kept talking around. That Cormac had gone too far to save this time. Nothing we said or did would ever erase that moment.

We walked a few more paces, and I changed the subject. "Why wouldn't the judge set bail?"

He scowled. "Espinoza doesn't want to take a chance on him getting away. Heller's right, those militia wingnuts do have a history of jumping bail. It's a case of them looking at the facts they want to and not the ones that matter. There might be some past history there that's coloring her judgment."

That brought up a whole other set of questions. We'd reached the car by then. "So what is all that about Cormac and the Mountain Patriot Brigade?"

Ben kept on, almost like he hadn't heard, climbing into the car and not looking at me. I'd started the engine before he finally said, "I'm not going to answer that."

"Why not? You know those guys are practically neo-Nazis?"

"I won't argue with that."

I couldn't fit that and Cormac in my mind at the same time. "And?"

"And I don't think the group even exists anymore. It's some guy in a basement running a Web site."

"How do you know this? How are you two even involved?" My voice was becoming shrill.

"I don't owe you an explanation."

That just pissed me off. "Oh, really?"

He glared at me, and I bristled. That was just what we needed. A fight. Posturing. A pissing contest. I didn't want to rile up his wolf any more than it already was.

I put the car in gear and pulled out of the parking lot.

The movement of the car, driving down the highway back to the cabin, settled us down. Ben didn't want to tell me, and that was his right, I supposed. But I had other ways of finding information. We had a lot of other problems to deal with right now.

A few more miles of ranch land sped past us when he said, "I want to get a hotel room in Walsenburg, to be closer to the courthouse."

We packed that night, and in the morning found a place to make camp for the duration.

The next day saw Ben working on building his case. Mostly, this involved talking to people, legwork, phone calls. He went to Alice, Joe, Tony, and Sheriff Marks. They were Cormac's defense. I offered to come along, but Ben said no. Cormac's lawyer needed to handle this, he said. My being there would muddy the issue. Remind them of their biases. Maybe he was right. Cormac told me not to let Ben out of my sight. But I let him go.

Besides, I had a research project of my own.

The public library, a couple of blocks down from the courthouse, had several computer terminals. I went to one and started searching. After a half an hour, I took my notes to the reference desk.

"Do you have copies of the *Denver Post* from these dates?"

The nice lady at the desk set me up at a microfiche machine, and away I went. It took about three hours of hunting to find the whole story.

Starting about fifteen years ago, a group of Front Range ranchers began protesting new restrictions and higher fees for grazing their cattle on public lands. Millions of acres across the West were owned by the government, and ranchers had been given access to those lands. To a lot of people, federally owned was the same as public, and anything that barred their access to those lands impinged on their rights as citizens. Some of them did the sane thing: they lobbied Congress, lodged complaints, took the issue to court. Others, though, turned to militias. They stockpiled arms and began to prepare for the violent overthrow of the government they saw as inevitable.

A man named David O'Farrell showed up in a series of articles. This was Ben's father, who at the time owned a ranch near Loveland. He was arrested several times on illegal weapons charges and went straight to the top of the list of people suspected of being the head of the Mountain Patriot Brigade, one of a network of paramilitary groups that gathered and trained in the backcountry, with the ultimate goal of defending by force their right to use public lands. Through the early nineties they had almost constant confrontations with local law enforcement—except in a few cases where local law enforcement happened to be members.

Eight years ago, after lengthy FBI surveillance and a carefully prosecuted case, Ben's father had been convicted on various felony weapons violations and conspiracy charges. He was still in prison.

The name Cormac Bennett didn't show up in conjunction with the Mountain Patriot Brigade in any of the articles and references I found. He'd never been arrested or suspected of any wrongdoing as part of the group. Espinoza's information about him came from FBI and police reports about the group. Young Cormac didn't rate the attention that the group's leaders did. He hadn't been considered a threat. But the association was there, especially since he was David O'Farrell's nephew.

I found another newspaper article, from a couple of years earlier than all the Mountain Patriot Brigade business, that featured Cormac. It reported on the strange death of Douglas Bennett. The coroner reported that the forty-eight-year-old had been mauled by an animal, possibly a bear or a very large dog. The police, on the other hand, claimed that he'd been murdered by a deranged assailant. Douglas's sixteen-year-old son, Cormac, had witnessed the attack, and shot dead the assailant. The police had the all-too-human body, with Cormac's rifle bullet in its head and Douglas's flesh between its teeth. The shooting was deemed a case of self-defense. No charges were filed against Cormac, who went to live with his aunt's family, the O'Farrell clan. His mother had died in a car accident when he was five.

It was déjà vu, this disagreement between the witnesses and the coroner's report. And Cormac had been in this situation before. Cormac had killed his first werewolf when he was sixteen years old. I didn't even know what to think about that. Once, I asked Cormac how he'd become a werewolf and vampire hunter, where he'd learned the tricks of it. He said it ran in the family. Which might explain why Douglas was in a position to get mauled to death in the first place, and why Cormac was there to witness it: Douglas had been training him.

I wondered what his mother would have thought of that, if she'd been alive to see it.

I printed off that article and a dozen or so others. By then, it was dinnertime. I called the hotel room, but no one answered. That meant Ben was either off being lawyerly— I hoped—or he was moping. I took a chance and picked up a pizza and beer for dinner.

When I got back to the room, Ben was there. Doing a little of both, it seemed: my laptop was on, plugged into the phone jack, and papers were spread over the table and half the bed. But he sat in the chair, staring at the wall. I couldn't even say that he was thinking hard. He was back in that fugue state.

He jumped when the door opened, clutched the arms of his chair, his mouth open slightly, like he was about to growl. He calmed down almost immediately, slouching and looking away. Tense—just a little.

"Hungry?" I said, trying to be nonchalant.

"Not really."

"When was the last time you ate?" He only shook his head. "You ought to eat something."

"Sure, Mom." He gave me the briefest flickers of a glance—half accusing, half apologetic. I must have glared at him. I didn't appreciate the label. I didn't appreciate having to behave like that label.

He cleared a spot on the table where I deposited the pizza.

I pulled my stack of papers out of my bag and set them between us. I'd put the one about Cormac's father on top. A grainy, black and white picture of the man occupied the middle of the page. He'd been lean and weathered, with short-cropped, receding hair. In the picture, a candid snapshot, he was smiling at something to the left of the camera, and wearing sunglasses.

Ben stared at it a moment, his expression blank. I thought I knew him pretty well by now, but I couldn't read this. He was almost disbelieving. Then, his lips quirked a smile.

Finally, he said, "I'd forgotten about that picture. It's a good one of him. Uncle Doug." He shook his head, then looked at me. "You've been busy."

"Yeah. It's funny how much of your family's history is plastered all over the newspapers."

He started shuffling through the articles. "Real busy."

"Just remember that the next time you think you can keep a secret from me."

"Why go to the trouble?"

"I wanted to make sure that you and Cormac aren't bad guys. I have to say, you have kind of a creepy past. When you say this stuff doesn't matter, I really want to trust you."

"I'm not sure that's such a great idea. You might be better off on your own. Get out of Dodge while the getting's good."

We were pack. I'd see this through. "I'll stick around."

"I haven't seen my father in over ten years. We had a throw-down screaming match over this Patriot Brigade garbage. I was twenty, first one in my family to go to college and so full of myself. I was educated." He gave the word sarcastic emphasis. "I knew it all, and there I was to throw it back in the face of my poor benighted father. And he was so full of that right-wing nut-job rhetoric... I left. Cormac was still there, helping him work the ranch.

That's the only reason he got tangled up with that crowd, was because of my father. When I left, so did he. I still don't know if it was something I said that convinced him. Or if we'd just spent so much time looking out for each other—we were already kind of a team, then.

"Dad called me right before that last trial. I'd just passed the bar. He wanted me to represent him. I said no. I'd have said no even if we were on good terms. He really needed someone with experience. But all Dad heard was that his only son, his own flesh and blood, was turning his back on him. The funny thing about it all, I wanted to convince him he was wrong. There wasn't a government conspiracy out to get him, I wasn't trying to sell him down the river. But everything that happened, from the FBI wiretaps to me walking out on him, confirmed everything in his mind. He's too far gone to come back."

"You haven't been to see him. You haven't talked to him at all," I said. "Do you want to? Do you think you should?"

He shook his head. "I made a clean break. We're all better off if it stays that way. Cormac and I always kind of knew that something he'd done in the past would come back to haunt him. I didn't think it would be this." He tossed the printouts back on the table.

"Where's your mom?"

"She divorced my dad after thirty years of marriage, sold the ranch to pay his legal expenses, and is now working as a waitress in Longmont. And that's the whole story of my sordid, screwed up family." He shook his head absently. "You know what's always gotten to me? My dad and I aren't that different. It's where we came from, that whole independent rural culture. I remember telling him, yeah, sure, take back the government, put it back in the hands of the people. That's great. But you're not going to do it with a stockpile of dynamite and hate speech. Me—I went to law school. Thought I'd work the system from the inside, sticking it to the man." His smile turned sad. "Maybe we were both wrong."

I wanted to hug him and make silly cooing noises. That Mom thing again. He had this traumatized look to him. Instead, I hefted the grocery bag. "I brought beer."

"My hero," he said, smiling.

We settled down to beer and pizza. "What have you been working on?"

"Precedents," he said. "You'd think in a state where half the population totes around guns in their glove boxes this sort of thing would have come up before. We have a Make My Day law for crying out loud. But there isn't too much out there to cover if you shoot something thinking it's a wild animal, then it turns out to be a person."

"Except for the werewolf that killed Cormac's dad."

"Which isn't going to help Cormac's case at all if the prosecutor digs it up, so I'd really appreciate it if you didn't draw anyone's attention to it. Judges get nervous when weird things keep happening to the same person."

I turned an invisible key at the corner of my mouth. "My lips are sealed."

He gave me a highly skeptical look. I wanted to argue—then realized I couldn't, really. We fell into a moment of silence, eating and drinking. He stared at the computer screen as if it would offer up miracles.

"How did the rest of your day go?" I asked, not sure I wanted to know.

"Pretty well, I think," he said, but the tone was

ambivalent, and he still looked exhausted instead of fired up. "Tony's going to stick around to give a statement, Alice is downright enthusiastic about testifying. She seems to think she owes you a favor. But you know what? I keep running into that same problem."

"What problem? I don't see a problem. Eyewitnesses, that's what you need, that's what you have. Isn't it?" I had the feeling he was about to tangle me up in some legal loophole.

"Why were we all there in the first place?" he said.

I wasn't sure I could explain it anymore. It seemed so long ago. "We were going to remove Alice's curse. Tony said he had a ritual."

"Magic. Witchcraft," he said curtly. "So how do you convince the legal system that this is real? That when Tony and Alice talk about casting their spells, they're serious, and it's real. That they're not crackpots. I'm afraid Espinoza's going to use that angle to discredit their testimony. He'll say, of course a couple of people who are out in the woods at dusk lighting candles and burning incense are going to think up some story about how this woman really turned into a wolf. Of course they'll say that even shot through the chest and dying she was a threat because she was a skinwalker. He'll say they're as deluded as Miriam was and therefore their testimony is suspect."

He was twisting the words, manipulating the story. Just like a lawyer. Just like Espinoza. Ben was thinking of all the angles, but none of them seemed to work in our favor.

"So you can't use their testimony."

"Oh, I'm going to use it and hope for the best. Maybe I'm wrong and Espinoza won't shoot them down."

This was looking grimmer and grimmer. Grasping

at straws. "What about Marks? He had it in for me in the first place—*that's* why we were at the cabin when Miriam attacked. Can't you use that to discredit him as a witness?"

"If you want to sue Alice and Sheriff Marks for harassment, I'm all for it. I think you have a good case against them. You don't even have to bring up magic to prove that leaving dead dogs in someone's yard is harassment. But it's a different case. I'll certainly bring it up, but the judge might decide that a suit against Marks doesn't have any bearing in the case of Miriam Wilson's death."

The pizza had gotten cold and I'd lost my appetite. Ben wasn't eating either.

"The whole thing seems rigged," I said. "It's not fair."

"Welcome to the American justice system." He raised his bottle of beer, as if in a toast.

"Cynic." I pouted.

"Lawyer," he countered, grinning.

"Ben. Drink your beer."

I went to see Sheriff Marks the next morning. I told Ben I was taking a walk to the grocery store for donuts.

Carefully, I approached the front desk at the sheriff's department like it was a bomb. I asked the woman working there, a nonuniformed civilian, "Hi, is Sheriff Marks in? Could I speak to him?"

"Yes, I think he is. Do you have an appointment?"

"No," I said, wincing. I fully expected Marks to refuse to see me. But I had to try.

The receptionist frowned sadly, and I tried not to be

mad at her. She was just doing her job. "Then I'm afraid he probably won't be available, he's very busy—"

"It's all right, Kelly." Marks stood in the hallway to the side, just within view. His expression was guarded, pointedly bland, like he'd expected me to be here all along and didn't mind. He knew his place in the world and I couldn't shake it. "I'll talk to her. Send her back."

He turned and went down the hall, presumably to his office.

"Go on back," Kelly the receptionist said. I did.

Marks disappeared through a doorway halfway down the hall, and I followed him into a perfectly average, perfectly normal cluttered office: a desk with a computer sat against the wall. There was an in-box overflowing with papers and files, bookshelves, also overflowing, certificates and plaques on the wall, along with a huge map labeled Huerfano County. Colored pins marked various spots; a red pin was stuck about where I guessed my cabin was.

Marks sat at the desk and gestured me toward a couple of straight-backed plastic chairs by the opposite wall.

"Thanks" I said, sitting. "I didn't think you'd even talk to me."

He gave an amiable shrug, donning the persona of a friendly small-town cop. "I figure the least I can do is hear you out."

"The least you can do is let Cormac go."

"Have you seen that guy's file? You know what he's done? He should have been locked up years ago."

"And if he had, I'd be dead, and so would you and four other people." I matched him, glare for glare. "He saved my life, Sheriff. That's all I'm paying attention to right now."

His glare set like stone, unrelenting. "That man's a killer."

Yes, but… "You can't deny he saved my life."

"That girl couldn't have really hurt anyone," he said, giving a huff that was almost laughter.

"Didn't you see what she did to me?"

"You had a few cuts," he said.

Then I realized, maybe he hadn't seen. It had been dark; I hadn't even known how bad it was until I got inside and saw all the blood. Marks simply might not have seen it. Once again, I kicked myself for not taking pictures.

I said, "Then you don't believe she really turned into a wolf. You're buying the 'insane woman in a wolf skin' version." He answered with a cold stare that said it all. "How can you believe in werewolves but not in skinwalkers? How can you believe in magic enough to curse my house, but not enough to believe what she was? You just want to put Cormac away because you can, without giving him the benefit of the doubt or anything!"

"Ms. Norville, I think we're done here."

"You're a hypocrite—you've broken the law yourself, in the name of protecting people, when you did those things to me. Well, Cormac was doing the same thing."

Marks leaned forward, hand on his desk, his glare still hard as stone. Nothing could touch this guy, not when he was like this. "He shot and killed an injured, dying woman in cold blood. *That's* what he's being charged with. Goodbye, Ms. Norville." He pointed at the door.

I glared at him, my throat on the edge of a growl, and he couldn't read the stance. All he saw was an angry, ineffectual woman standing before him. And maybe that was all I was.

I left, gratefully slipping out of his territory.

* * *

I went back to the hotel, where Ben greeted me with, "Where are the donuts?"

I'd forgotten. Crap. I shrugged and said, "Didn't get them. Got lost."

"In Walsenburg?" Clearly, he didn't believe me. I just smiled sweetly.

Later, we returned to the county jail to see Cormac. I hadn't had a chance to talk to him, not after the attack, not before or after the hearing. It had been frustrating, sitting five feet away in the courtroom and not being able to say anything to him.

I had hoped Marks would be there to meet us. That he'd have seen the error of his ways and come to make amends by releasing Cormac. That all this would just go away. Wishful thinking. He wasn't there, and Cormac was still locked up.

"Has Marks talked to you?" I asked Ben. "Maybe changed his mind about all this?"

"Are you kidding? He's not even returning my calls."

So much for my grand speech at him having any influence and giving us that Disney happy ending.

Still, Ben had a plan. "I have to go to New Mexico. Talk to people who knew Miriam Wilson. Find out if they knew what she was, and if she killed anyone there. Espinoza's not going to have to dig too much to prove that Cormac's a dangerous man. So I have to prove that he didn't have a choice but to kill her."

"He didn't," I said. "Did he?"

"That's what I have to prove."

A deputy ensconced us in a windowless conference

room, like a thousand others in police stations and jails all across the country. I bet they all had the same smell, too: dust and old coffee. Strained nerves. Ben got me in by claiming I was his legal assistant. Then the deputy brought Cormac.

Ben and Cormac sat across from each other. I hid away in the corner. I both did and didn't want to be there. I hated seeing Cormac like this. I didn't know exactly what *this* meant. Objectively, he looked the same as he always did, half slouching, appearing unconcerned with what went on around him—moving through the world without being a part of it. That orange jumpsuit made him look *wrong,* though.

Ben had a pen and paper out, ready to take notes. "I need to know everything that happened while you were gone. Between the time you left the cabin in Clay and when you got back in time to shoot her."

"I told you before."

"Tell me again."

"I got in my Jeep, I drove all night to Shiprock. Stopped to get some sleep at a rest stop. Went back to the place where we'd gone to bait them." As in, the place where Ben was attacked. "I spent a lot of time just looking around. I honestly didn't think she'd leave the area. That was her territory."

"Except she wasn't a lycanthrope. She didn't have a territory."

"Sure, we know that *now.*"

"Go on."

"I talked to the werewolf's family. The people who hired me. The Wilsons. Trying to find out more about the second one. They wouldn't tell me anything. They wouldn't believe me when I said there was a second one running around. They thanked me for freeing their son from his curse, and that was it. End of story. I didn't know anything about Miriam. I didn't know they were related."

I hadn't intended on interrupting, but I did. "You shot this guy and nobody said anything. Nobody hauled you in on murder charges there."

"No one reported it. No one witnessed it. Bodies just vanish out there."

That was just weird. But I'd never understood Cormac's "profession."

"They didn't mention their daughter?" Ben asked. "Not once?"

"Not once. I spent a couple more days looking. Then I got your message."

"Not checking your phone?"

"I was in the backcountry most of the time. I didn't have reception. I came back as soon as I did get it. I don't think she followed us. How could she?"

"You heard what Tony said. She was a witch. It may have taken her a few days, but she found us."

Then Cormac asked, "What are the odds they can pin this on me, Ben?"

Ben shook his head. "I don't know. The primary witness has it in for you, Espinoza's a hot young prosecutor who'd love to land a Class One felony conviction. We don't have a whole lot in our favor."

"We have a bunch of witnesses," I said.

"And Espinoza will do everything he can to discredit them."

"You'll figure something out," Cormac said. "You always do."

Ben's shoulders bent under the weight of Cormac's trust. "Yeah, we'll see about that," he said softly.

After an awkward moment, Cormac said, "What happened back there, at the hearing—should I be worried? Are you up for this?"

They stared at each other, studying each other. "If you want to get someone else—"

"I trust you," he said. "Who else is going to understand this shit?"

Ben wouldn't look at him. "Yeah. I'll be fine. Somehow. Not getting bail was a setback, but you'll be okay."

He didn't sound confident, but Cormac nodded, like he was sure. Then he made a sour-faced grimace and muttered, "I can't believe they dug up that Brigade shit."

I jumped on him. "Yeah, what the heck is up with that? Those guys are insane. It just doesn't seem like your style."

"And what would you know about it?" Cormac said.

Before I could fire back, Ben said, "She spent yesterday in the library digging up every article the *Denver Post* ever printed on the Brigade. Got the whole story."

"Talk too much, and you're nosy as hell," he muttered.

"I also found the story about your father," I said, almost chagrined at the confession, because when he put it that way, it did seem like going behind their backs. But what else was I supposed to do when no one would tell me anything? "I'm really sorry, Cormac. About what happened to him."

He waved me away. "That was a long time ago."

"And now she knows everything about our dark, secret past," Ben said.

"Shit, I was having fun being all mysterious."

"Now you're just making fun of me," I said. "The Brigade. Start talking."

"So. You want to know why I spent a couple of years running around with a bunch of gun-toting wannabe skinhead maniacs?"

"Uh. Yeah. And you can't dodge, 'cause I'm going to sit here until... until—"

"Until what?"

Until you convince me you aren't crazy. I looked away.

Then, he spoke almost kindly. "I was working on my uncle's—Ben's dad's—ranch. He got caught up in it, and I tagged along. I was just a kid, must have been nineteen or so. I didn't know any better. Those guys—I was still getting over losing my dad, and I thought maybe I could learn something from them. But they were playing games. They weren't living in the real world. They hadn't seen the things I had. I left. Quit the ranch. Spent a couple years in the army. Never looked back."

Simple as that. I knew as well as anybody how a person could get caught up in things, when that pack mentality took over. He'd been a kid. Just made a mistake. I bought it.

"Why are you worried about it?" he said, after my long hesitation.

I didn't know, really. After seeing what Cormac was capable of, it seemed strange to find him involved, however tangentially, with such garden-variety creepiness. I said, "I keep finding out more things that make you scarier."

And I had trouble balancing both liking him and being scared of him.

He stared at me so hard, so searching, like it was my fault we'd never been able to work out anything between us. Which one of us hadn't been able to face that there was anything between us? Which one of the three of us? Because Ben had dropped all those hints. He'd known. And now it was Ben and me, with Cormac on the outside, and all three of us locked in a room together.

He'd run, and that wasn't my fault. He scared me, and maybe that was my fault.

Then the spell broke. Cormac dropped his gaze. "It still cracks me up, that you're a goddamned werewolf and you can talk about me being scary."

"It's like rock-paper-scissors," I said. "Silver bullet beats werewolf, and you've got the silver."

"And cop beats silver bullet. I get it," he said, and he was right. Almost, the whole thing made sense. Cormac turned to Ben. "What's the plan?"

"I'm going to go to Shiprock to learn what I can about Miriam Wilson. There's got to be someone willing to testify that she was dangerous, that it was justifiable. We'll decide our strategy when I get back."

"Has Espinoza said anything about a plea bargain yet?"

"Yeah. I told him I didn't want to talk about it until I had all my cards in hand. Hearing's on Wednesday. We'll know then, one way or the other."

He nodded, so it must have sounded like a good plan to him. "Be careful."

"Yeah."

Ben knocked on the door, and the deputy came to take Cormac back to his cell.

"I hate this," Ben said when he was gone. "I really, really hate this. We've never gone as far as a preliminary hearing. I want to tear into something."

I took his arm, squeezing to offer comfort. "Let's get out of here."

We'd only just stepped outside, into the late-morning sunlight, when we were ambushed. Not really—it was only Alice, lurking across the parking lot and then heading straight for us on an intercept path. My heart raced anyway, because all I saw was someone half running, half trotting toward me. I stopped, my shoulders tensing, and only an act of will forced me to smile.

Ben grabbed my arm and bared his teeth.

"Hush," I whispered at him, touching his back to calm him. "It's okay. It's just Alice."

He froze, seemingly realizing what had just happened. His features shifted; he didn't relax much, but he didn't look like he was going to pounce anymore.

Strange how I was still getting used to this new Ben. He was a new Ben—strangely, subtly different, slightly less steady, slightly more paranoid. As if he were recovering from some sort of head injury. Which maybe he was. Maybe all of us who'd been infected with lycanthropy were.

"Kitty! Kitty, hello. I'm so glad I caught you." She smiled, but stiffly, as you do in awkward social situations.

"Hi, Alice."

"I just came to give another statement to the sheriff. I thought it might help your friend. Even Joe gave another statement, said that if he hadn't come along—well, I don't know what would have happened."

I did, or I could guess. It really wasn't worth describing to her. "Thanks, Alice. I'm sure it can't hurt."

I was about to say goodbye, to get out of there before I said something impolite, when Alice spoke.

"I wanted to give you this. I've been thinking about what Tony said, about how much we all might still be in danger. It's not much, but I want to help." She offered her hand, palm up. "Tony may be right, I may not know what I'm doing most of the time. But this came from the heart, and I can't help but think that means something."

She held a pendant to me, a clear, pointed crystal about as long as my thumb. The blunt end of it was wrapped with beads, tiny beads made of sparkling glass and polished wood, strung together in a pattern and bound tightly to the crystal. A loop of knotted cord woven into the beadwork had a string of leather through it, so it could be worn around the neck. It was a little piece of artwork. It glittered like sunlight through springtime woods when I turned it in the sun.

"I usually use silver wire to string the beads," she said. "But, well, I didn't this time. I used silk thread."

It was so thoughtful I could have cried. If only it hadn't been too little, too late.

Did I trust it to actually work? A talisman made by Alice, who'd cast that horrific curse against me—and cast it badly, gutlessly, so that it hadn't worked. Had that one come from her heart as well? Did I trust her?

At the moment, it didn't cost me anything to pretend that I did.

"It's beautiful," I said. "Thank you."

She stood there, beaming, and I hugged her, because I knew it would make her feel better. Then I put the pendant over my head, because that would make her feel better, too.

She went to her car, waving goodbye.

"It's hard to know where to draw the line isn't it?" Ben said. "About what to believe and what not to believe. What works and what doesn't."

I sighed in agreement. "She's right, though. If it comes from the heart, it has to count for something."

chapter 14

We set off in the morning. We had five days until the hearing, when Cormac had to enter a plea. Ben had to find evidence on Cormac's behalf that would get the case thrown out.

The weather was on our side; it felt like a small advantage. I hadn't had to work very hard to talk Ben into letting me go with him. I didn't know how much help I'd be in hunting down the information he needed to shore up Cormac's defense, but that wasn't the argument I'd made.

I had to be there to keep Ben sane.

"*Wolf* Creek Pass," he said when we passed the highway marker over the mountain. We had a couple more hours until we reached New Mexico. "Am I the only one who thinks that's funny?"

"Yes," I said, not taking my eyes off the road ahead. Too many signs advertising local motels and gift shops had featured pictures of fuzzy, howling wolves. The Wolf Creek ski area was doing a booming business.

I let him drive the stretch that took us over the pass. Just over the mountain, cruising into the next valley and toward the junction that turned onto the highway that led to New Mexico, a zippy little sports car with skis in a rack on the back roared up behind us, gunned its engine, swerved around us, and nearly cut us off as it pulled back into the right line, obviously expressing great displeasure at our insistence at driving only five miles an hour over the speed limit.

Ben clenched the steering wheel with rigid fingers and bared his teeth in a silent growl. Something animal crawled into his eyes for a moment.

"Ben?" I spoke softly, not wanting to startle him. Not wanting to startle the wolf that adrenaline had brought to the surface for a moment.

"I'm okay," he said. His breaths were rough, and his body was still more tense than the stress of driving mountain roads warranted. "How many days?"

"How many days?"

"Full moon," he said.

"Sixteen," I said. Keeping track had become second nature.

"I thought it was sooner. It feels sooner."

I knew the feeling. The wolf wanted to break free, and it let you know. "It's better if you don't think about it."

"How do you not think about it?" His voice cracked.

"Do you want to pull over and let me drive?"

He shook his head quickly. "Driving gives me something else to think about."

"Just don't let the jerks get to you, okay?"

He pushed himself back in the seat, stretching his arms, making an effort to relax. After another ten miles or so he said, "I started smoking in law school. It was a crutch, a way to get through it. You feel like you're going crazy, so you step outside for a cigarette. Everything stops for a couple of minutes, and you can go back to it feeling a little bit calmer. Quitting, though—that's the bitch. 'Cause as much as you tell yourself you don't need the crutch anymore, your body isn't convinced. Took me two years to wean myself off them. That's what this feels like," he said. "I want to turn wolf like I wanted a cigarette. That doesn't make any sense."

"Like any of this makes sense," I muttered. "You don't have to wait until the full moon to Change. The wolf part knows that. It's always trying to get out."

Watching him, I could almost see the analytical part of him trying to figure it out—the lawyer part of him on the case. His eyes narrowed, his face puckered up with thought.

He said, harshly, "Where does the part about that side of it being a strength come in?"

I could have said something cutting, but our nerves were frayed as it was. He needed a serious answer. "Being decisive. Sometimes it helps seeing the world as black and white, where everyone's either a predator or prey. You don't let details muddy up your thinking."

"That's cynical."

"I know. That's what I hate about it."

"You know what the trouble is? We all see this case— what they're doing to Cormac—as black and white. But we're looking at white as white and Espinoza's looking at white as black. Does that make any sense?"

"When maybe if we all saw it as gray we'd be able to come to some sort of compromise."

"Yeah." He tapped the steering wheel as he lost himself in thought.

It started snowing as we left the mountains.

* * *

Northern New Mexico was bleak, windswept, and touched with scattered bits of blowing snow from the storm. Stands of cottonwoods by the river were gray and leafless. All the colors seemed washed out of the landscape, which was barren desert hemmed in by eroded cliffs and mesas.

We didn't have much to go on. The woman's name, the missing person report. We arrived in Shiprock in time to stop at the police department—Tribal law enforcement. Shiprock was on the Navajo Reservation. The town's namesake, a jagged volcanic monolith rising almost two thousand feet above the desert, was visible to the south, a kind of signpost.

Ben spoke to the sergeant on duty at the front desk, while I lurked in the back, peering at them with interest.

"I'm looking for information about Miriam Wilson." He showed them a picture from the coroner's office. A terrible, gruesome picture because half her face was pulped, but the other half still showed recognizable features. Her cheeks were round, her large eyes closed. "A missing person report was filed on her about three months ago. I don't know if the Huerfano County sheriff's department sent you the news that she was killed in Colorado."

"Yeah, we got word," said the man behind the counter, a Sergeant Tsosie according to his nameplate. He had short black hair, brown skin, dark eyes, and an angled profile.

"You don't seem concerned."

"She won't be missed."

Ben asked, "Has her family been notified? The coroner up there hasn't received any instructions about what to do with her body."

"He's not likely to, either. She's not going to have anyone asking about her. Trust me."

"Then who filed the missing person report on her in the first place? Families who don't want to find out where their kids went don't normally do that."

"This isn't a normal family," Tsosie said, almost smiling.

"What if I went to talk to them?"

"Good luck with that. The Wilsons are impossible to deal with."

The officer looked nervous. He kept glancing around—over his shoulder, toward the door, like he expected someone to come reprimand him. "You want some advice? Stop asking about her. She was bad news. That whole family's bad news. You keep going on about this, you won't like what you find, I guarantee it."

"Bad news," Ben said. "Would you be willing to testify to that in court?"

The officer shook his head quickly—fearfully, I might have said. "I won't have anything to do with it."

Ben leaned forward and almost snarled. "I'm the defense attorney for the man who shot her. I need to show that it was justifiable, and you need to help me do that."

Tsosie's lips pressed together for a moment while he hesitated. Then he made a decision. I could see it settle on his features. "Hold on a minute."

He went to a filing cabinet off to the side of the room. He opened the top drawer and flipped through a few folders, drew one out, and studied the top sheet for a moment. Then he brought the whole folder over and lay it open in front of Ben. "Take it," he said. "Take all of it. And your client? You thank him for us."

"Yeah. I'll do that," Ben said, a little breathlessly. "Thanks. Look, it would really help him out if I could get a statement. Just a signed statement."

"I'm not sure a judge would look twice at anything I could say about her."

"Anything'll help."

He got the statement. One paragraph, vague, but it was on the department letterhead and had a signature. It was a start.

Tsosie watched us leave, an unsettling intensity in his eyes.

"What was that all about?" I said as we returned to the car. I drove this time, while Ben studied the folder's contents.

"We just witnessed what happens when a police force wants a person put away, either behind bars or with a bullet, but they don't have any right to do it themselves. Miriam pissed somebody here off real good, but for whatever reason—no evidence, no real crime committed—they couldn't touch her. Tsosie here has expressed his gratitude that somebody was able to do it."

"Then why won't he testify on Cormac's behalf?"

"If they don't have any evidence against her, then he's just a bitter cop bitching about some local nobody liked."

"What did she do?"

"That's the million-dollar question." He turned a page over, studied it. "Looks like she's got an arrest record. Drunk and disorderly, disturbing the peace, vandalism. Typical juvenile delinquent–type stuff. A bad kid heading for trouble. Nothing unusual. But here's something." He shuffled a couple of pages aside and studied a typed report. "A little family history. Her older sister Joan died about three months ago."

"How?"

"Pneumonia. Natural causes. She was only twenty-three."

"Then what's it doing in a police file?"

"Someone thought it was important. It happened right before the missing person report was filed. Maybe there's a connection. Maybe that's what caused her to snap. And here's her brother John's death certificate. Two gunshot wounds. No investigation conducted."

"Does that seem weird to you?"

"It seems like no one was too sorry to see him dead, either. They must have made quite a pair. Here it is: Lawrence Wilson, her grandfather. He's the one who filed the missing person report."

"Just her grandfather. What about her parents? What would they say?"

He studied the file for a moment. "There's an address. It might be worth dropping in on them. We can do that tomorrow. Let's find out if my car got towed."

Ben had left his car in the parking lot of the motel in Farmington, some thirty miles away from Shiprock, where he and Cormac had stayed during their ill-fated hunting expedition. After two weeks, the sedan still lurked in the parking lot, unnoticed. It was the kind of place that might slowly sink into the ground without anyone thinking to panic. The motel was part of a national chain, but that couldn't remove the veneer of age and fatigue that rested over it. Over this entire region.

"Now let's see if the windows are broken and the radio's gone," he said, wearing a thin smile.

They weren't. He'd locked his laptop and other belongings in the trunk. But the tires were slashed. All four wheels sat on their rims.

He stared at them for a long minute. "I'm not going to complain. I am absolutely not going to complain. This is fixable."

I had to agree. When something was fixable, you didn't complain.

He retrieved his belongings, then went to get us a room.

The walls of the building couldn't keep out the weird taint in the air. It was like I could hear howling, but it was in my head. No actual sound traveled through the air.

Ben stayed up late refamiliarizing himself with the contents of his briefcase and laptop. More online searches, more note-taking. I wanted him to come to bed. I wanted to be held.

Then I remembered it was Saturday, and I turned on the clock radio by the bed.

"You're listening to Ariel, Priestess of the Night."

Like I needed to make myself even more depressed. I lay on the bed, staring at the ceiling. Ben scowled at me.

"Do you have to listen to that?"

"Yes," I said bluntly. He didn't argue.

Ariel droned on. "Let's move on to the next call. I have Trish on the line. She's trying to decide whether or not to tell her mother that she was infected with lycanthropy and became a werewolf two years ago. The kicker: her mother has terminal cancer. Trish, hello."

Strangely, I suddenly understood the attraction of a show like this, and why people listened to my show. There was always somebody out there who had bigger problems. You could forget about your own for a while. Or secretly gloat, *At least it's not me.*

"Hi, Ariel." Trish had been crying. Her voice had a strained, worn-out quality.

"Let's talk about this, Trish. Tell me why you think you shouldn't tell your mother what happened."

"What's the point? It'll upset her. I don't want to upset her. If it's true—if she doesn't have much time left—I don't want her to spend that time being angry with me. Or being scared of me. And once she's gone... it won't matter. It doesn't matter."

"Now, why do you think you should tell her?"

Trish took a shaky breath. "She's my mother. I think... sometimes I think she already knows that something's wrong. That something happened to me. And what if it *does* matter? What if when she's gone, there is something after? Then she'll know. She'll die and her soul will be out there and know everything, and she'll be disappointed that I didn't tell her. That I kept it secret."

"Even if you know it'll upset her now."

"I can't win, either way."

"Is there anyone else in your family you can talk to? Someone who might be able to help you decide what's best for her?"

"No, no. There's not anyone. No siblings. My parents are divorced, she hasn't spoken to my father in years. I'm the only one taking care of her. I've never felt this alone." She was on the breaking point. I was amazed she could even speak coherently.

"What's your first impulse? Before you started second-guessing yourself, what were you going to do?"

"I was going to tell her. I'm thinking—it's like everyone talks about how you should work things out before it's too late. But she's so sick, Ariel. Telling her something like this wouldn't be working anything out, it would be torturing her. It's easier to keep quiet. I want to try to make this time as comfortable and happy for her as I can. My problems, my feelings—they're not important."

"But they are, or you wouldn't be calling me."

"I suppose. Yeah."

Ariel said, "It's commendable, your wanting to put your feelings aside for your mother's sake. But you're not convinced it's the right thing to do, are you?"

"No. No, I've always talked to Mom about these things. And I'm not going to have her anymore. I don't want to face that." Finally her voice broke. My heart went out to her. I was almost crying myself.

Ariel spoke gently, but firmly. "Trish, if you're looking for me to tell you what to do, or to give you permission to do one thing and not another, I'm not going to do that. This is a terrible situation. All I can tell you is, listen to your heart. You know your mom better than anyone. You should think about what she would want."

I hadn't intended to do it this time. I was too tired to be snarky. But I found myself digging out my cell phone.

Ben noticed. "What the hell are you doing?"

"Shh," I hissed at him.

I fought through the busy signal and got to the gate-keeper. I explained my reason for calling—that I could speak to Trish's situation. Then I found myself telling him my name. "Kitty."

The guy didn't say anything. Why should he? I wasn't the only person in the world named Kitty. He didn't have any reason to think that Ariel's radio rival would call in to her show.

I wasn't angry this time. I wasn't frustrated and lashing out. I really had something to say.

Ben watched me, kind of like he might watch a train

wreck on TV. I had turned down the radio, but he'd moved it over by him and was listening with it up to his ear. I paced the room along the foot of the bed and ignored him.

The call with Trish had drawn to a close. Then Ariel spoke to me. "Hello. Why have you joined me this evening?"

"Hi. I just wanted to tell Trish that she should tell her mother."

"Why do you say that?"

I wished I were in charge here. I wished Trish had called into my show so I could have told her directly. So I knew she was listening. For the first time in weeks, I really wished I were doing my show.

I said, "Because I told my mother that I'm a werewolf, and it was the right thing to do. I didn't mean to. It just kind of slipped out. But once I did, she wanted to know why I hadn't told her sooner. And she was right, I should have. I didn't give her enough credit for being able to handle it. She was upset, sure. But she's still my mom. She still wants to be there for me, and the only way she can do that is if she knows what's going on in my life. In the long run it meant I could stop making stupid excuses about where I was on full moon nights."

"How long ago did you tell her?"

I had to think a minute. "It's been a year or so."

"And you have a good relationship with your mother?"

"Yeah, I think I do. We talk at least once a week, usually." In fact, I should probably give her a call. I should probably tell her what was really going on in my life. "This is going to sound trite, but if Trish doesn't tell her mom, she'll always regret it. If she tells her now they still have a chance to talk it out. If she waits, she'll be telling it to her mother's grave for the rest of her life, hoping for an answer that isn't going to come."

An uncharacteristically long pause followed. Radio people were trained to shun silence, to fill the silence at all costs. Yet Ariel let maybe five seconds of silence tick by.

Then she said, without her usual sultry, sugary tone, "Wait a minute. You said your name is Kitty. Is that right?"

Damn. Caught. Now would be the time to hang up. "Uh, yeah," I said instead.

"And you're a werewolf."

"Yes. Yes I am."

"That's not a coincidence, is it? There couldn't possibly be two werewolves named Kitty. That would be... ridiculous."

"Yes. Yes it would."

"You're Kitty Norville. What are you doing calling in to my show?"

"Oh, you know. Stuck at home on a Saturday night, feeling kind of bored—"

"But you listen to my show. That's so cool."

Huh? "It is?"

"Are you kidding? You're such an inspiration."

"I am?"

"Yeah! You're so down to earth, you make it so easy to talk about things. You've changed the way everyone talks about the supernatural. You inspired me to try to build on that. Why do you think I started this show?"

"Uh... to cut in on my market share?"

She said, horrified, "Oh, no! I want to expand what you've done. Add another voice, make it harder for the critics to gang up on us. And now you're calling me. I hardly know what to say."

Neither did I. To think, I'd wanted to sue her, and here she was sounding like one of my biggest fans. I could have cried. "Thanks, I guess."

"So why are you sitting at home bored and not doing *The Midnight Hour*?"

"Let's just say I've had a rough couple of months."

Again, she hesitated, just a moment this time. She came back, almost shy. "Do you want to talk about it?"

Did I? On the air? But I had to admit, she was good. She knew the trick of making the caller feel like it was just the two of you having a chat over a cup of tea. Maybe I could talk a little.

I glanced at Ben, still listening to the radio turned way low. He kind of looked like he was suppressing a grin.

"A friend of mine was attacked and infected with lycanthropy a couple weeks ago. I've been taking care of him, and it's been tough. Another friend just got arrested for something he did to save my life. He's being charged with a felony. It's complicated. It also feels like the last straw. No matter how much you try to do the right thing, you get screwed over. Makes it easy to just drop out. To give up."

"But not really. Life gets hard, but you don't just run away."

"Except there's this thing inside me, the wolf side of me, and all she wants to do is run away. I'm really having to fight that."

"But you've always won that fight. I listen to your show. That's one of the great things about it, how you always tell people to be strong, and they listen to you. You understand."

"I'm flying by the seat of my pants most of the time."

"And that's gotten you this far, hasn't it?"

Was sultry Ariel giving me a pep talk? Was it working? I was a bit taken aback, that here was this person I didn't know, out on the airwaves, rooting for me.

Maybe I'd forgotten that anyone was rooting for me.

I smiled in spite of myself. "So what you're saying is I just have to keep going."

"Isn't that what you always tell people?"

"Yeah," I murmured. Nothing like having that mirror held up to you, or your words thrown back at you. "I think you're right. I just have to keep going. I never thought I'd say this, Ariel. But thanks. Thanks for talking to me."

"I'm not sure I really said anything."

"Maybe I just needed someone to listen." Someone who wasn't depending on me to keep it together. "I'll let you go back to your show now."

Ariel said, "Kitty, I'm really worried about you."

"How about I give you a call in a couple of weeks and let you know how it's going? Or you could give me a call."

"It's a date. Take care, Kitty."

I shut off the phone and sat on the edge of the bed.

I felt Ben staring at me, but I didn't want to look back. Didn't want to face him and whatever snide thing he was about to say. But the room was too small for us to avoid each other for long. I looked at him.

He said, "You really need to get back to doing your show. The sooner the better. You're too good at it not to."

I wanted to cry. What I couldn't say—not to Ariel, not to him, not to anyone—was that I was too scared to go back. Scared that I couldn't keep it going anymore. I felt like I'd rather quit than fail.

Slowly, I walked over to him, putting a slink in my step

and a heat in my gaze. I needed distracting. I sat on his lap, straddling him, pinning him to the chair, and kissed him. Kissed him long and slow, until he put his arms around me and held me tight. Until his grip anchored me.

"Come to bed, Ben," I breathed, and he nodded, kissing me again.

We went to visit the Wilsons in the morning.

The family lived west of Shiprock, on a flat expanse of desert scrub and sagebrush. The police report left directions. We turned off the highway onto a dusty track masquerading as a road. A couple of miles along, we found the house. Some run-down rail and post fencing marked corrals, but nothing lived in them. The house was one story, plank board, small and crouching. It didn't seem big enough to serve as a garage, much less house a family. A couple of ancient, rusting pickup trucks sat nearby.

We parked on the dirt road and walked the path—a track lined roughly with stones—to the front door.

"If it were anyone but Cormac I wouldn't be doing this. I'd write the whole case off," Ben said. "I have to go in there and ask these people to help me defend the man who killed their daughter. This kind of thing didn't used to bother me but now all I want to do is growl and rip something apart."

I started to say something vague and soothing, but I couldn't, because I felt the same way. Every hair on my body was standing on end. "There's something really weird about this place."

We'd reached the door, a flimsy-seeming thing made

of wood. Ben stared at it. Finally, I knocked. Ben took a deep breath and closed his eyes, opening them as the door opened.

A young woman, maybe eighteen, looked back at us. "Who are you?" The question and her stance—the door was only open a few inches—spoke of suspicion. Maybe even paranoia.

"My name's Ben O'Farrell. I'm trying to find information about Miriam Wilson. Are you her sister?"

Of course the girl was. I'd only ever seen Miriam dying and dead, but they had the same round face, large eyes, and straight black hair.

The girl stole a look over her shoulder, into the house, then said, "She's gone. Been gone a long time. I don't have anything to say about it."

Ben and I glanced at each other. Did she know her sister was dead? Surely someone had come to tell her, when the police here found out.

"What's your name?" I said.

She shook her head. "I don't want to tell you my name."

Names had power, yadda yadda. Okay, then. We'd do this the blunt way.

"Miriam's dead," I said, "She was killed near Walsenburg, Colorado. We're trying to learn as much as we can about her so we can explain what happened."

Some expression passed over her. Not what I expected, which was grief or sadness, or resignation at learning the truth after months of uncertainty. No, the girl closed her eyes and the release of tension softened her features. It was like she was relieved.

She said, "You're better off letting it go. You're better

off forgetting about it. Let it end here." That was the same thing Tony had said. And Tsosie.

"We can't do that," I said. "It's not over. Don't you want to know what happened?"

"No." She started to close the door.

"Is there anyone else who'd be willing to talk to us about her? Are your parents here?"

"They don't speak much English," she said. A convenient shield.

Ben spoke up. "Would you be willing to translate for us?"

"They won't talk. My sister—my oldest sister died before Miriam disappeared, my brother died a couple of weeks ago. We've had a hard time of it, and we're trying to move on. I have to go now."

Ben put his hand out to stop the door from closing. "How much of that did they bring on themselves? They hired my client to kill your brother. He did it, then Miriam came after him. He's in jail now, and you know as well as I do he doesn't deserve to be there. Where did this whole thing get started?"

She was lost, cornered, staring at us with a panicked expression, unable to close the door on us and unable to speak.

"Please," I said, "talk to us."

The words seemed to war inside her, like she both did and didn't want to speak. Finally, the words won. "Joan was murdered. No matter what anyone else says, she was murdered. But the more we talk of these things, the more likely we are to bring more curses upon ourselves."

You got to a point where one more curse wasn't going to make a difference.

"Louise, who are you talking to?" a male voice shouted from within. The father who didn't speak much English, I bet.

"Nobody!" she called over her shoulder.

The door opened wide, revealing a short man with desert-burnished skin aiming a rifle at us.

I wondered if he knew that he'd need the bullets to be silver.

"My daughter's right," he said in perfectly decent English. "We've had enough. Get out, now, before you bring more evil with you."

It seemed to me that we weren't the ones carrying evil around with us. We just kept finding it. I had the good sense not to say anything. Funny how a loaded gun can shut you up.

"Well. Thanks for your time," I said. I took Ben's arm and pulled him away from the door. Slowly, we backed along the path, until the door to the house slammed shut.

Ben's muscles were so tense they were almost rigid, like he wanted to pounce. "Keep it together, Ben," I whispered.

"What a pack of liars."

"Does this surprise you? This is the family that produced John and Miriam Wilson. Both confirmed monsters."

"Okay, but you're living proof—in fact you've based your whole career on the belief—that being a monster doesn't make someone a... a..."

"A monster," I finished, grinning wryly. "A fucked-up family's a fucked-up family, whether or not werewolves are involved."

"You think I'd have figured that out by now," he said.

"You know, I'm sick and tired of people pointing rifles at me."

"That was a shotgun, not a rifle."

For some reason, that didn't make a hell of a lot of difference to me.

We got back in the car and pulled out on the dirt track. We didn't speak. Another door had closed, figuratively speaking. One less chance to boost Cormac's defense.

"Kitty, wait, look." Ben pointed to a figure running toward us, from the Wilson house. Small against the landscape, it looked like it fled something terrible. It was Louise, her black hair tangling in the desert breeze.

I hit the brakes and waited for her to catch up. I didn't see anything chasing her, but I wondered.

I'd started to unbuckle and climb out, but Ben said, "Wait. We may have to drive out in a hurry."

He was probably right. I left the car running while Ben got out and waited for her. She reached us more quickly than I expected—she was fast, and we hadn't gone far. The house was still visible. I wondered if her father would show up in a minute with his shotgun.

Sliding to a stop, she leaned on the car's trunk. Her dark eyes were wide, wild. She seemed too flustered to speak, but she said in a rush, "Let me in. I'll talk to you, but we have to go."

Ben put the seat down so she could climb in the back, then he returned to the front.

"Go, now, hurry," Louise commanded. I was already driving, before Ben even closed the door.

I glanced at her in the rearview mirror. She perched at the edge of the seat, her hands pulling at the fabric of her jeans. Her gaze never rested. She looked around, out both side windows, over her shoulder to the back window, ducking to see out the front. Like she was worried something might follow us. She had the look of someone who was always afraid that something was following her.

I said, "Do you always jump into strange people's cars and tell them to drive? How do you know we're not murderous psychopaths?"

Her gaze settled on me, briefly. "I know a murderous psychopath when I see one."

"A murderous psychopath like Miriam?"

"Yes."

"Miriam was a skinwalker," Ben said.

"*Yee naaldlooshii.* Yes."

"What else can you tell us?"

"Not here. Someplace safe. We'll talk someplace safe."

"We're in a car driving forty miles an hour," I said, annoyed. "What could possibly get at us?"

She gave me a look that clearly pitied my ignorance. "You never know what could be listening. Waiting."

I wanted to laugh, but I couldn't. I said, "If we're not safe driving, where do you want to go?"

"There's a place close by. I'll tell you where to go. Turn right on the highway."

Her directions steered us farther away from Shiprock, then off the highway. I feared for the car's suspension. Many miles out, a dirt track led down a slope to a ravine—gullies and dry riverbeds like this cut across the desert. I never would have found this cleft in the hills if I hadn't been guided here. It was very well hidden.

Ahead of us, toward the end of the ravine, was a hut made of logs sealed with mud. It was octagonal—almost round—ancient-looking, with a low-sloping roof.

We all climbed out of the car, and Louise hurried ahead of us.

She said, "This hogan belonged to my family years ago, in the old days. Everyone's forgotten about it. But I found it again. It'll keep us safe."

"Safe from what?" It seemed like the obvious question.

She gave me a look over her shoulder.

Ben was the one who said, "If you have to ask, you haven't been paying attention."

"Just trying to make conversation."

He took my hand and squeezed it quickly before letting it go and walking on. A brief touch of comfort.

The scene we were walking into was from another world, something out of a tour book, or maybe an anthropology textbook: the desert, the cold wind, the round hut that might have been sitting there for decades. I looked up, expecting to see vultures. I only saw crisp blue sky.

Louise pushed aside a faded blanket that hung over the door and invited us in with her intent stare.

The hogan was dark, windowless, except for a hole in the ceiling, through which a shaft of sunlight came through. My lycanthropic sight adjusted quickly. The single room was almost bare. Toward the back, to the right, a blanket lay spread on the floor. A couple of wooden trunks sat by the wall nearby, along with a pile of firewood. Clearly, this wasn't a room for living in. It was a sanctuary. I could feel it, the way the walls curled around me, the way that I was sure that even though only a blanket hung over the doorway, nothing could get in. No curses, no hate. I felt a great sense of calm.

Even Louise seemed calm now, confident in the hogan's security. She knelt in the center of the room and struck a match to light the fire that was already built there. The kindling lit, glowed orange, and flames started tickling the firewood. The air smelled of soot and ash, of many previous fires that had burned themselves out. The smoke of this one rose up through the hole in the roof.

She showed us where to sit, on the ground to the right of the blanket.

She sat on the blanket. Before her, spread on the ground, was a sandpainting.

The pattern showed a complex and highly stylized scene. The colors were earth tones—brown, yellow, white, red, and black—yet vivid. In the firelight, the figures seemed to move.

Four birds, wings outstretched, marked the four quarters of the picture. Their clawed feet pointed inward, toward a circle at the center of the painting. In the middle of the circle stood a figure, a woman: black hair streamed from her square head, and she held arrows in both hands. Crooked white lines—lightning, maybe—rose up from her feet. Her eyes and mouth were tiny lines, hyphens, making the figure seem expressionless. Sleeping. The whole picture was bounded on three sides by rainbow stripes ending in bunches of what must have been feathers. The fourth, unbounded side faced the door. All of it was symbolic, but the symbols eluded me, except for one: the dark-haired woman at the center of great power, armed for battle.

Louise picked up a plastic dish, an old margarine tub. She took a pinch of something out of it: a white, powdery sand, or some other finely ground substance, which she sprinkled onto the image. I didn't know how she got the lines so straight. Her movements added bolts of lightning radiating out from the circle, between the soaring eagles.

"Tell me how Miriam died," she said.

Ben looked at me. I was the talker. But I didn't feel much like telling the story. "She attacked me. Our friend shot her."

"Friend. The same man who shot John."

"That's your brother. The werewolf."

She said, "John and Miriam were twins. They were destined to be killed by the same man. It all happened so quickly. I didn't expect it to happen so quickly."

"What happened, Louise? How did this all start?"

She continued adding to the painting as she spoke. "John went to work in Phoenix. When he came back—he was different. That must have been when it happened. When he became the monster. He wouldn't talk to anyone but Miriam. They'd go off together, for days at a time. Then Joan died. Then John. Then Miriam." Her voice never cracked, her expression never slipped. She'd lived this over and over in her mind for weeks now. "I knew," she said. "Somehow I knew what had happened, that Miriam took Joan. This magic, this evil has lived in the land since the beginning of the world. My family has been part of it, on both sides. I've learned what I can, but I've had no one to teach me the right way. The way of harmony. The old ways are gone.

"My father believed that because John brought a new evil from outside, an outsider should stop it. He knew someone who knew of a wolf hunter—your friend. The wolf hunter came and did his work. But it didn't stop the evil. It only made it stronger."

The flickering light from the fire made the figures in the painting waver and move. I blinked, flinching back, bidden by an animal instinct to escape. My eyes watered, and I shifted so my arm touched Ben's. He felt shaky, nervous.

Like me. Louise caught the movement, understood the way Ben and I stared at the picture on the ground.

"This is for Joan. She didn't die; she was killed. There's no one to help her find her way to the next world. No one else cares. I don't know how, but I have to try to help her with what I know."

It came from the heart, Alice had said. That had to count for something.

"She's still here. She hasn't traveled on. Maybe she'll talk to you. Maybe she'll tell you what happened."

"How will we know?" I said. "How will we know if she's talking to us?"

Ben muttered, "If she can't testify or sign a statement, what's the point?"

I elbowed him in the side.

"Joan?" Louise sat at the head of her painting, hands on her knees, gazing unfocused at the painting, or the light, or phantoms of her own imagination. She had the voice of a little girl calling in the dark. "I'm here."

Then she spoke a phrase in another language—Navajo, each sound punctuated, melodic.

The fire dimmed suddenly to embers.

Ben tensed; I felt for his hand, gripped it. He squeezed back. I expected the sudden spike of fear to rouse the Wolf. Any sense of danger always woke her, sparked her instinct, made her want to fight. I expected that instinct to kick in, but it didn't. This space, this weird timeless feeling, soothed her somehow. She slept, even though my brain was firing. It gave me a strange, disembodied feeling, like I wasn't really here. Like I couldn't feel the ground under me anymore.

After a long silence, Louise said, "She is telling me the story to tell to you. I can tell you like she's telling me."

An aura of blue light glowed around Louise, like some kind of static charge danced around her. No—she was backlit. The light was coming from behind her. I wanted very much to move around her, to see what was behind her. I stayed put.

"I was outside, mending one of the fences after a wind knocked it down. Miriam came to me. She called my name. I looked, and she stood right behind me. She held a powder in her hand and blew it into my face. I knew what it was, anyone would know what it was: corpse powder. She cursed me. She killed me, but no one would ever know. I grew sick. The doctors had a name for it, called it a disease, tried to heal me—but they couldn't, because it was witchcraft. Miriam stood by my bed at night—my last night—and told me what she would do: she would cut my heart out, take the blood, and put it on the wolf's skin. Take my soul and use its power for herself. I could see it, see her cutting out my heart, holding up the dripping fist of muscle, and I thought, *This is my heart, why can I see it? It should be hidden. My heart should be hidden, safe, but she has taken it from me.*"

I choked on a gasp, feeling my own heart suddenly. It wasn't me, it was her. I told myself it was only a story.

Louise shook her head, and when she spoke next, her voice was hers again. "Joan died of pneumonia, that's what the doctors said. But Miriam killed her. Miriam took her heart. I found her spirit crying in the desert, searching for her heart. But I'll help her find it. I'll help you, Joan."

She reached out, like she would clasp someone's hand, but there was no one in front of her. The glow faded, and she was left holding a point of light in her hand. She closed her fist around it before I could see more. As it was, it might have been my imagination.

In fact, a second of dizziness and a slip of time changed the look of the whole room: the fire burned again, as it always had. Louise held her hand over the painting, as if she'd just finished dropping the last grain of color into place.

None of it had happened. I was sure that none of it had happened. Except Ben still held my hand in a death grip. His hand was cold, his face pale. He swallowed.

Louise looked at us, her dark eyes shining. "I'll sign your statement. She wants me to sign your statement, to tell you what I know. To tell her story."

She swiped her hand through the painting, smearing the image, blurring the colors, stirring the ground until it showed a galaxy swirl of dark sand, and nothing more. Odd grains of quartz sparkled in the light like stars.

She sat back, closed her eyes, and sighed. "Let's go."

We scooped sand over the fire to put it out. Louise put her things—matches, the little containers of colored sand—into the trunk against the back wall. She drew something out as well, but tucked it into her fist so I couldn't see.

Pulling back the blanket over the door, she ushered us out of the hogan. She paused, looking back to scan the interior, as if searching for something. Or waiting for something. Then she slipped out, letting the blanket fall back into place behind her.

Walking back into the sun was like being in another world, a too-bright sunlit world where birds chirped and a fresh breeze smelled of dust and sage. Surely a world where nobody killed anybody.

Ben said, "I'll put together that statement."

Louise nodded. Ben gave a thin smile in acknowledgment, then went to the car. His hands were buried deep in his pockets, his shoulders bent against a cold wind that wasn't blowing. I was shivering as well. I hugged myself against the cold that came from inside rather than outside.

Louise and I waited, standing halfway between hogan and car. Her tangled hair made her look tired, older than when we'd started out. She looked up and around, studying sky, ground, distant trees, eyes squinting against the sun. For a moment she reminded me of a wolf taking in the scents.

I finally said, "Did you know what would happen in there? Has she ever talked to you before?"

She shook her head. "I didn't know if it would work with outsiders watching. Most people, if I said that Joan talks to me, they'd laugh. Or they'd feel sorry for me. They wouldn't think it was real. But you believe. I think that's why she came."

"I've had my own conversations with the dead."

"Some people aren't ready to go when they die."

I choked on a lump in my throat. "Yeah."

"I'm afraid—I'm afraid Miriam might come back. She was angry all the time. I'm afraid that might hold her to this world."

That damned cabin was going to be haunted forever. I didn't want to go back there to find out if Miriam's ghost was hanging around or not. Let someone else deal with it.

I said, "When she died, a man was there, a *curandero*. He was afraid of the same thing. He did something—I don't know exactly what. I think it was to keep her from coming back."

"Then maybe it'll be okay." She gave a smile that seemed brave and hopeless all at once.

Ben called us over to the car. He used the hood as a

desk and transcribed while Louise told a straightforward version of the story. She signed it where Ben indicated. It seemed like such a slim thing to pin any hopes on. We were grasping at straws. After she'd signed, Ben packed away his briefcase.

"Can we give you a ride back?" I said.

"No thanks. I'm not in too much of a hurry to get back. The walk'll do me good."

The walk was something like fifteen miles, but I didn't argue. I understood the urge to walk yourself to exhaustion.

She drew something out of her pocket, holding it in a tight fist. She kept her face lowered. "I have something for you. The questions about Miriam, the thing she was and what you're looking for—it's dangerous. You should leave, you should go back and forget about it all. But I know you won't, so you need these."

She opened her hand to show two arrowheads tied to leather cords lying on her palm.

I took them from her. They were warm from her clutching them tightly. She must have sensed my hesitation, because she pulled at a length of leather around her own neck. An arrowhead amulet had been hiding under the collar of her shirt.

"Why do you think that I, out of all my sisters and my brother, am still alive?"

She had a point there.

"Thank you," I said.

She smiled and seemed calmer. Less fearful. Sometimes rituals weren't about magic. They were about helping people deal with events. Deal with life. She walked away from the road, heading into the scrubland between here and the town. Didn't look back.

I gave one of the amulets to Ben. Back in the car, I opened the glove box and pulled out two items: the leather pouch Tony had given me, and Alice's crystal charm. I lined them up on the dashboard above the steering wheel, added Louise's arrowhead to the collection, and regarded them, mystified.

Ben looked at me looking at the amulets. "Does this make you super-protected? The safest person in the world?"

I frowned. "I'm thinking they might all cancel each other out. Like red, green, blue light making white."

"Which do you pick?"

"Local color. I'll bet Louise knows what she's talking about." I took the arrowhead, slipped the cord over my head, and put the others back in the glove box. Ben put on his arrowhead. There we were—protected.

We left. Ben sat with his briefcase on his lap, his head propped on his hand, looking frustrated.

"Will her statement help?" I said.

He made a vague shrug. "Maybe the court will believe it, maybe not. When you get right down to it, there's an official death certificate saying Joan Wilson died of pneumonia. Louise is the only one saying Miriam killed her. Hearsay and ghost stories. I don't know, I'll take whatever I can get at this point." We trundled along in silence for a few minutes, when he added, "As dysfunctional goes, this family's really got something going."

I snorted a laugh. "No joke. Where to next?"

"The grandfather. Lawrence Wilson. See what he has to say about Miriam, since he was the only one who cared to look for her."

"After the rest of the family, I'm afraid to see what he's like."

"Tell me about it."

The sun had dipped to the far west, and a cold wind bit from the desert. We were nearing the turn to the highway. We'd have to pick one direction or another. I had a thought.

"You want to wait to see him until tomorrow?"

"If small-town gossip works here the way it works everywhere else, he's probably gotten word that someone's wanting to talk to him. It'll give him a chance to go to ground."

"Yeah, okay. But it's almost sunset. Call me chicken, but I don't really want to be out after dark. Not around here."

He thought, lips pursed, watching the desert landscape slide by. "Then back to the hotel it is."

I turned east, back to Farmington.

chapter **15**

No, Mom. I'm in New Mexico now."

I'd returned to the motel room to find a message from Mom on my phone. As usual, the timing was not the best.

"What are you doing in New Mexico?"

Trying to track a dead killer without any evidence or witnesses? "I'm looking for some information. We'll only be here for a couple of days."

"We?"

Crap. I wasn't going to be able to talk my way out of this. "Yeah. I'm with a friend."

"Oh. Anyone I know?" She spoke brightly. Trying to draw me out.

I thought of the white lies and half-truths I could tell her. Then I remembered the phone call to Ariel last night. Be straight. Tell the truth. "By reputation. It's Ben O'Farrell. I'm helping him with a case." This was going to worry her. This was going to make her pry further. No information was better than too little information. I shouldn't have told her anything.

"Well, be careful, okay?" She just let it go. Like she actually trusted me to take care of myself.

"I will."

The rest of the conversation went pretty much as usual. Except for the part where Ben was sitting there smirking at me.

"I hope you're not planning on taking me home to meet the family."

I smiled sweetly at him. "Do you want to meet the family?"

He didn't answer. Just shook his head, with an expression like he was close to laughter. "That just sounds so damn normal."

Yeah, it did. And we weren't. Muddied everything up.

The honeymoon was over. That night, Ben and I lay in bed, holding each other, but it was as two people shored up together against the fears of the dark. He twitched in his sleep, like he was fighting something in his dreams. I whispered to him, stroked his hair, trying to calm him. We were near the new moon, on the downhill slide toward the full moon, when the pressure built, when the Wolf started rattling the bars of the cage. I'd forgotten how hard it was to resist when it was all new. I'd had over four years of practice keeping it under control. This was new to him. He was looking to me for guidance, which was perfectly reasonable. But I felt out of my depth most of the time.

Take this place for example. This magic. A family that decided it was okay to hire a bounty hunter to kill their son and pretend like their daughter didn't exist. A family so steeped in magic that all its members were terrified of each other. I didn't understand it.

* * *

We thought out loud during the drive back to Shiprock the next day.

"What's the series of events?" I said. "John comes back from Phoenix and he's different. A werewolf. We know how that can mess with someone. Then their oldest daughter, Joan, dies. Then Miriam disappears. They hire Cormac to hunt John."

"It sounds like John coming back from Phoenix as a werewolf was the trigger. Everything else happened after that," he said.

"What was it Tony said? A witch has to make a sacrifice to become a skinwalker. So Miriam cursed Joan, killed her, became a skinwalker."

"But why? Why did she want to do that? And why at that moment?"

"She wanted John to have a pack," I said softly. She didn't want her brother to be alone. It actually made sense, from a twisted point of view. I knew how hard it was to be alone.

"Why didn't she just let him bite her?" Ben said.

I thought about it a moment. Some people wanted to become lycanthropes. They sought it out, got themselves bitten. Why wouldn't Miriam have been one of those?

"Control," I said. "She wanted to be able to control it. She probably saw how it affected John. He wasn't able to control it. She wanted the power without that weakness."

He winced thoughtfully, his face lined with thought. "Thus begins their reign of terror. God, it almost makes sense. But we still can't prove she was dangerous. We need proof that she killed her sister. No one's willing to pursue the connection. Maybe they're afraid she'd take revenge on them. Curse them, kill them—"

"But she's dead. She can't do anything now."

"I'm not sure that changes anything in some people's minds."

Spirits lingered. Evil spirits continued to spread evil. If they—Louise, her family, Tony, others—believed that, I couldn't argue.

Miriam's immediate family may not have lived on a beautiful estate, but at least they had a house, a bit of land, an aura of normality.

Lawrence, on the other hand, lived in an honest-to-God shack, with weathered planks tied together for walls and a corrugated tin roof that seemed to just sit on top, without anything holding it down. It looked like he'd been living this way for years, because the place was actually several shacks attached to each other, as if he'd been adding rooms over the years whenever the mood struck him. The desert scrub around his place was covered with junked equipment, including several cars, or objects that had once been cars. The place was isolated, out on a dirt road, behind a hill, invisible from the town.

The question remained, did he live like this because he had to, or by choice?

"I have a bad feeling about this," Ben said, staring at the desolate house.

"Let's get it over with." I left the car, and Ben slowly followed.

I was afraid to knock on the front door. It looked like a deep sigh would knock it in. I tried it, rapping gently. The walls around it shuddered, but nothing broke.

No one answered, which wasn't entirely surprising.

This didn't seem like the kind of place where people threw open the door and welcomed you with hugs. In fact, I kind of expected to hear rattlesnakes or yipping coyotes in the distance.

I knocked again, and waited for another minute of silence. "Well?"

"Nobody's home?" Ben shrugged. "Maybe we can come back later."

We didn't have a whole lot of time to wait. We also didn't have a whole lot of choice. What could we do, drive all over town asking random people where to find Lawrence?

"What do you want?" A man spoke with an accent, as if English wasn't his first language.

We had turned to leave, when the man leaning against the farthest corner of the building spoke. He was shorter than me, thick without being heavyset. He was old, weathered like stone, rough and windblown. His hair hung in a long gray braid.

"What do you want?" he said again, the words clipped and careful.

Ben said, "Are you Lawrence Wilson? Miriam Wilson's grandfather?"

He didn't answer, but Ben stayed calm, and seemed ready to wait him out.

"Yes," the old man said finally. For some reason the word was earth-shattering.

"I don't know if the police have told you—Miriam's been killed."

He nodded, his expression unchanging. "I know."

"We're trying to find out what she did before then."

Did Lawrence smile, just a little? "What is it you think she did?"

"I think she killed her oldest sister."

He slipped past us and opened the front door. It wasn't latched, locked, or anything. It just opened.

"You have proof?" he said.

"Still looking for it."

"And you came here to find it?"

"You filed the missing person report. The rest of her family seems happy enough forgetting about her. But not you. Why?"

Lawrence stood in the doorway, gripping the edge of it. I thought maybe he'd slam the door shut, after a good hard scowl. But he stayed still, watching us with hard, dark eyes.

"If I'd found her first, I could have helped her. I could have stopped her. That's why I filed the report."

"But she never turned up. You didn't find her."

"She didn't want to be found."

He went inside, but he left the door open. Like an invitation.

Ben and I glanced at each other. He gave a little shrug. I followed Lawrence inside, into the cave of the house. I sensed Ben come through the door behind me.

I'd never seen anything like it. The floor was dirt. The place wasn't sturdy. The planks had weathered and warped so that sun showed through the cracks between them, and dust motes floated in the bars of light that came in. In this weird, faded haze, I could make out the room's decorations: bundles of dried plants hung by the stems. Sage, maybe, fronds of yucca, others I couldn't identify. Along the opposite wall hung furs. Animal skins. Eyeless heads and snarling, empty mouths looked at me: the pale hide of a coyote; a large, hulking hide that covered most of the wall—a bear; a sleek, tawny, feline hide of a mountain lion. And a large canine, covered with thick, black fur. Wolf. One of each. His own catalog.

I couldn't smell it. At least, I couldn't smell what I expected. I should have scented the fur, dried skin, herbs, the stuffy air. But all I smelled was death. The stench of it masked everything. And it didn't come from the skins, from the room. It came from Lawrence. I wanted to run screaming.

"You're one, too," I said. "A skinwalker. You taught her."

He stood at the far side of the room, which looked somewhat functional: a table held a camp stove and cooking implements. Lawrence lit a pair of candles, which did nothing to brighten the place.

"No," he said. "She learned. She watched. I was careless. I let her learn."

"You couldn't stop her?" Ben said.

"Couldn't you? You aren't the only one who's been hunting her."

"If you knew what she was, if you taught her—then you had the power to stop her, and you didn't." His voice rose, along with his anger.

"I don't owe you any answers." He went to a box on the floor, a wooden crate that might have held fruits or vegetables for shipping, and pulled out a can. He started cutting it open with an old-fashioned, clawlike can opener.

The wolf skin on the wall had dark, curved claws intact.

"Yes, you do," Ben said. "A man may go to jail unless I bring the court evidence of what she was and what she did."

Lawrence looked at us coldly. "The man who killed my grandson? The man who killed Miriam?"

The strangeness of this place smothered my own anger. I felt strangely calm. "He saved my life when he killed her."

Lawrence was busy lighting the stove and pouring the can of soup into a pot. "You're lucky to have a friend who will kill for you."

So. I once had a friend who died for me, and now one who killed for me. Why didn't I feel lucky?

Ben turned his back on Lawrence and hissed at me. "We're not getting anywhere. He's not going to tell us anything."

"What do you want me to tell?" Lawrence said, and Ben flinched—he thought he'd been whispering. "That she was evil? That I am evil? Do you expect me to tell everything I know as some kind of atonement? What's done is done. Nothing will change it. Nothing will make it better. The dead don't come back."

"Wouldn't bet on that," I muttered.

"I don't have any proof for you. I can tell you that Miriam killed Joan, but the police have no record of it. The doctors say it was natural, not witchcraft. Three of my grandchildren are dead, but you won't find anyone here who will admit that they were ever alive. That's what it is to be a witch here."

"Then why do it? If it makes you disappear." If it made you live in a place like this, isolated, other.

"It never starts out that way. But the line between medicine man and witch, *curandero* and *bruja,* is very thin. The magic comes from the same place. The danger comes with the spells that pull you one way or another. Miriam saw what her brother became, and she wanted it. Donning the coat of a wolf, tasting blood—it pulls you toward the darkness. You understand this. Both of you. You live in the dark because it's what you are."

I did understand, and hated that I did. Wolf seemed to prick her ears up at the very mention of the word blood. Beside me, Ben stood frozen, staring. His eyes weren't his own, not entirely. Something wolfish swam in them. I had to get him out of here. But I wanted more answers.

"Why did she kill Joan?"

"She had a sister to spare? I don't know. Didn't anyone warn you about asking too many questions around here?"

"Who did you kill in trade for your powers?"

He hid a smile with a bowed head. "It's a good thing for a witch to have a large family."

My stomach lurched into my throat; I wanted badly to throw up. I took hold of Ben's arm and squeezed too hard.

Lawrence continued. "Bodies disappear out here. You go out to the desert, a body gets dried up and covered with sand in a day. In a month it's nothing but bones. You tell anyone you were coming out here?"

"Let's go." I wrenched Ben's arm and steered him out of there. The door to Lawrence's shack slipped closed behind us.

Back in the open air, I felt light-headed, giddy—free. I almost ran to the car.

Ben was stewing. Fuming. His shoulders hunched, his fists closed. He kicked the dirt on our path.

"He knows, but we'll never get him into court. He knows Cormac did the world a favor putting a bullet in her. Hell—that guy probably needs a bullet put in him."

"Calm down. We'll figure something out. We still have leads." But we were running out of them. I tried to stay positive.

I stopped a few paces from the car. Something wasn't right. A sound tickled my throat—the start of a growl.

"Kitty." Ben's voice was tight. He moved toward me, so our shoulders touched. Side by side, protected—but from what?

A mountain lion leapt onto the roof of my car.

It had dodged around us in a couple of strides and made the jump without effort, so quickly I hadn't sensed it coming. Or maybe it had simply been able to slip by without us noticing. The thing was huge, solid, with thick limbs and a wedge-shaped face. It sat tall, its tail wrapped around its paws, looking for all the world like a house cat surveying its domain. Its tan fur was flat and slick, and dark smudges marked its eyes. Red eyes, bright as garnets.

Like somebody in a slapstick comedy, I looked back to the shack, then back at the mountain lion. And yes, the shack's door stood open.

"Kitty..." Ben murmured, taking my hand.

"Me or it?"

"Not funny."

We backed away.

The lion jumped off the car and stalked toward us, head low, tail flicking like a whip. Red eyes flashed.

Had to think of a plan. Had to do something. Couldn't just let this thing hypnotize me with its terrible gaze. All I wanted to do was scream. But I recognized the freezing terror that was numbing my limbs. I'd felt this when Miriam attacked me. Had to break out of the witch's spell somehow.

I whispered, "Ben, I'm going to break left. Try to draw him off while you get to the car and call for help."

"I was going to say the same thing, but with me drawing him off and you calling for help."

"No, I can fight him if I have to. I can take him."

"Just like you took Miriam?"

Details...

Both of us spoke quickly, breathily, on the verge of panic. I wondered how he was doing with his wolf. I still held his hand, which strained with tension. But no claws had started growing.

The mountain lion took another set of steps and opened its mouth to show thick, yellowed teeth, sharp as nails. It made a sound that was half growl, half purr, grating and skull rattling. Ben and I kept backing, until I slipped on the gravel. His grip on me kept me upright.

The monster crouched, its muscles bunching, gathering itself to jump at us.

"It jumps, we break," I murmured. Ben nodded.

But instead of jumping, it paused, stared at us, blinking those red eyes. It bowed its head. Then, its whole body seemed to collapse. Like the air went out of it. The face crumpled, and the eyes went dead.

A human hand reached out from under the lion's body and pulled off the tawny skin, revealing a naked man crouching in the dirt. A long gray braid draped over his shoulder.

Lawrence Wilson looked up at us and smiled.

"Louise got to you first. Lucky. Very lucky."

I touched my chest, feeling the hard shape of the arrowhead under my shirt. It worked. The damn thing worked.

"Let's get the hell out of here," I muttered to Ben.

Carefully, cautiously, we circled around the old man. Watching us, he stood, but didn't make another move toward us. Quickly we slipped into the car.

The tires kicked up a rain of gravel in my hurry to drive

us out of there. Lawrence watched us go, standing at the side of the dirt road. He seemed to hold my gaze in the rearview mirror until we were out of sight. The mountain lion's skin hung limp in his hand.

Around the hill and out of sight, I snuck a glance at Ben. He sat straight against the back of the seat, staring ahead, expressionless.

"You okay?"

After a pause he nodded. "Yeah. I think I am."

We made it off the dirt road and onto pavement. "Good."

Another dusk had fallen by the time we returned to the motel. The sky had turned deep blue, and a cold wind blew across the parking lot. It smelled dry, desiccated, and wild. Wrong. Like something out there was looking for us, and meant us harm. It might have been paranoia. Or not.

We had police reports, death certificates, coroner's reports. We had a couple of statements, a couple of newspaper articles. Tales of crimes that might have happened, of the bad reputation of a certain family, and people who wanted nothing more than the rumors and fear to go away. We didn't have hard evidence that Miriam was anything other than a highly disturbed young woman, or that Cormac had had no choice but to kill her.

We got out of the car. Ben slammed shut the door, lingered, then leaned on the hood and kicked the tire. And kicked it again.

"Would you stop kicking my car?" I said.

Hands on the hood, he leaned over, breathing hard. His anger was getting the better of him, which meant his wolf was getting the better of him.

"Are you okay?"

If he started shifting, I didn't know what I'd do. He didn't have experience keeping it together, when everything around you poked the creature awake. When all you wanted to do was run.

"Ben?"

He turned his head, glancing at me over his arm. He was sweating, despite the cool air. He was so tense he was shivering. I was afraid if I touched him, he'd jump out of his skin. "This place is getting to me. I hate it. I completely fucking hate it."

Sort of like I hated a certain hiking trail where I'd gotten stranded one full moon night, some four and a half years ago.

"Ben, keep it together."

"Will you stop telling me that? It's not helping."

Anything I said now would just be patronizing. "I know it's hard. It'll get easier. It gets easier."

"I don't believe you."

"Look at me. If I can hang on this long, so can you."

He straightened, left the car, and started pacing. Pacing was a wolf thing, a nervous thing, the movement of an animal trapped in a cage. I wanted to grab him, to make him stop.

He said, "No. I don't think so. You're stronger than me."

"How can you say that?" I almost laughed.

"Because you are. You're the one knocking on doors, you're the one keeping me moving. Me—I can't get my hands to stop shaking. I can't get my head on straight. If it weren't for you I'd have shot myself by now. Cormac wouldn't have had to do it."

He hadn't broken yet. I was so proud of him because he'd made it through one full moon and hadn't broken. But he still could. Years from now, he still might.

I said, "You didn't see me after I was attacked. I was the same way you are now."

Looking out across the desert, away from me, he said, "You deserve better than to get stuck with a guy like me." He spoke so softly I almost didn't hear him.

Pain filled the words. A gut-wrenching, heart-stabbing kind of pain. Like his heart was breaking. We were pack; his pain became my pain. I thought I knew what caused it: he wanted us to stay together, and he didn't think we could. Didn't trust that I would stay with him.

I had to make a joke—I wanted to keep things light. To not face what was happening. I couldn't even articulate what was happening, it was all gut. Gut and heart. If I didn't make a joke, I'd burst into tears.

My voice caught. "Are you sure it isn't more like you deserve better than to get stuck with a girl like me?"

"You could have anyone you want," he said. He turned back to me. At least he looked at me.

I didn't feel like a good catch. I didn't feel like I had that much power. "Yeah, that's why I've been way single since before I got out of college."

"You're still young. Plenty of time."

"You're not exactly falling into your grave."

"Feels like it some days. After thirty you start looking back and realizing you haven't done a damn thing with yourself."

I wanted to tell him that he was worth the world. That

he shouldn't have any regrets. But I'd really only known him for a year. I was only beginning to understand the baggage he carried.

Before I could say another word, he was walking to the door of the motel, leaving me behind.

Ben worked into the night, sitting at the room's tiny table, staring into his laptop, typing in notes, shuffling through papers, writing on them. His work spread out to the foot of the bed. I lay under the covers, trying not to disturb him. Not even pretending to sleep. I let him work instead of trying to get him to come to bed, like I wanted. I wanted to jump him and *make* him relax. I wanted him to forget about work, at least for a little while. I wanted him to believe he was worthwhile.

I flipped through some of the pages that had fallen within my reach. One of them was the coroner's photograph of Miriam's body. I studied it, trying to figure out who she had been. What had been going on in her mind, what had made her think that killing her sister and becoming a shape-shifter was a good idea. What had she been like as a girl. I tried to imagine the four siblings in better days: three sisters and a brother kicking a ball or playing tag in the dusty yard of that house we'd been to. I tried to imagine a young Louise before she'd become so frightened and desperate, laughing with a young Miriam who wasn't dead. Little girls in black pigtails. I could imagine it—but what I couldn't imagine was what had brought them to where they were today.

What brought any of us to where we ended up?

Ben sat back and blew out a heavy sigh. His hair was sticking out from him running his hands through it over and over again. His shirt was open, his sleeves rolled up, and the job didn't seem to be getting any easier.

He left the table and stalked across the room. At first I thought he was heading to the bathroom. But he went to the door.

I sat up. "Ben?"

The door opened and he left the room.

I lunged out of bed, yanked on a pair of sweatpants, and shoved on my sneakers.

"Ben!" I called down the hall at him.

He didn't turn around, so I followed him. He'd already disappeared outside. I trailed him to the parking lot in time to see him take off his shirt and drop it behind him. He continued past the parking lot, through a trashed vacant lot to the desert beyond.

He was going to Change. His wolf had taken over.

We were too close to town. I couldn't let this happen.

"Ben!" I ran.

He was so focused on the path before him, on what was happening inside him, he didn't see me pounding up behind him. He wasn't in tune with those instincts yet, the sounds and smells, the way they bend the air around you and tell you something's wrong.

I tackled him.

I wasn't sure I could take him in a fight. He was stronger than I, but he hadn't had much practice. I half hoped he'd panic and freeze up. I jumped, aimed at the top half of his back, and knocked him over.

Probably wasn't the smartest way I could have handled that.

On the ground now, I sat on top of him, pinning him down, and tried to talk reason. I didn't get a word out before he growled at me—a real, deep-lunged, wolfish growl, teeth bared. His bones slipped under his skin—he was shifting.

"Ben, please don't do this. Listen to me, listen to me—"

Had to keep him on the ground. This had turned into a wolf thing, and this was how the Wolf would handle it. Keep him on the ground, keep on top of him, show him who's in charge.

I much preferred talking things out with the human Ben. The real Ben. But I couldn't argue that this *was* Ben—him with all the frustrations of the last couple of weeks coming to the fore, finally gaining expression and taking over. Deep down I couldn't blame him.

Screaming a cry of pain and frustration, he struggled, his whole body bucking and writhing. I couldn't hold him. I almost did, but then his arm came free and he swiped. He struck, and wolf claws slashed my face. I gasped, more at the shock of it than the pain.

He broke away. In the same movement, the rest of the shift happened, his back arcing, fur rippling across his skin, thick hind legs kicking off his trousers.

"Ben!" My own scream edged into a growl.

This was only his second time as a wolf. He stood, and his legs trembled. He shook himself, as if the fur didn't sit quite right on his body. He looked back at me, and his body slumped, his tail clamping tight between his legs, his ears lying flat. A display of submission. I held the side of my face, which was slick with blood. His slap had cut deep. His wolf was sorry.

I was frozen. Wolf wanted to leap at him. His struggle

called her out, and she wanted to run. Keep our pack together. But I was so angry. Anger burned through every nerve and radiated out. She was the alpha and she wanted to prove it.

He ran. The wolf knew better than to stick around to see what I'd do next, so he leapt around and ran, body stretched out, legs working hard.

I sighed, the anger draining out of me. I ought to just let him go. Except that I couldn't. Had to keep him out of trouble.

I wiped blood off my face, wiped my hands on my sweats, and ran after him.

chapter **16**

I could run faster and for longer than someone who wasn't a lycanthrope. But I couldn't hope to keep up with a lycanthrope in wolf form. I could only track him, hope he knew I was following, and that maybe he would think about slowing down. Fortunately, his instincts led him true: away from town, into the open desert.

The night was clear, the air crisp, but the moon was absent. The world was dark. *Let me go, let me come out, I can see better in the dark.*

No.

I smelled prey here—jackrabbits, quail. Ben had smelled it, too, and it slowed him down. I spotted him ahead, trotting now, his head low, his mouth open, and his tongue hanging.

He must have been tired. Afraid. His movements weren't assured. A wolf's trot should have been graceful, swinging, able to cover miles without effort. His feet were dragging, his tail hung low. He wasn't used to this—lucky for me.

"Ben!"

He froze, lifted his head, his ears pricked forward. Then he turned and ran again.

I leaned on my knees, gathered my breath, and set off after him.

We must have gone on like that for half the night. He wasn't going toward anything. If I hadn't been chasing him, he might have stopped to try to hunt—I seriously doubted his ability to catch anything in his current state. But he was just running away, and I just followed. My face bled for a long time; I kept wiping the blood away and didn't think of it. I only noticed that I hadn't touched my face in a while when it started itching—scabs had formed and the healing had started. I could only concentrate on my lungs working overtime.

I'd lost sight of him, but his scent—musk and fear— blazed a trail. As long as I kept breathing, I could find him.

He came into view again when he slowed to a walk. I stopped following him then. Instead, I cut over obliquely from his trail. Like I'd stopped paying attention. Like I was circling back. I made a wide loop, and watched him out of the corner of my eye.

As I'd hoped, my change in behavior caught his attention. Now, I just had to tell him I was a friend. I almost wish I'd Changed so I'd have the throat to vocalize it. But I did what I could. I moved slowly, relaxed as much as I could manage, my gaze down and limbs loose. Just out for a stroll.

He watched, ears forward, interested. I kept walking, not moving toward him, not doing anything threatening. He should have been able to smell me—I should have smelled familiar, safe. *Come home, Ben. Please.*

He started trotting, taking a path that was parallel to mine. I walked a few more steps, then crouched and watched him. He circled me, not looking at me, swinging along, pretending I wasn't there. But his circles grew smaller, and he came closer. I didn't move, not even to watch him over my back.

Then, he stopped. He was off to my right. We stared at each other. This wasn't a challenge. Both his head and his tail drooped. Our hackles were down. I made a conscious effort to keep my arms and shoulders relaxed. We were asking each other: *Well? What's next?*

He gave the smallest, tiniest whine. A lost and tired breath wheezing through his throat. I stepped forward, crawling on all fours, and I wished I had a tail to hold out to tell him it was okay, that I'd take care of him. "It's okay, Ben. It's going to be okay." I'd been telling him that for two weeks now. I didn't know why he should believe me now.

He reached forward, stretching his body low, and licked my chin. I let him, closing my eyes and touching his shoulder. His fur was hot, his ribs still heaving with the effort of his run. I pressed my face to his neck and breathed deep. He leaned into me, whining softly with each breath.

I just kept saying, *It's okay.*

The wolf lay down, curling up next to me right there in the dirt—I was going to have to teach him how to find a safe place to bed down. But I supposed he figured that settling in next to me was safe enough. He fell asleep quickly. He dreamed, his breaths whining, his legs kicking out a couple of times. Chasing rabbits. Still running.

I'd taken it upon myself to look after him. To take care of him. So I did, staying awake while billions of stars arced overhead, against a velvet-black sky. More black and more stars than I'd ever seen, with no city lights to wash them out. All the clichés you could think of about the humbling vastness of the universe, the awe-inspiring sweep of sky and stars, seemed true now. The two of us might have been alone in the world.

The night was freezing cold, but I had a warm bundle of fur lounging against me and didn't mind so much. I buried my hands in his coat and watched the stars. Enjoyed the moment of peace, and hoped it would extend past this night.

I hummed to pass the time, something slow and classical. Slowly, Ben shifted back to human. This was almost gentle compared to the shift in the other direction. There, the wolf tore out of its human skin. But this, the wolf seemed to slip away, fading, limbs growing, hair thinning until only skin showed. By then, dawn had come, the sky growing pale. A bird sang, a series of high, watery notes—an incongruous beauty in the middle of the cold desert. Even in this desolate place, something lived and thrived.

Ben's skin looked gray, stonelike in the early light. Sitting close to him, I kept my hand on his shoulder, sheltering him. I sensed the moment he awoke; his arm twitched. He snuggled, pillowing his head more comfortably into my lap, which made me smile. I played with a strand of his hair, brushing it back from his forehead. He was awfully cute like this.

He opened his eyes.

"Oh, God." He squeezed them tightly shut again.

"Morning, sunshine," I murmured.

He rubbed a hand over his face, shifted uncomfortably on the hard ground. "What happened?"

"What do you remember?"

He thought for a moment, his brow furrowing. "Getting up. I thought I was going to the bathroom—but I just kept going, didn't I?"

I smiled wryly, brushing damp hair out of his face. That he remembered so little surprised me. I could usually track to the moment I shifted, even though I might forget everything after that. But he hadn't been in control at all.

"Yeah. At least you made it out of the parking lot before you shifted."

He groaned again, sitting up. He touched my sweatpants and shirt, which were smeared with blood. So was my hair, which had gone all dried and crunchy. I didn't want to know how I looked.

He said, "You're bleeding. You're hurt."

"Not anymore. All healed up."

"Did I do it?" I nodded. "God, I'm sorry."

"You can make it up to me later. Take me out for a nice steak dinner."

He thought for a moment, pursing his lips. "We've never even been out on a real date, have we?"

I hadn't thought of it. We'd fallen together by chance. But I didn't believe that anymore, not really, because something pulled at me. Something that kept me from looking away. I couldn't turn away from him.

I shrugged. "No sense in being all traditional."

"Why did you even bother coming after me?" He tilted his head to look out at the horizon. "Why did you bother staying?"

I touched his face. I couldn't not touch him. I held him, made him look at me, made him see my smile. This was another one of those situations that as a human seemed too weird, too strange to even consider. Sitting in the middle of the desert at dawn, me in pajamas, him naked. But it didn't feel strange. Sitting beside him, pulling him into my arms, felt right.

"You're afraid it's just the lycanthropy. That I wouldn't be here if we weren't both werewolves. You should know, I wouldn't have come after just anyone. I wouldn't have taken care of just any new werewolf that showed up on my doorstep. I wouldn't have sat out in the desert all night with just anyone."

He leaned his head against mine. "You're not just saying that to make me feel better?"

"I don't know, do you feel better?" He made an indecisive grumble. "Ben, you're naked. I can't lie to a naked man."

He took my hand, where it rested on his thigh. He studied it, rubbing the back of it with his thumb. "If you can't lie, this is when I should ask you anything. Anything I want to know, now's my chance."

This was the kind of conversation new couples had the morning after sex. I was sure I had no secrets from him— he was my lawyer, for crying out loud. But conversations like this were also tests. Uneasy, I said, "Sure."

"Did you and Cormac ever get together?" He gave a little shrug.

"No. Got close a couple of times. He kept running away."

He nodded, like this didn't surprise him. Like it was the story of Cormac's life. Then he asked, "If I hadn't come along, would you two have eventually gotten together?"

These were questions I was afraid to ask myself.

"I don't know. Ben, why do you need to know this?"

"I'm afraid I've messed things up for him. Again. But

it's all 'what ifs' now, isn't it? No way to tell what might have happened."

No. No way at all to tell. Those "what ifs" followed us our whole lives, didn't they? What if I hadn't been at that hiking trail on a full moon night. What if I hadn't met Cormac. What if he hadn't brought Ben to me but shot him instead. What if I'd invited him back to my apartment that one night...

I had Ben here with me, not "what ifs." Had to move on.

"You didn't mess anything up. Cormac never had the guts to say anything about it to me."

"Ironic. He's always been the tough one."

Ben had his own kind of toughness. I smiled. "What about you? Are you with me because you want to be, or because you're a victim of circumstance?"

He kissed me gently, a press of warm lips. Took my face in his hands, holding me for a moment. And I felt safe with him.

I stood, rubbing the pins and needles out of my legs, and tugged on his hand. "Come on. We've got a long walk back, and you have no clothes."

He covered his eyes and groaned. "It's just one damn thing after another, isn't it?"

Slowly, he got to his feet, and we walked back, side by side, arms around each other.

We found his clothes on the way back to the motel, which was good. Then we discovered that we'd both left our keys in the room.

Just one damn thing after another.

chapter 17

We spent the morning replacing the tires on Ben's car. Then, he wanted to run an errand. He asked me to come along, and I did. He drove, and I didn't bother to ask where we were going or what he was doing until we ended up on yet another dirt track that led us miles into the desert. We stopped at the bottom of an arroyo, covered with tall scrub, more vegetation than I was expecting to find. Lots of places to hide. This was the kind of area where ranchers grazed herds of sheep, and where wolves liked to run.

I'd never been here, but I recognized it. He didn't have to tell me where we were. He stopped the car, shut off the engine, and looked out, staring hard. He gripped the steering wheel like he was clinging to a lifesaving rope.

"Is this where it happened?" I said.

"Up past the curve there. Cormac drove the Jeep into the clearing. I don't really recognize it in the daylight."

I couldn't guess what he was thinking, why he'd wanted to come here. Wanting to come full circle, hoping to find closure. Something pop-psychological like that.

"You want to get out?" I said.

"No," he said, shaking his head slowly. "I just wanted to see it. See if I could see it."

"Without freaking out?"

"Yeah, something like that. I wondered if there'd be more to this place. If I'd feel something."

"Do you?"

He pursed his lips. "I think I just want to go home." He turned the ignition and put the car in gear.

On the way back to town I said, "I've never been back to the place where it happened to me," I said. "Just never saw much point in going back."

"That's because you've moved on."

"Have I? I guess it depends on what you call moving on. Sometimes I feel like I'm running in circles."

"Do you want to go back? I'll go with you if you want to see it."

I thought about it. I'd replayed that scene in my mind a hundred times, a thousand times, since that night. I realized I didn't want to see the place, and it wasn't because I was avoiding it, or because I was afraid.

Ben was right. I'd come so far since then.

"No, that's okay."

We had lunch at a local diner before heading back to Colorado. We'd be caravanning back in separate cars. I was half worried that Ben might take the opportunity to drive through a guardrail and over a cliff, or into oncoming traffic, like he was still regretting not making Cormac shoot him.

But he seemed okay. He was down, but not out. Some

life had come back into his eyes over the last week or so. Even though we were leaving New Mexico with stories, but no hard evidence. Statements, but no witnesses. Nothing to keep Cormac out of court.

Ben slouched in his side of the booth, leaning on the table, his head propped on his hand. "Everybody he's killed—every *thing* he's killed—deserved it. I have to believe that. I have to convince the court of that."

With a sympathetic judge, a less gung-ho prosecutor, or just one person from Shiprock willing to come testify, this probably would all go away. Lawrence had called us lucky, and maybe we were, but only to a point.

What it all came down to in the end: Cormac had shot an injured woman dead in front of the local sheriff, and nothing we could say changed that. And my opinion of Cormac was definitely colored by the fact that the first time we met, he'd been coming to kill me.

"Cormac's not clean, Ben. We both know that."

"We've spent half our lives looking out for each other. I guess it blinds you. I know he's killed people. The thing is, you drop a body down a mine shaft far enough off the main drag, nobody'll ever find it. And nobody's looking for the people he's killed."

Like what Lawrence said about bodies in the desert. Every place had its black hole, where people disappeared and never came back again. It made the world a dark and foreboding place.

"That's how the pack took care of things," I said. "T.J. ended up dumped in a mine shaft somewhere. I hate it."

"Me, too." He stared at nothing, probably mentally reviewing everything we knew, everyone we'd talked to, every fact and scrap of evidence, looking for something he'd missed, waiting for that one piece to slide into place that would fix everything. The check arrived, and I took it—Ben seemed to not notice it. I was about to go pay it when he said, out of the blue, "I should just quit."

"Quit what?"

"The lawyer gig. Too complicated. I should go be a rancher like my dad. Cows and prairie."

"Would that make you happy?"

"I have no idea."

"Don't quit. It'll get better."

A slow smile grew on him. "I won't quit if you won't."

"Quit what?" Now I just sounded dumb.

"Your show."

I hadn't quit. I'd just taken a break, why didn't people understand that?

Because it looked like I quit. Because if I wasn't making plans to go back to it, it meant I'd quit.

"Why not?" I said, feeling contrary. "They have Ariel, Priestess of the Night, now. She can handle it."

"There's room for both of you. You love your show, Kitty. You're good at it."

We were both leaning on the table now, within reach of each other, our feet almost touching underneath. Proximity was doing strange things to me. Sending a pleasant warmth through my gut. Making me smile like an idiot.

It was getting very hard for me to imagine not having Ben around.

I bit my lip, thought for a moment. Grinning, I took a chance. "Better be careful. You keep saying nice things about me I might fall for you or something."

He didn't even hesitate. "And you're cute, smart, funny, great in bed—"

I kicked him under the table—gently. "Flatterer."

"Whatever it takes to keep you coming after me when I go around the bend."

I touched his hand, the one lying flat on the table. Curled my fingers around it. He squeezed back, almost desperately. He was still scared. Getting better at hiding it, at overcoming it. But still scared, at least a little.

"Of course I will. We're pack."

He nodded, picked up my hand, brought it to his lips. Kissed the fingers. Then without a word he grabbed the check, slid out of the booth, and went to the front counter to pay.

Bemused, I followed.

Back in Walsenburg the next day, Espinoza was late for our meeting. The last meeting before the hearing. The last chance to convince him to drop the charges against Cormac. Ben had shaved, gotten a haircut, and looked as polished as I'd ever seen him. He had on his best suit this time. Even I put on slacks and a blouse and put my hair up. He paced along the wall with the window, in a conference room in the courthouse. Slowly, with measured steps. Not an angry, desperate, wolfish pacing. Just nerves. He held a pen and tapped it against his opposite hand, glanced out the window as he passed it.

I sat in a chair by the wall and watched him. He was a handsome, competent, intelligent, determined man. And none of that was enough to help Cormac.

The door opened, and the young prosecutor blazed in, like a general in wartime.

"Mr. O'Farrell, sorry to keep you waiting." He glanced at me, his look questioning.

Ben was right on top of things. "No problem. This is Kitty Norville, she's helping me with the case."

Espinoza nodded, and his smile seemed more like a smirk. "The infamous uninjured Kitty Norville."

"I heal fast."

"Real fast, apparently."

"Yeah."

"Too bad for Mr. Bennett. If you'd ended up in the hospital he might have had a case."

Of all the low, blunt, arrogant, shitty things to say . . .

"That kind of talk isn't really appropriate," Ben said, the picture of calm professionalism.

"Of course. I'm sorry, Ms. Norville."

My smile felt wooden.

"If you don't mind, I'd like to get moving on this," Ben said, handing Espinoza a written report.

Ben explained the report, a formal, legalistic retelling of everything we'd found in Shiprock. Somehow, between then and now, between his abrupt shape-shifting and our night in the desert and the drive back, he'd compiled our adventures into a narrative that sounded dry, believable, and even logical. He said that according to the local police Miriam had had a reputation for violence, that her younger sister Louise believed that Miriam killed her older sister Joan, that we'd been threatened by her grandfather Lawrence—in short, that the family's history and Miriam's character suggested that she was prone to murderous violence and it was entirely reasonable to assume that her motives here—against me and the others who'd witnessed the encounter—were violent. That Cormac had had no choice but to stop her.

Espinoza seemed to consider all this. He studied the report, tapping a finger on his chin, and nodded seriously. Then he said, "And what of the fact that she had only her bare hands as a weapon? Was a naked woman dressed in a wolf skin really that threatening?"

That was where Ben's scenario fell apart. We had no way to prove that she wasn't just a woman in a wolf skin.

Ben said, "You have four signed statements from witnesses who swear she would have killed someone. Two more statements from Shiprock. All of them saying that she was more than a woman in a wolf costume."

"Four people at night whose perceptions were muddled by fear and the dark, rendering their testimony somewhat unreliable."

They were testing each other, I realized. Practicing the arguments they'd have to use against each other in court. This was a practice run, to see if each really had a chance of beating the other.

Espinoza tapped the pages. "You've got hearsay. You've got nothing."

"I have enough to raise a reasonable doubt in front of a jury. You'll never land a murder one conviction."

"None of this is verified. I'll have it all disallowed. As I said—you've got nothing, and I will land the conviction. Your client's use of excessive force removes any protection under the law he might have had."

Ben turned away and crossed his arms. He was through arguing. I waited for a growl, a snarl, a hint that the wolf was breaking through. His shoulders hunched a little, like hackles. That was it.

"Mr. O'Farrell, for what it's worth, I believe you," Espinoza said, his tone turning sympathetic. I couldn't help but feel it was false sympathy—he was getting ready to bargain, softening Ben up. "I believe *this*. The skinwalker story, all of it. I grew up in this area, I've seen things that make no sense in the light of day. But you know how it goes in court. No judge is going to let you stand there and say she was a skinwalker, and that's the only way you can justify why Mr. Bennett did what he did."

Ben turned back to him. "If you believe, then this doesn't have to go to court. A judge never has to see it. Drop the charges. You know the truth, you know he was justified. Drop the charges."

Espinoza was already shaking his head, and my gut sank. "Sheriff Marks is standing by his testimony. If I won't prosecute, he'll find someone else to do the job."

Ben said, "Marks threatened my client. He's a biased witness."

"That's for the judge to decide," Espinoza said, giving no doubt how he thought the judge would decide. "If both sides' witnesses are discredited, it'll come down to the coroner's report." The coroner's report that said Cormac shot a woman in the back, then killed her when she was already dying.

"So I guess that's it," Ben said curtly.

"No." Espinoza produced a paper of his own and handed it across the table. Ben read it while the prosecutor explained. "I can offer a plea agreement. It's very generous, and I think based on the circumstances it's the best any of us will get out of the situation."

Espinoza didn't seem to be in a hurry. He sat back and gave Ben plenty of time to read the document. Ben must have read it half a dozen times. I could hear the electric hum of the clock on the wall.

"Any questions?" Espinoza said.

Ben lay the paper aside. "You're right. It's generous. I'll have to talk it over with my client."

"Of course. Mr. O'Farrell, Ms. Norville." He gathered up his things and took his leave.

I waited another minute. Ben still hadn't moved. "Ben? You okay?"

He tapped the tabletop, then pressed a fist into it. Seemed to grind his knuckles into the wood. "I'm trying to figure out what I did wrong. I keep trying to figure it out."

My guess was he hadn't done anything wrong. Sometimes you did everything right and you still lost.

We went to the jail to visit Cormac.

The three of us sat in a small, windowless room, on hard, plastic seats, around a hard, plastic table, saturated with fluorescent lights and the smells of old coffee and tired bodies. Ben had his briefcase open, papers spread in front of us, everything we'd found in New Mexico, everything Espinoza had laid out for us. Cormac read through them all.

"Espinoza will lower the charge to manslaughter in exchange for a guilty plea. Two to six years max. Otherwise, the charge stays first-degree murder and we go to trial. Mandatory life sentence if convicted." Ben explained it all, then finished, spreading his hands flat on the table, like he was offering himself as part of the evidence.

The silence stretched on forever. No one would look at anyone. We stared at the pages, but they all said the same thing.

Then Cormac said, "We'll take the plea bargain."

Immediately Ben countered. "No, we have to fight it. A jury will see it our way. You didn't do anything wrong. You saved everyone there. We're not going to let them hang you out to dry."

Cormac took a deep breath and shook his head. "Espinoza's right. We all know how this is going to look in court. Everyone may be willing to sit here and talk about skinwalkers and the rest of it, but it won't hold up in court. The law hasn't caught up with it yet."

"Then we'll make them catch up. *We'll* set the precedents—"

Still, he shook his head. "My past's caught up with me. We knew it would sooner or later. This way, they put me away for a couple years, I get out and keep my nose clean, I'll get over it. If this guy pins murder one on me, I'll be in for decades. I've taken too many risks. I've gambled too much to think I can win this time. Time to cut our losses."

"Think about it, a felony conviction on your record. Don't—"

"I can handle it, Ben."

"I won't let you do this."

"It's my choice. I'll fire you and make the deal myself."

Ben bowed his head until he was almost doubled over. His hands closed into fists. Anger—anger made the wolf come to the surface. I half expected claws to burst from his fingers. I didn't know what we'd do if Ben shifted here, how we'd explain it to the cops. How we'd get him under control.

Ben straightened, letting out a breath he'd been holding.

"Don't think you have to do some kind of penance because of what happened to me."

"It's not about you. If I hadn't taken that last shot…" He shook his head. "This is about folding a bad hand. Let it go."

"I feel like I've failed."

"You did the best you could. We both did."

Ben collected his papers, shoving them into his briefcase, not caring if they bent or ripped. I didn't know what to do or say; I was almost bursting, wanting to say something that would hold everyone together. That would somehow make this easier. Fat, hairy chance.

Ben said, "The hearing's in an hour. We'll enter a guilty plea. The judge will review the case and pass sentence. We've got Espinoza's word, six years max. They try anything funny, we'll file a complaint, get this switched to another jurisdiction. They'll be coming to get you in a couple of minutes. Is there anything else? Anything I've forgotten? Anything you need?" He looked at his cousin, a desperate pleading in his eyes. He wanted to be able to do more.

"Thanks, Ben. For everything."

"I didn't do anything."

Cormac shrugged. "Yeah, you did. Can I talk to Kitty alone for a minute? Before the goons come back."

"Yeah. Sure." Gaze down, Ben gathered up his things, threw me a quick glance, and made a beeline out the door.

That left the two of us alone, him in his orange jumpsuit sitting at the table, arms crossed, frowning. His expression hadn't changed; he still looked emotionless, determined. Though toward what purpose now, I couldn't guess.

I hugged my knees, my heels propped on the edge of the chair, trying not to cry. And not succeeding.

"What's wrong?" Cormac said, and it was an odd question coming from him. Wasn't it obvious? But it was an acknowledgment of emotion. He'd noticed. He'd been watching me closely enough to notice, and that fact was somehow thrilling.

Thrilling, to no purpose.

"It's not fair," I said. "You don't deserve this."

He smiled. "Maybe I don't deserve it for this. But I'm no hero. You know that."

"I can't imagine not being able to call you for help." I wiped tears away with the heels of my hands. "Cormac, if things had been just a little different, if things had somehow worked out between us—"

But it didn't bear thinking on, so I didn't finish the thought.

"Will you look after Ben for me?" he said. "Keep him out of trouble."

I nodded quickly. Of course I would. He slowly pushed his chair back and stood. I stood as well, clumsily untangling my legs. We didn't have much time. The cops would open the door any second and take him away.

Face-to-face now, we regarded each other. Didn't say a word. He put his hands on either side of my face and kissed my forehead, lingering a moment. Taking a breath, I realized. The scent of my hair. Something to remember.

I couldn't stop tears from falling. I wanted to put my arms around him and cling to him. Hold him tight enough to save him.

He lightly brushed my cheeks with his thumbs, wiping

away tears, and turned away just as the door opened, and the deputies came at him with handcuffs.

Ben and I waited in the hallway, side by side, watching them lead Cormac away, around the corner, and out of sight. Cormac never looked back. I held Ben's arm, and he curled his hand over mine.

We'd lost a member of our pack.

Epilogue

I had to admit, being back at a radio station felt like coming home again. Like meeting a long-lost friend. I thought I'd be scared. I thought I'd dread the moment when that ON AIR sign lit. I discovered, though, that I couldn't wait. I had so much to talk about.

We'd set up the show in Pueblo, as far north as I dared to go. I'd packed up the house in Clay and left for good. It was time to head back to civilization. I had a lot of work to catch up on. Even Thoreau hadn't stayed at Walden Pond forever.

I held the phone to my ear but had stopped paying attention to the voice on the line. I was too busy enjoying the dimly lit studio, taking it all in, the sights and smells, the hum of jazz playing on the current music program.

". . . don't take too many this time, let yourself get back into practice." Matt, the show's original sound guy from back in Denver, was talking at me over the phone. Giving me a pep talk or something.

"Yeah, okay," I rambled.

"Are you even listening to me?"

"Yes." I was unconvincing.

Matt sighed dramatically. "I was saying you shouldn't

take too many calls. Don't overwhelm yourself. You should spend most of the time on your interview."

For tonight's show I had scheduled a phone interview with Dr. Elizabeth Shumacher, the new head of the Center for the Study of Paranatural Biology, now organized under the auspices of the National Institute of Allergy and Infectious Diseases. I liked her a lot—she was smart, articulate, and much more forthcoming than the Center's previous director.

Next week was going to be even better: I'd convinced Tony and Alice to come in to talk about what had happened in Clay. They'd talk about where each of them learned their particular brands of spellcraft, and I'd get to tell my own personal ghost stories.

I hadn't yet found anyone willing to come on the air to talk about skinwalkers. I planned on running my mouth about it and hoped someone called in with a good story.

Yeah, *The Midnight Hour* was back, just like the old days.

Matt was *still* talking. I should have been more responsive.

I interrupted. "How about I take a lot of calls, but let Dr. Shumacher deal with them? I'll just referee."

He paused for a beat, then said, "I'm not sure that's such a great idea."

"Stop worrying, Matt. I'll be fine. You know if it gets really bad I'll break for station ID anyway."

"I just keep thinking that one of these days you'll break for station ID and not come back."

"Come on, I always come back."

"Then if you're all set, I'll hand it over to the local crew."

"We'll be fine."

Ben came into the room then. I beamed at him and waved. He smiled tiredly and sat in a chair by the wall.

"I can stay on the line to help out if you think—"

"Matt—we're fine. If we need you we'll call."

"Okay. If you're sure."

"I'm sure. Thank you, Matt."

"I'll talk to you later."

We hung up, and I turned my attention to Ben.

He'd just come from Cañon City where he'd checked on Cormac, who now and for the next four years resided at the Colorado Territorial Correctional Facility. The very thought of it was gut-wrenching. But it could have been so much worse. That was what we'd all ended up telling each other. It could have been worse. This way, he'd be out in no time. We'd see him again soon.

I'd just have to make sure I kept out of trouble until then.

Ben looked exhausted. His hair had that sweaty, spiky look that meant he'd been messing it up for hours. A nervous habit. Then I noticed he carried a thick stack of paper, bound together by a rubber band, under his arm. It was the manuscript for a book. *My* book.

I'd finished it. I'd given it to him to read. Now, I wasn't sure I wanted to talk to him. I didn't want to know.

Yes, I did.

"Well?"

"Well, he's doing okay. Says the food stinks, but what do you expect? Says he's catching up on his reading." In fact, Cormac—the bastard—had asked me for a reading list, since I was always saying nobody read anymore. "I'm wondering if maybe the time off will do him some good. Does that sound weird?"

I felt bad that I'd really been asking about the book. I gave him a sympathetic smile. "No, it doesn't. You want him to find something else to do with himself. Give up the hunting."

"This all does seem kind of like a sign in that direction, doesn't it?"

"What would he do if he didn't do the bounty-hunting thing?"

"I don't know. He grew up on a ranch, like me. His dad was an outfitter, guided hunting expeditions and that sort of thing. Cormac used to work with him. Yeah, I guess I'm thinking that spending some time without a gun in his hand will give him the idea that he can do something else."

I was torn between agreeing with him, and writing the whole idea off as silver lining bullshit. I wanted Cormac out. I wanted him free.

Even with Ben here, even with everything that had happened to build the bond that now existed between us, part of me still asked, *What if.* What if Cormac hadn't run off, what if we'd managed to make a connection—

"I already miss him," Ben said. "My phone rings and I keep hoping it's his number on the caller ID. Even though I know better."

"Yeah," I said. "You know what he said, at the end of that last meeting in Walsenburg?" Ben raised a questioning brow, and I answered, "He asked me to take care of you. To keep you out of trouble."

"Did he, now?" Ben said, smiling. "He said the same thing to me about you."

I might have blushed. I did look away. It was almost like Cormac was giving us each a mission, to keep our minds off him.

I said, "Does he have so little faith in our ability to take care of ourselves?"

"Can you blame him?"

No, I couldn't. "Is he going to be the same when he gets out?"

"I don't know. He's been through worse than this. But who knows? Am I the same? Are you the same? I wonder sometimes what you were like before the lycanthropy, if we would have had the time of day for each other. I guess—some of him'll be the same, some'll be different. We'll just have to see what stays and what doesn't."

Like peeling back the bandages after surgery, hoping it worked. Praying it isn't worse. It made me feel so out of control.

"How did you do?" What I meant was: how did his wolf do.

"I kept it together. But I hate how that place smells."

I bet he did. I didn't want to think about how it smelled. "So. What did you think of it?" I gestured to the manuscript in his lap.

Idly, he flipped through the top half of the pages, around the rubber band, wearing a studious expression. He made some noncommittal noises that might have expressed a positive or negative opinion. My anxiety increased. If the whole thing was crap, I wasn't sure I could start over.

"I have to admit, I especially like the chapter called 'Ten Ways to Defeat Macho Dickheadism.'" I couldn't tell if he was joking or not. Or if the joke was at my expense.

I felt like I was eight years old and begging. "But what

about the whole thing? Did you like it? Is it any good? Should I just give it all up and go into accounting?"

He chuckled and shook his head. Then, he set his joking manner aside. "It's good. It's not what I was expecting... but it's good. I think it'll go over like gangbusters."

It hadn't turned out the way I was expecting either. The publisher came to me wanting a memoir, a look back at my past experiences. It had ended up being more about the present, and a little about the future.

"Thanks—I mean, thanks for reading it. I really needed you to read it since you and Cormac ended up in it, at least a little bit."

"Yeah, that's what I wasn't expecting. But it's subtle. You don't use our names, but it's all there. I don't know how you got some kind of message, some kind of optimism out of that mess."

"Don't you know I'm an idealist?"

"God help us all."

The producer from the station, a young woman, the usual public radio night owl staff, leaned in the doorway and said, "Kitty, you've got one minute. We have Dr. Shumacher on the line."

"Thanks," I said to her, and she ducked back out. To Ben I said, "You going to stay and watch?"

"Sure, if you don't mind."

I didn't. I was glad to have him around. I found the headphones, adjusted the mike, checked the monitor, found my cue sheet. I didn't think I'd listen to Matt; I'd take as many calls as I wanted. Because when I got right down to it, everybody was right: I loved this. I'd missed it.

The ON AIR sign lit, and the music cued up, guitar

chords strumming the opening bars of CCR's "Bad Moon Rising." Sounded like angels. And there I was, just me and the microphone. Together again. Here we go—

"Good evening, one and all. I'm Kitty Norville, bringing you an all-new episode of *The Midnight Hour,* the show that isn't afraid of the dark or the creatures who live there…"

About the Author

CARRIE VAUGHN survived the nomadic childhood of the typical Air Force brat, with stops in California, Florida, North Dakota, Maryland, and Colorado. She holds a master's in English literature and collects hobbies—fencing and sewing are currently high on the list. She lives in Boulder, Colorado, and can be found on the Web at www.carrievaughn.com.

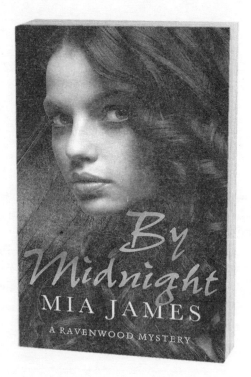

IN A WORLD SURROUNDED BY THE LIVING DEAD, WHAT DO YOU LIVE FOR?

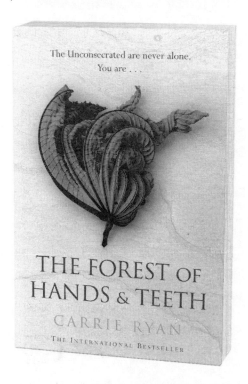

In Mary's world there are simple truths. The Sisterhood always knows best. The Guardians will protect and serve. The Unconsecrated will never relent.

But Mary's truths are failing her. When the fence that surrounds and protects her town from the Unconsecrated is breached her world is thrown into chaos and she must choose between her village and her future - between the boy she loves and the one who loves her.

For more information, proof giveaways, exclusive competitions and updates please visit: **www.orionbooks.co.uk/gollanczya**

NEW GIRL.
NEW SCHOOL.
SAME OLD MONSTERS.

As the new girl at the elite St. Sophia's boarding school,
Lily Parker thinks her classmates are the most monstrous things
she'll have to face. When a prank leaves Lily trapped in the catacombs
beneath the school, she finds herself running from a real monster.
This is a world of magic, vampires, demons and secrets.
Get ready to join the Dark Elite.

GOLLANCZ Y/A
Fierce fiction for young adults

For more information, proof giveaways, exclusive competitions and
updates please visit: **www.orionbooks.co.uk/gollanczya**

WHAT IF EVERYTHING YOU TOUCHED WAS CURSED?

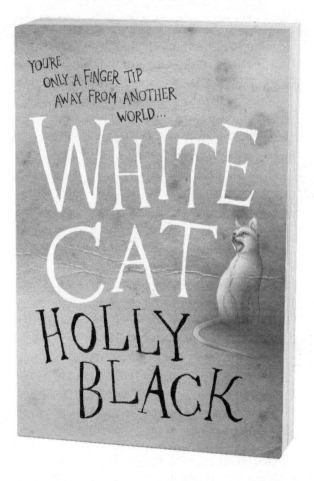

Cassel is cursed. Cursed by the memory of the fourteen year old girl he murdered. No-one at home is ever going to forget that he is a killer or that he isn't a magic worker. But Cassel is about to discover a dangerous family secret that will change everything.

www.orionbooks.co.uk